LEGEND OF THE GALACTIC HEROES

VOLUME 6
FLIGHT

YOSHIKI TANAKA

HAIKA SORU

SAN FRANCISCO

LEGEND OF THE GALACTIC HEROES

VOLUME 6
FLIGHT

WRITTEN BY
YOSHIKI TANAKA

Translated by Tyran Grillo

Legend of the Galactic Heroes, Vol. 6, Flight
GINGA EIYU DENSETSU Vol.6
© 1985 by Yoshiki TANAKA
Cover Illustration © 2007 Yukinobu Hoshino.
All rights reserved.

English translation © 2018 VIZ Media, LLC

Cover and interior design by Fawn Lau and Alice Lewis

HAIKASORU
Published by VIZ Media, LLC
P.O. Box 77010
San Francisco, CA 94107

www.haikasoru.com

Library of Congress Cataloging-in-Publication Data

Names: Tanaka, Yoshiki, 1952- author. | Grillo, Tyran, translator.
Title: Legend of the galactic heroes / written by Yoshiki Tanaka ; translated
   by Daniel Huddleston and Tyran Grillo
Other titles: Ginga eiyu densetsu
Description: San Francisco : Haikasoru, [2016]
Identifiers: LCCN 2015044444| ISBN 9781421584942 (v. 1 : paperback) | ISBN
   9781421584959 (v. 2 : paperback) | ISBN 9781421584966 (v. 3 : paperback) | ISBN
   9781421584973 (v. 4 : paperback) | 9781421584980 (v. 5 : paperback) | ISBN
   9781421584997 (v. 6 : paperback)
   v. 1. Dawn -- v. 2. Ambition -- v. 3. Endurance -- v. 4. Stratagem -- v. 5. Mobilization --
   v. 6. Flight
Subjects: LCSH: Science fiction. | War stories. | BISAC: FICTION / Science
   Fiction / Space Opera. | FICTION / Science Fiction / Military. | FICTION /
   Science Fiction / Adventure.
Classification: LCC PL862.A5343 G5513 2016 | DDC 895.63/5--dc23
LC record available at http://lccn.loc.gov/2015044444

Printed in the U.S.A.
First printing, April 2018

MAJOR CHARACTERS

GALACTIC EMPIRE

REINHARD VON LOHENGRAMM
Emperor.

PAUL VON OBERSTEIN
Secretary of defense. Marshal.

WOLFGANG MITTERMEIER
Commander in chief of the Imperial Space Armada. Marshal. Known as the "Gale Wolf."

OSKAR VON REUENTAHL
Secretary-general of Supreme Command Headquarters. Marshal. Has heterochromatic eyes.

FRITZ JOSEF WITTENFELD
Commander of the Schwarz Lanzenreiter fleet. Senior admiral.

ERNEST MECKLINGER
Deputy manager of Supreme Command Headquarters. Senior admiral. Known as the "Artist-Admiral."

ULRICH KESSLER
Commissioner of military police and commander of capital defenses. Senior admiral.

AUGUST SAMUEL WAHLEN
Fleet commander. Senior admiral.

NEIDHART MÜLLER
Fleet commander. Senior admiral. Known as "Iron Wall Müller."

HELMUT LENNENKAMP
Alliance resident high commissioner. Senior admiral.

ADALBERT FAHRENHEIT
Fleet commander. Senior admiral.

ARTHUR VON STREIT
Senior imperial aide. Vice admiral.

HILDEGARD VON MARIENDORF
Chief imperial secretary. Treated as captain. Often called "Hilda."

FRANZ VON MARIENDORF
Secretary of state. Hilda's father.

HEINRICH VON KÜMMEL
Hilda's cousin. Baron.

HEIDRICH LANG
Chief of the Domestic Safety Security Bureau.

ANNEROSE VON GRÜNEWALD
Reinhard's elder sister. Countess von Grünewald. Archduchess.

JOB TRÜNICHT
Former head of state for the Alliance.

RUDOLF VON GOLDENBAUM
Founder of the Galactic Empire's Goldenbaum Dynasty.

DECEASED

SIEGFRIED KIRCHEIS
Died living up to the faith Annerose placed in him.

FREE PLANETS ALLIANCE

YANG WEN-LI
Commander of Iserlohn Fortress. Commander of Iserlohn Patrol Fleet. Marshal. Retired.

JULIAN MINTZ
Yang's ward. Sublieutenant.

FREDERICA GREENHILL YANG
Yang's aide. Lieutenant commander.
Retired.

ALEX CASELNES
Acting general manager of rear services.
Vice admiral.

WALTER VON SCHÖNKOPF
Commander of fortress defenses at
Iserlohn Fortress. Vice admiral. Retired.

EDWIN FISCHER
Vice commander of Iserlohn Patrol Fleet.
Master of fleet operations. Temporarily
laid off.

MURAI
Chief of staff. Rear admiral. Temporarily
laid off.

FYODOR PATRICHEV
Deputy chief of staff. Commodore.
Temporarily relieved of duty.

DUSTY ATTENBOROUGH
Division commander within the Iserlohn
Patrol Fleet. Yang's underclassman. Vice
admiral. Retired.

OLIVIER POPLIN
Captain of the First Spaceborne Division at
Iserlohn Fortress. Commander.

ALEXANDOR BUCOCK
Commander in chief of the Alliance Armed
Forces Space Armada. Marshal. Retired.

LOUIS MACHUNGO
Julian's security guard. Ensign.

KATEROSE VON KREUTZER
Corporal. Often called "Karin."

WILIABARD JOACHIM MERKATZ
Veteran general. Commander of the Yang
fleet's remaining troops.

BERNHARD VON SCHNEIDER
Merkatz's aide. Commander.

JOÃO LEBELLO
Prime minister.

DECEASED

IVAN KONEV
A coolheaded ace pilot who died in the
"Vermillion War."

PHEZZAN DOMINION

ADRIAN RUBINSKY
The fifth landesherr. Known as the "Black
Fox of Phezzan."

NICOLAS BOLTEC
Acting governor-general.

BORIS KONEV
Independent merchant. Old acquaintance
of Yang's. Captain of the merchant ship
Beryozka.

ARCHBISHOP DE VILLIERS
Secretary-general of the Church of Terra.

*Titles and ranks correspond to each
character's status at the end of *Mobilization*
or their first appearance in *Flight*.

TABLE OF
CONTENTS

PROLOGUE:

A CHRONICLE OF EARTH'S DOWNFALL

I

"HUMAN CIVILIZATION AS WE KNOW IT began on this planet called Earth. And now, it is expanding its reach to other heavenly bodies. Someday, we can expect Earth to be one of many inhabited worlds. This isn't prophecy. It's only a matter of time before it becomes a reality."

So proclaimed Carlos Sylva, fifth-generation director of the Ministry of Space for the Global Government, after an exploration team took the first step in interplanetary colonization when it set course for Pluto in the year 2280 AD. Sylva was a capable businessman, but he wasn't the most philosophical or creative thinker. His speech was little more than a recasting of what was then commonly held knowledge.

Before the reality of which he spoke took shape, however, humankind would need to spill the blood of its brethren, only to drink it in massive quantities like some unholy communion. It wasn't until nearly seven centuries after Sylva's address that the political nucleus of civilization would relocate to another planet.

The Global Government was formed in 2129 AD. A world exhausted from ninety years of conflict believed that purging its worst creation—sovereign nations—would forever liberate humanity from the folly of laying millions of lives on the altars of the powerful. The global cross fire of thermonuclear weapons known as the Thirteen-Day War reduced the major cities of both parties involved—the Northern Condominium and the United States of Eurafrica—to radioactive wells: a morbid retribution for abuses of military power. Nor were minor powers caught in the middle of this carnivorous savagery spared harm and suffering. The Northern Condominium and United States of Eurafrica alike, fearing the other might suck those minor powers dry of resources so that they might continue to fight, launched their weapons of mass destruction at neutral countries. That both sides were destroyed as a result was one small comfort to those few who came out alive. To avoid such tyranny's resurgence, a strong, united system would be necessary. Without it, the world was bound to spiral into a destruction from which it might never recover.

In the long run, it was a matter of uniting a complex of power structures into a single overarching one. But cynicism abounded, and some people were less than optimistic about putting their faith in politics. "Even if there were no more world wars," they said, "we'd still have civil wars." Perhaps they weren't entirely misguided, but such rhetoric wasn't fatalistic enough to make people turn a deaf ear to its warning. In any case, given that the world's population had been reduced to about one billion, and food production had slowed to a crawl, there was hardly enough energy to sustain a civil war anyway.

The Global Government's capital was set up in Brisbane, a city in northeastern Australia facing the Pacific Ocean. Its location in the southern hemisphere, where damage from the war was minimal, made it ideal as a political center. It was also a hub for the largest economic bloc on the planet, rich in natural resources, and geographically far removed from offending nations.

A major consequence of the Global Government's establishment was a sharp decline in the influence of religion. Try as they might, traditional religious organizations had ultimately failed to put an end to the age of conflicts that was at last resolved by birth of the Global Government. If anything, religiosity was a primary factor in fomenting enmity and prejudice between opposing sides. Private armies representing various religious sects rampantly killed the women and children of heretics, all in the name of their almighty God. In the wake of the Northern Condominium's destruction, the minor "Order Nations" defending local authority across the North American continent transformed this vast industrial power once known as the pinnacle of reason and republican government into a wasteland of metal, resin, and concrete, while infecting survivors with viruses of superstition and exclusion.

In the end, their God did not intervene, their messiah did not appear, and people barely managed to pull the world up by its bootstraps from an abyss of ruin.

Reconstruction proceeded quickly. The remnant population put their all into projects large and small, building up the new capital and revitalizing wasted lands, yet with always one foot forward into the frontier of outer space.

As one popular doctrine had it: "He who owns the frontier will never be counted among the weak." Prior to the Global Government's establishment, humanity had left its mark as far as Mars, but by 2166 AD, humans had traversed the asteroid belt to build a developmental base on Jupiter's satellite Io. The Ministry of Space was the Global Government's most active department at that time. Its headquarters was located on the moon's surface, where it functioned as the nerve center for all divisions, including navigations, resources, facilities, communications, management, education, science, exploration, and shipping. The vastness of its scale was in proportion with the times, and by the mid-2200s its population surpassed that of Brisbane.

Brisbane, some said, might have been the capital of Earth, but Luna City was the capital of the entire solar system.

At first, any terraforming activities conducted off planet remained confined to the solar system. In 2253 AD, the first interstellar exploratory vessel made way for Alpha Centauri, but when it failed to return twenty years later, people started doubting whether their dreams of colonizing undiscovered worlds would ever be realized. The population was still hovering around four billion, however, so the solar system alone promised to provide more than enough living space.

In 2360 AD, a team of space engineers and their leader, a Dr. Antonel János, became saviors of the entire human race when faster-than-light travel was at last realized. At first, warp travel worked only at short distances. More importantly, it brought about remarkably adverse effects on the human body, especially regarding female fertility. But by 2391 AD, full implementation was in effect. This widened the scope of exploration to the extent that, in 2402 AD, a habitable planet was discovered in the Canopus star system. And with that discovery, the era of interstellar migration was under way.

With this new technology, however, came the first cracks in the "single authority" system under which the world was now governed. In 2404 AD, even as the first team of interstellar emigrants set out for the navigations base on Io to enthusiastic acclaim, Global Government leaders in Brisbane were butting heads over an elliptical debate: Just how much autonomy *should* they grant those settlements as they established themselves farther and farther away from Earth? Should they be allowed total independence, abide by Earth's laws and regulations without compromise, or operate somewhere between those two extremes?

Over the course of eight decades, the organization modestly founded as the Ministry of Space Navigation Safety Department was promoted to the Ministry of Space Department of Public Peace, which then became Space Defense Command under the vice undersecretary of defense, and finally Space Force. Space Force was of an entirely different disposition than the NCASF, or Northern Condominium Aerial Space Force, which threatened and overpowered weaker countries from the air before the Global Government came into being. Space Force's intended purpose was to guarantee the safety of citizens traveling through space by protecting civil liberties and economies against any wrongdoing that might undermine those privileges. With the advent of interstellar travel came near-total amnesia over the fact that any army touting an emphasis on peaceful protection at home was inevitably running wild with invasions and offensive campaigns abroad, where its actions ran relatively unchecked by the central powers that were.

Time and time again, any student of subsequent history will have encountered proof that an army is a nation's most powerful and most violent organization, that there can be no military groups outside any nation claiming to unite all of humanity. And so, despite a minimum sufficiency of military power, Space Force continued to expand its manpower and material resources.

By 2527 AD, this significantly enlarged military organization was showing signs of internal degeneration, but a section meeting on disarmament and arms control at the Unification Congress drew cynical complaints from all sides. One such testimony described the situation in the following terms:

"Are high-ranking military men nothing more than armed nobility under another name? As an example, let's take a good look at the extravagant life of Arnold F. Birch, captain of *Dixieland*, the carrier attached to fourth company HQ. His quarters consist of an office, a living room, a bedroom, and a bathroom for a total area of 240 square meters. But let's compare that to the soldiers' living quarters on the level below him, where we find ninety men crammed into the same area. With respect to labor, it's only natural for a captain to have an aide attached to him, but he has a private secretary (a female officer), six orderlies, two personal chefs, and a private nurse on call to meet his every need. Of course, their salaries are all siphoned from the people's taxes, but the greater indignity is that an infirm man in need of a private nurse is commanding an entire fleet."

This indictment became a target of heated criticism. The military already had enough spokespeople within congress and the press to handle the situation.

Interstellar travel had approached a ceiling in terms of technological innovation and effective range, and any prospect of limitless development was withering away. By 2480 AD, humanity's sphere of influence had reached a radius of 60 light-years, with Earth as its center. By 2530 AD, that radius had expanded to 84 light-years; by 2580, it had crept up to 91 light-years; and by 2630, 94 light-years. And while expansion had clearly plateaued, the military and bureaucratic organisms supporting these increasingly futile efforts were growing to gargantuan proportions.

Even as scientific advances were coming to a standstill, economic injustices were flourishing. Earth had already folded its agricultural and industrial mining industries, staking capital instead to control its more than one hundred colonies, greedily siphoning profit and resources in return. Any governmental autonomy nominally bestowed upon the colony planets did nothing to alleviate their subservience to Earth. A Pan-Human Congress was established in the hopes of alleviating some of these concerns. But while the Pan-Human Congress had every good intention of doing so, 70 percent of its delegates had been elected from Earth. And because amendment of any bills put to congress required 70 percent approval, there was no chance of the colonies' concerns being fairly represented. At one point, a delegate elected by the Spica star system called attention to the uneven distribution of Earth's abundant natural and financial resources. He was answered by the Global Government's ruling National Republican Party secretary-general, Joshua Lubrick:

"Any destitution suffered by the colony planets can be due only to their own incompetence and nothing else. To insist that Earth is to blame is the very definition of a slave mentality, one that shows a lack of independence and ambition."

Sentiments such as these were sparks that sent wildfires of indignation blazing across the colonized planets. Earth's monopoly had forced the colonies into adopting monocultures by buying out their crops well below actual value and pushing those producing them to the brink of starvation. As a result of these and other injustices, interactions with Earth went cold.

According to historian Ivan Sharma, "At that time, Earth lacked resources, just as its inhabitants lacked imagination. There's no question the latter fueled their present deterioration."

Earth's lack of imagination was manifested in its stubborn allegiance to elitist dogma. The powerful only grew to the heights they did because they were so deeply invested in notions of ancestral wealth and military strength that to even think of questioning either was to risk undermining the very foundation of terrestrial power. Earth plundered its colonies, and via their abundance fortified its own military prowess. The people of the colonies had, in effect, supported the very soldiers who surveilled and oppressed them.

By the year 2682 AD, the colonies had reached a breaking point. Joining together, they made the following demands. First, Earth was to slash her overgrown military. Second, the number of representatives elected to the Pan-Human Congress was to be redistributed to reflect the actual proportions of interplanetary populations. Third, Earthly capitalism was to cease its interference in the economic affairs of her colonies. To those making the demands, these were natural, if modest, hopes. But to those of whom they were being made, they were difficult to fulfill. Either way, what right did *they* have to make such demands in the first place? Those barbarians of the frontier barely knew their place, yet they dared make demands of the suzerain superstate of Earth as if they were equals?!

The honeymoon was over. Earth stopped paying its dues to the Pan-Human Congress, but not without attempting to strike a deal.

Historian Ivan Sharma looks through a glass darkly at this turn of events:

"At this historical juncture, Earth's moral slump was deeper than it had ever been. The people of Earth were determined to guarantee her manifest rights, even if that guarantee flew in the face of justice. But how were they ever going to exercise said rights as a first step toward advancement and progress?"

Contrary to Sharma's speculative outlook on the past, the people of whom he writes no longer cared about advancement and progress. And so, Earth resorted to conspiracy and brute military force to suppress the discontent of her colonies. The Sirius star system government went on the offensive, taking it upon itself to spearhead a nascent anti-Earth faction.

Earth began spreading disinformation, claiming that Sirius was criticizing her at every possible opportunity. This was not because Sirius sought equality, but because it aspired to rule over all humanity in Earth's place. From the point of view of Sirius, Earth was to be universally feared, as its policies had eroded every last hope of amiable relations with her colonies. Not every colony planet had cause to blame Earth so brazenly. Their discontent was not, some said, connected at all to Earth's ruin, but to the possibility that every colony might have to forfeit its own freedom and future in subservience to a maniacal Sirius. Sirius had now become a common enemy to both Earth and the other colonies. Its very existence was a danger to all. Before anyone knew better, Sirius had amassed incredible national power and armaments, and had even put a spy network in place to protect its clandestine interests. Before long, the slogan "Watch out for Sirius!" was on everyone's lips.

When confronted with these developments, the leaders of Sirius laughed away any such accusations of tyranny. Other colony leaders laughed with them, if only defensively, in sincerest hopes that Earth had merely been spreading rumors for the purpose of affirming hegemony.

Thus, Sirius became officially recognized by Earth as an enemy nation. They were a controllable enemy, a miserable villain that could only yield and beg for mercy if Earth chose to display her true power. But even as Earth was propagandizing Sirius's threat and might on the universal main stage, an unforeseen development was brewing behind the scenes.

Many good citizens began to believe that Sirius's power and intentions surpassed those of Earth. All other autonomous nations, including Sirius, followed suit.

At first, and with malicious delight, Earth had magnified a false image of Sirius, only to watch as the mirage took on three-dimensional form as a fearful reality in people's minds. The colonies were in awe of Sirius's apparent power and convinced themselves that all would end well if push came to shove with Earth. There were also those who held to more cynical views, as famously exemplified by a journalist named Marenzio:

"Last night, a local road was flooded when a major underground water line broke. We have every reason to believe that a spy from Sirius was behind the incident. This morning, a man was arrested for a series of arsons in F Block. Authorities suspect he may have been brainwashed by that same spy into committing these crimes. Make no mistake about it: Sirius's devilish scheming can be traced back to all those ships that have gone missing in the Bermuda Triangle, the genocide of indigenous peoples, and even Eve's eating of the forbidden fruit. Alas, Sirius, thou wilt loom over history as a universal evil."

Not surprisingly, this emblematic piece of hyperbole incurred the anger and hatred of security agencies across the board. Because they couldn't very well punish its author openly for simply expressing his opinion, they instead threatened his boss and had him demoted to an undisclosed location on the frontier, where he was never heard from again.

Meanwhile, Earth's plot to paint Sirius as the enemy of her own propaganda brought about a most ironic consequence when several colony planets, harboring animosity toward Earth, began cozying up to Sirius in hopes of being on the winning side. Indeed, Earth had made them believe that casting their lot with Sirius was the only way to shore up their defenses against Earth's despotism.

The situation quickly deteriorated for Earth as one colony after another joined forces with Sirius. And even as Earth's government was fretting over the backfiring of its seemingly foolproof plan, Sirius spearheaded a vigorous anti-Earth campaign in response to mounting pressures. In 2689 AD, fearing Sirius's precipitous military expansion, Earth decided to teach her most self-sufficient colony a harsh lesson in provocation.

Sirius gathered every colonial garrison at its disposal to carry out joint military exercises, promising heavy artillery provisions. Seeing that these activities were being mounted on such a grand scale, Earth's military forces used this as a pretext to launch a preemptive strike. Their blitzkrieg tactics were a resounding success. Sirius's homeworld, the sixth planet of Londrina in the Sirius Starzone, was overtaken by the so-called Global Forces. All colonial populations involved, beginning with that of Sirius, fled into space, leaving the surfaces of their planets in ruins.

Despite having saved their planet from annihilation, discipline and morale among Earth's troops had degenerated to an abominable level.

Local headquarters took to crunching the enormous numbers involved in cleanup. On the one hand, the amount of confiscated materials was underreported, while the remainder went into the roomy pockets of Earth's highest-ranking officers. On the other hand, enemy casualties were drastically exaggerated. The actual number of those killed in action, who totaled 600,000, had been inflated to 1,500,000. In order to make that number seem more plausible, not only did Space Force massacre innocent civilians by the thousands, but they also quietly carried out the barbaric act of dismembering corpses to make it seem as if those body parts belonged to a greater number of war dead. Space Force officials also underreported the number of casualties among their own so that officers could embezzle those salaries that would have gone to the dead had they still been alive.

The climax of this hideous farce took place at a military tribunal held in February of the following year, 2690, in the Earth capital of Brisbane. There, a journalist who'd risked his life on the battlefield to report from the front lines was indicted for bringing to light the atrocity of Earth's civilian massacre. Flying in the face of his hard-won information, only military officers took the witness stand. No one from the side of the victims was brought in to testify. The perpetrators, of course, denied their complicity in the matter. They waxed patriotic about having fought so bravely for the honor of their motherland and fellow countrymen, only to have their motives questioned while they were still licking their wounds. How unconscionable it was, they said through forced tears, that some ignorant journalist should ride in on his moral high horse and seek to defame them as a publicity stunt. The court exonerated the defendants and slapped a judgment of libel on their accuser, barring him from practicing military-related journalism at any point in the future. The victors, riding on the shoulders of their comrades-in-arms, marched down the capital city's central avenue, chorusing war songs at the top of their lungs. As the verses of "Under the Banner of Justice," "Guardians of Peace," "My Life for Honor," and "The Hero's Triumphal Return" rose from their lips, their supremacy felt more secure than ever.

All of which only further whetted the appetite of Earth's military forces. No matter the cruelty, they distorted the truth under a delusion that they could get away with anything. With no accountability to show for their actions, they saw it as a disadvantage *not* to commit crimes for personal gain. Slaughtering civilians en masse, raping women, destroying cities, and looting came far more naturally, and more easily, than the challenge of battling a worthy foe. From this sinful turn, they stood only to gain. The military had gone from a group of soldiers to a band of thieves, and their hearts burned with romantic idealism for the next battlefield.

That is, until the Raglan City Incident.

While remnants of defeated colonial armies had fled into Raglan City, weapons and all, of greater importance to Global Forces was that Raglan, as the center of production and distribution for the planet Londrina's abundant natural resources, had amassed great wealth from both above- and belowground. Global Forces mobilized its infantry, using fifteen mechanized field divisions to make a wall of troops around the city's perimeter. In addition, they readied four aerial assault units and six urban warfare units to storm the city. The first wave of attack was planned for May 9 but was postponed twice—the first time because Raglan's mayor, Massaryk, had overextended himself in his negotiations to avoid war, and the second time because within Global Forces, a certain Vice Admiral Clérambault, second in command at the Command Headquarters Strategic Division, had repeatedly downplayed tactical plans on the part of local forces toward preventing acts of barbarism. His efforts came to naught, however, when, on the night of May 14, ten units stormed the streets of Raglan City from land and air.

The invasion did not go at all as planned. Under siege by a massive force and gripped by panic, some of the remnant soldiers in Raglan City, thinking they might neutralize an attack by giving themselves up to Global Forces, scrambled to organize vigilante squads and began hunting down insurgents. But the hunted had their own agenda, and because they had weapons, they would not simply allow themselves to be flushed out. Shoot-outs erupted across the city, and at 8:20 p.m., soldiers watched from the perimeter as the Western Block's liquid hydrogen tanks went up in flames. They took this as their cue to launch an offensive in what would come to be known as the "Blood Night."

Their orders were harsh, to be sure:

"Anyone bearing arms will be shot on sight. No questions asked. Anyone *suspected* of bearing arms, and those who *appear* to be resisting, escaping, or hiding, will be punished accordingly."

By giving its troops free license to kill, the military had effectively openly condoned indiscriminate killing.

Those who stormed the city were hungry for the slaughter and destruction they'd been authorized to carry out, feverishly raping and pillaging wherever they could. Such actions were not officially sanctioned but were quietly tolerated nevertheless. Paintings and jewels were stolen from the city's museums, and rare books were kicked into the flames by soldiers who understood nothing of their inestimable worth.

The city's Northern Block was home to its diamond refinery, as well as processing plants for gold, platinum, and other precious minerals. Naturally, it, too, became a target of attack by the overzealous Global Forces, whose second air assault and fifth land units accidentally killed some of their own in their zeal for destruction. Fatalities amounted to approximately 1,500 on both sides, but an investigation conducted on the following day revealed that the stomachs of over sixty bodies had been cut open, presumably to seize the raw diamonds they'd swallowed. Among the civilian casualties, such victims numbered a hundredfold those of the troops. Old men had their jaws cut open with military knives and their gold teeth pulled out, and women taken by force had their ears cut off for their valuable earrings and their fingers cut off for their rings.

The Blood Night lasted ten hours. In that time, nearly one million inhabitants of Raglan City were killed by Global Forces, while damages from destruction and plunder totaled fifteen billion units of common currency. Local headquarters kept a substantial portion of stolen goods for themselves and informed their home base on Earth that, after a fierce battle, enemy forces had been eliminated and the city successfully occupied.

In his grief, Clérambault grabbed a pen and vented his anger in his diary over failing to prevent his comrades' barbarism:

Nothing in human society is so egregious as an army without shame or self-restraint. And the force I serve in has become exactly that.

Back at command headquarters in the capital, military leaders chatting idly before their comm screens with whisky glasses in hand sobered up at the loathsome voice of a veteran admiral named Hazlitt.

"You all look pretty pleased for a bunch of men who've just sent other people's cities up in flames. Does that thought excite you? Does it bring you joy? I guarantee you that, ten years from now, our capital will face the same fate. Mark my words. Should we not at least be prepared for that eventuality?"

But those who criticized their allies' misdeeds were forever in the minority. Two such dissenters were met with derision and retired from active duty.

A Rear Admiral Weber, who worked as chief press secretary, made the following initial statement:

"I can say with confidence that no single instance of massacre or pillaging was carried out in Raglan City. Those who claim as much should be branded as rebels whose only goal is to fabricate history and thus wound the honor of Global Forces."

Three days later, the military changed its tune:

"After careful internal examination, we have determined that massacres and pillaging did in fact occur, albeit on a much smaller scale than originally reported. Casualties were, at most, twenty thousand. Furthermore, the perpetrators of these heinous acts were not Global Forces, but anti-Earth guerilla extremists hidden in the city. They pinned their own crimes on Global Forces in an attempt to incite anti-Earth sentiments. You can be sure these heinous crimes will be met with suitable punishment."

Military spokesmen never divulged the reasoning or investigative processes by which they'd arrived at such a quick about-face regarding their position on the Raglan City skirmish. Actions, they continued to stress, were more important than words. It was their responsibility to brutally punish these armed insurgents who'd destroyed the lives of civilians, and public order along with them. Carrying out said duty to its fullest, they claimed, would require them to conduct another search-and-destroy operation in Raglan City.

What on the surface seemed a swift act of recompense in reality allowed Global Forces to go back for those material goods they'd failed to pillage the first time around, eliminate any lingering eyewitnesses who might compromise the credibility of their story, and thoroughly suppress anti-Earth efforts. But Global Forces, as Clérambault had predicted, lost control of themselves and went on a rampage. If their fourth objective was to seed fear toward the anti-Earth faction and dampen enthusiasm for the resistance, it never worked. If anything, they courted further hatred and hostility. Their little "cleanup" operation cost another 350,000 lives.

Even their cruel hands of oppression, however, let a few small grains of sand fall unseen through their fingers, much to the regret of the Global Government and the delight of the colonies. These grains, it turned out, were the first of what would grow into a mountain of historic proportions.

A twenty-five-year-old solivision journalist named Kahle Palmgren was beaten unconscious with laser rifles and left for dead when he refused a material inspection by the military. When he came to, he discovered that he'd been thrown atop a pile of corpses. Seeing that the mound had been doused with rocket fuel and set ablaze, he managed to escape through the thick cloud of smoke before the fire could add him to its victims.

There was also Winslow Kenneth Townsend, a twenty-three-year-old accountant for a metallic radium mine and labor union secretary, who was watching the army marching by from his apartment window when he was shot at from below by a drunken soldier. The gun's ray beamed straight into the forehead of his mother, who was standing next to him. He was utterly ignored when he pressed charges against military authorities, who responded by accusing him in turn of killing his mother himself. Knowing it was futile to take the case any further, he fled into the mines, shaking off pursuit until he'd gone completely off the radar.

Then there was Joliot Francoeur, a twenty-year-old student of herbal medicine at the institutional affiliate of a medical school, who with his two thousand–page medicinal reference guide split open the head of an Earth soldier for raping his girlfriend. This left him no choice but to slip into the underground sewers as a fugitive. Only after his successful escape did he come to learn that his girlfriend had killed herself.

And finally, there was nineteen-year-old Chao Yui-lun, who had interest in neither politics nor revolution, and who'd been studying composition at a music conservatory. After losing his brother and sister-in-law, who'd raised him in place of his parents, to the random gunfire of safety corps officers, he grabbed his three-year-old nephew and fled the burning city of Raglan.

These four survivors went on to great renown. Unlike them, most others who vowed to take revenge against Global Forces as they watched their streets go up in flames died trying and ended their lives in obscurity. For this fateful quartet, resistance was more than a matter of principle. It was the means to survive.

"Raglan City has burned to the ground," went the official report, "leaving behind massive carbonized ruins, 1.5 million dead, 2.5 million injured, 4.5 million prisoners of war, and four avengers."

"Avengers" wasn't the most accurate way of putting it, for what motivated Palmgren, Townsend, Francoeur, and Chao wasn't merely a desire to oust Global Forces from their easy chair of authority and glory fourteen years later, but to see the phantoms of the razed city rise soundlessly from the depths of their ideals and ideology, overtaking the ones who'd killed them like thieves in the night.

The four of them first gathered on Proserpina, fifth planet of the Proxima central star zone. The date was February 28, 2691 AD. It was the first time they'd come to know each other by name, although it was possible they'd crossed paths at the anti-Earth faction's base of operations without being formally introduced.

The subsequent division of roles among the four was a prime example of the right people being in the right place at the right time. Palmgren drew on his own ideals and worldview to unify anti-Earth factions and raise awareness among the public. These actions, combined with his natural leadership and rallying power, earned him status as the poster child for the anti-Earth movement. Using his keen sense of finance and administrative capacities, Townsend laid an ambitious economic foundation for what came to be known as the United Anti-Earth Front, thus engendering giant leaps forward in the potential of undeveloped colonies to boost domestic production on their own terms. Moreover, he successfully capitalized on his acumen in these matters to power an efficient distribution system. Francoeur, as supreme commander of a combative anti-Earth organization known as the Black Flag Force, mobilized a disorderly mob into a highly trained revolutionary faction, which he reorganized, regimented, led, and commanded. At the time, the Earth's governmental army boasted three superlative admirals in its ranks, along with an overwhelming abundance of material resources, so initially Francoeur failed to subdue them on more than one occasion. But in the tide-turning Battle of Vega, he succeeded in dividing the Earth fleet, winning all eighty-four engagements after unlocking the secret to their legendary invincibility. Meanwhile, Chao Yui-lun oversaw intel, strategy, and espionage. In his normal life, he'd been a reserved young man who wouldn't dare cheat so much as a bakery out of incorrect change, but when it came to toppling the Earth's governmental hegemony he granted no quarter. To ensure their leadership within the United Anti-Earth Front, they accused the indecisive old regime of being Earth spies and banished them at the outset, thus opening several black holes within factions on both sides and reducing the number of potential combatants by half.

The aforementioned admirals—Collins, Schattorf, and Vinetti—were extraordinarily rare tacticians who possessed both experience and theoretical know-how, but refused to cooperate and severed contact with one another during the Battle of Vega. Each lost to Francoeur's crushing tactics. It was Chao who took advantage of the dissonance borne between the admirals by this setback. His plan was devilish enough to have earned him a certificate of commendation from Mephistopheles himself. First, he forced Vinetti into a coup d'état, had Collins killed, and made the truth known to Schattorf, who had Vinetti captured and killed. He then pinned it all on Schattorf and incited Vinetti's former subordinates to kill Schattorf in revolt. After being riddled with dozens of bullets, Schattorf lived long enough to let one word escape his lips:

"Fools…"

And so, in 2703 AD, Earth, effectively cut off from its own food supplies, raw industrial materials, and energy sources, commenced a last-ditch attack. Earth's army, magnificent only in terms of equipment, was led by second-rate admirals devoid of talent and collaborative spirit. They were crushed repeatedly under Francoeur's tactical boot, especially in the Second Battle of Vega, in which an Earth fleet sixty thousand strong suffered shameful defeat by the Black Flag Force's mere eight thousand ships. By the following year, 2704 AD, Earth's army had lost control of the solar system. Using the asteroid belt as a last defense, Earth kept up its nearly futile resistance until it abandoned even the formality of protecting its own people, commandeering citizens' provisions and repurposing them for munitions use.

Within the Black Flag Force, which had been deployed as far as Jupiter, opinions were split between Commander Francoeur and Chao's political committee. Whereas Francoeur insisted on full-scale attack, Chao was all for a war of attrition. The only options left for Global Forces were to surrender or starve to death. Assuming they were too stubborn to surrender, Earth's surface would be reduced to a graveyard soon enough.

A compromise was reached, and Earth got the worst of it. The Black Flag Force cut off all supply channels to Earth, and after two months of siege commenced an all-out attack.

The tragedy at Raglan City was reenacted on a scale many times over.

In the wake of this unilateral slaughter, Global Forces representatives, along with over sixty thousand high military officials, were executed en masse as war criminals. Following this, Sirius's—that is to say, the Raglan Group's—sovereignty was established. The Earth's power and authority had turned to ashes in an all-consuming conflagration, and the four who'd unified an angry mob of anti-Earth forces would surely be the ones to replace them. But the "Age of Sirius" would amount to nothing more than a flash in the pan.

Two years after the Sirius War, in 2706 AD, Palmgren, the living embodiment of revolution and liberation, died suddenly at the age of forty-one. A touch of cold had been exacerbated by inclement weather when he'd attended a cornerstone laying for an emancipatory war museum on a rainy day. Immediately after the ceremony, the cold had quickly escalated into acute pneumonia, which had kept him bedridden until his death.

"If I die now," he said to his trusted doctor, "this new system we've created will come apart at the seams. If only death would give me five more years…"

Not three months after his passing, opposition between Prime Minister Townsend and Defense Minister Francoeur on the matter of Sirius's victory came to a head.

Francoeur was upset that Townsend hadn't dismantled the so-called Big Sisters, corporate giants funded by the Earth's former regime, choosing instead to absorb them into the new economy.

Francoeur was a realist on the battlefield, demonstrating superb flexibility in planning and implementation, but stuck to his conceptual principles when it came to politics and the economy. When he suggested they tear down the power of the transplanetary capital of the Big Sisters, Townsend curtly refused. He couldn't afford to lose that privilege, without which his power meant little to him.

At first, Chao Yui-lun looked on as if at deep-sea fish from far above sea level. When he saw with his own eyes the degradation of Earth's system of authority into cruelty, one could say his own part to play was finished. He'd already been withdrawing from the political front lines, and this was the last push he needed to divorce himself completely from their downward spirals. Once the new system was in place, he was offered the dual seats of vice prime minister and internal secretary, but he refused the positions and the authority that came with them on grounds of personal principle, returning instead to his recovering hometown of Raglan to fulfill his lifelong dream of opening a music conservatory. Working as board chairman, dean, and administrator, he found renewed contentment in teaching organ music and songs to a generation of children who, more than ever, needed the hope that only the arts could provide. As far as he was concerned, he'd finally recovered from both the fever of revolution and the epidemic of politics, and had gone back to who he used to be. Who he'd always been *meant* to be.

The children were very attached to him. No one among them would ever imagine that their beloved, kindhearted dean would, in two or three years, be deceived by a cruel and bitter opponent, and be either assassinated or driven to suicide, thereby bringing about the ruin of Earth's governmental authority. The young dean's pockets were always filled with chocolates and candies for the children, much to the chagrin of mothers worried about cavities. A sign, perhaps, of his naïveté when it came to securing the future of those he cared for most.

With Chao no longer claiming affiliation, the dispute between Townsend and Francoeur reached a tipping point. At first, Francoeur had tried to legally acquire the highest authority. When he realized it was impossible to sway the influence of a man like Townsend, rooted as he was in bureaucratic and economic soil, Francoeur decided to resort to a coup d'état. Townsend avoided disaster by a matter of seconds, as an officer once dismissed for disobeying Francoeur's orders exposed the former tactician's plan. The consequences of this dismissal played out one morning in Francoeur's bedroom, when a Public Safety Bureau member kicked in the door and shot Francoeur dead just as he was reaching for his visiphone to order the coup.

Meanwhile, the Black Flag Force became a faithful watchdog of the Townsend regime and was reorganized under a stern policy of purging and oppression. Among the so-called Ten Admirals under Francoeur's command, one had already died of natural causes, six had been executed, and another had died in jail. This left him with only two reliable men under his charge.

Townsend had emerged as the victor in this battle of authority. Like the man he'd overthrown, he believed in his own righteousness, which made them more alike than he cared to admit. Since whatever modicum of clout the Global Government possessed had already fallen by the wayside, from now on it would be necessary to rebuild resolution and order out of chaos and, for the sake of societal development and equilibrium in citizens' lives, to erase Francoeur from history like the dogmatic revolutionary he was. With Francoeur gone, Townsend had no doubt that a new society would be built in strict accordance with his plans and abilities.

The one remaining obstacle, it seemed to Townsend, was Chao Yui-lun. While on the surface Chao seemed more than satisfied teaching songs to children at his music conservatory, who knew whether he was secretly cultivating a desire for his power, like he'd done when his balls were up against the Global Forces' wall. Would he scoff at Townsend's strategy and attempt to bring him down? Was he, in fact, capable of something more ruthless than anyone could imagine?

Hardly a week after Francoeur's death, eight armed investigators from the Ministry of Justice's Public Safety Bureau were dispatched to Raglan City. An arrest warrant presented to Chao accused him of being responsible for the death of revolutionaries who'd been purged for once opposing the Raglan Group and its hegemony. After silently reading the warrant and mentally confirming its untruth, Chao turned to his nephew, now grown up and helping with his uncle's work while pursuing his studies.

"To me," said Chao to his nephew, who advised him to escape, "strategy is an art form, but to Townsend it's business. It was only a matter of time before I lost to him. There's no one to blame. This is simply what fate has in store for us."

He signed the payment ledger for the cost of the organ he'd recently purchased and handed it to his nephew. Twenty minutes later, a Public Safety Bureau worker who'd been awaiting orders in the adjacent room entered the dean's office, only to discover that Chao was unconscious from a knockout drug. Another twenty minutes passed, and the untimely death of the revolution's "elder statesman" was confirmed. One of the pupils had witnessed a sketchy-looking man exiting the dean's room clutching a wet handkerchief. When he told his parents back home, they went pale and kept silent, exhorting him to do the same, for the sake of their family's safety.

After thwarting Earth's tyranny on the planet Proserpina and vowing to emancipate the colonies, the Raglan Group was utterly annihilated in the following year, 2707. The eminently powerful Winslow Kenneth

Townsend, prime minister of Sirius and Pan-Human Congress chairman, got into a car to attend the anniversary of his victory against Earth, but when he was warned of a bomb planted on-site, he turned back toward his official residence, only to be killed by a microwave bomb en route.

This was one month after Chao's nephew Feng escaped the Public Safety Bureau's surveillance as a supposed criminal ringleader. Feng was never apprehended. Whether he'd gone on a crime spree or had been killed by an associate, no one could say for sure. In any event, he was never heard from again.

Neither was the bureau's investigation thorough enough to say for sure. The moment Townsend's body was blown to pieces, so too was the new world order that he'd strong-armed into place. Any bureaucratic loyalty toward Townsend had lost its cohesive power, left to percolate out of sight like all the blood that had been spilled to uphold that power in the first place. The Black Flag Force, for its part, had atrophied in the face of Francoeur's tragic death and the political purge that followed. These events had triggered an explosion of pent-up energy, splintering the group in a mess of bloody infighting to the point of total irreconcilability.

Had Palmgren lived just ten more years, the Space Era (SE) might have begun nine decades earlier. As the cards fell, however, it would take almost a century and the efforts of countless individuals before a "universal order, sans Earth" could be rebuilt after being demolished halfway through its construction when, in the year 2801 AD, the Galactic Federation of States established its capital on Theoria, second planet of the Aldebaran system.

Throughout the eight centuries that followed, humanity—with all its developments and setbacks, times of peace and times of war, tyranny and resistance, submission and independence, progress and regression—averted its gaze from Earth. Along with losing her political and military authority, this lone planet had lost any reason for its existence, and had no value worth noticing. For all the valiant (and not-so-valiant) efforts of her citizens, Earth had become nothing more than flotsam on a forgotten sea.

But a few stayed behind on this forgotten mother planet to keep her memory alive, hoping to touch the torch of their Earthly zeal to the unlit candles of the future…

CHAPTER 1:

THE KÜMMEL INCIDENT

I

TWELVE YEARS HAD PASSED—he'd been but a young man—since he'd witnessed a coronation. At the time, he had been just another student at the Imperial Military Elementary School, where he'd matriculated under the name Reinhard von Müsel. Standing against the wall of the grand reception hall, roughly ninety meters away, he had barely been able to make out the face of the one being enthroned. It would take him four thousand days to collapse that distance to zero.

"For every second that blond brat continues to breathe, he sucks up one ton of blood. Like a vampire, he's never satisfied."

Such were the sentiments of those who hated him. He'd come to accept even the severest criticisms with graceful silence. Exaggerated as they were, such negative comments were founded in certain truths. While throwing his weight around amid the horrors of war, Reinhard had lost many allies, consigning a hundred times as many enemies to oblivion along the way.

His subjects raised their arms and voices high.

"Long live Emperor Reinhard!"

"Long live the new Galactic Empire!"

It was June 22 of SE 799, IC 490, and year one of the New Imperial Calendar. Just one minute prior, he'd received a golden crown upon his golden hair to become the founding emperor of the Lohengramm Dynasty.

A twenty-three-year-old monarch. His ascendency to the throne was through no means of providence. He had gained the position and all the authority that went with it thanks to his own ingenious power. Nearly five centuries ago, Goldenbaum Dynasty founder Rudolf the Great's descendants, who had usurped the Galactic Federation of States and claimed the throne, were driven from it after their long and senseless monopoly on power. And it had taken thirty-eight generations, or 490 years, for usurpation to be repaid with usurpation. None before Reinhard had been able to change history in this manner. It was as if the stars had required perfect alignment to bring about his genius.

Reinhard stood up from his throne and met the jubilation of his many subjects with a simple raise of his hand. His uncannily natural gestures seemed to follow a melody of refinement that only he could hear. But while his elegance, along with his comparable talents in politics and war, was unsurpassed in his time, it was the impression of those ice-blue eyes as they scanned the crowd that those present would remember most. Even those among his subjects less prone to flights of imagination held those eyes in their regard as jewels of purest blue, forged in ultrahot flames and then frozen, ready to smite all of creation should even one lick of the unimaginable power therein breach its containment.

First to be reflected in those eyes were his highest-ranking imperial military officers in the front row. All of them were clad for the occasion in their finest dress, uniforms of black trimmed in silver; they were young men not unlike the emperor, men in the prime of their lives, notorious soldiers who'd valiantly aided the ascendancy of their young lord.

Imperial Marshal Paul von Oberstein was thirty-eight years old. His half-white hair made him look older than he was. Both of his artificial eyes were connected to an optical computer and emitted a brilliance that was not always easy to describe. Known as a cool and keen strategist, he'd been allowed to carve out a space in the shadow of Reinhard's supremacy. Whether valued or misunderstood, he saw no need to explain himself. No one among his colleagues or subordinates disliked him. Neither did anyone scorn him, for none doubted his achievements and abilities. He was never one to patronize or mince words with his lord out of self-interest. At the very least, he was instilled with a sense of reverence that served him well in every situation. He genuinely strove to accord common courtesy to all. In the new dynasty he'd been appointed secretary of defense, serving also in a ministerial position as an official military delegate.

Imperial Marshal Wolfgang Mittermeier, he of the unruly honey-colored hair and vivacious gray eyes, was thirty-one years old. If pushed to say, one might have called him diminutive in height, but he had the toned and well-proportioned physique of a gymnast and gave an impression of being just as agile. Known throughout the military by his other name, the "Gale Wolf," he was unparalleled in tactical speed. By all accounts, Mittermeier was the Galactic Imperial Navy's bravest general, and to prove it he had racked up significant deeds of arms during the Battle of Amritsar three years before (when he'd first entered Reinhard's direct command), the Lippstadt War, the occupation of Phezzan, the Battle of Rantemario, and the capture of the Bharat star system. Only the late Siegfried Kircheis and, of those still with them, Oskar von Reuentahl possessed comparable track records.

Von Reuentahl himself was thirty-two years old, a tall young officer with dark-brown hair and graceful features. But surely his heterochromatic eyes—the right black, the left blue—were the most impressive of those features. Along with Mittermeier, he was known as one of the "Twin Ramparts" of the Imperial Navy, a man of exceptional offensive and defensive capabilities. Yet when it came to winning without fighting, he was a man who thought outside the soldier's box. Once, he had recaptured Iserlohn Fortress after it was snatched away by the empire's sworn enemy, the Free Planets Alliance, and together with Mittermeier had subdued the alliance capital of Heinessen. These were but two of his many splendid military achievements. Mittermeier was his friend of ten years. And yet, whereas the "Gale Wolf" was a good family man, von Reuentahl was a notorious philanderer. In the new dynasty, as secretary-general of Supreme Command Headquarters, he oversaw the entire Imperial Navy as the emperor's proxy and worked closely with the emperor himself during official expeditions.

Outside of this formidable trio, who came to be known as the "Three Imperial Chiefs," there was Senior Admiral Neidhart "Iron Wall" Müller, praised by Marshal Yang Wen-li of the Free Planets Alliance as "a great general." There were also thirty-six-year-old Senior Admiral Ernest Mecklinger, who in addition to being a military man was renowned as a poet and watercolorist; thirty-seven-year-old Senior Admiral Ulrich Kessler, military police commissioner and commander of capital defenses; thirty-two-year-old Senior Admiral August Samuel Wahlen; and thirty-two-year-old Senior Admiral Fritz Josef Wittenfeld, a decorated general and commander of the Schwarz Lanzenreiter fleet.

Mingled among these starfarers, weaving her way through the cross fires of men, was a single youthful woman: Hildegard, also called Hilda, daughter of Count Franz von Mariendorf, who was now secretary of state under the new regime. Referring to the two as "Fraulein Mariendorf and her father," as long-serving heroes did, seemed accurate enough. This twenty-two-year-old woman, who kept her dark-blond hair short and dressed almost no differently from her male counterparts, might easily have been mistaken for an attractive and vivacious young man were it not for her lightly applied makeup and the orange scarf peeking out from her collar. She worked as Emperor Reinhard's chief imperial secretary and was treated like a captain by the military. She'd never commanded a single soldier, but as far as Mittermeier was concerned, she had enough gumption to run an entire fleet. Even as Reinhard had been waging a hard fight against Yang Wen-li in the Vermillion star system, she had come up with a way to save him. Hilda alone had paved the way to success by proposing capture of the alliance capital of Heinessen.

Compared to her illustrious accomplishments, most civil officials lacked luster against past brilliance, but now that Reinhard had taken the throne and had gone on to claim total domination over the Phezzan Dominion and achieve submission of the Free Planets Alliance, the time for change had come. Under the young emperor and his regime, orthodoxy was destroyed, and its progenitors made sure the new order established in its place would be the stuff of legend. The future was calling their names.

Secretary of State Count Franz von Mariendorf felt only modest satisfaction as the ceremony quietly evolved into a party. Although the ceremony reflected the former—that is, the Goldenbaum—dynasty's seemingly institutionalized extravagance and empty formalities, none of it was to his liking, despite it being within his duties as secretary of state to oversee ceremonies and festivals of national importance. He wanted every soiree and formal display to be as simple, yet thorough, as possible.

There were several reasons why the emperor should look upon him favorably. One of which was that, being the frugal man that he was, he hadn't made the ceremony any more lavish than it needed to be. And while some spoke ill of him behind his back, accusing him of putting on an act, most of the old-dynasty emperors had failed to respect the boundaries of the proscenium.

"You must be tired, Father," came a soft voice.

Count von Mariendorf turned to see standing there the only person who could rightly call him father. She offered him a wineglass.

"Not at all, Hilda, I'm fine. Although at this rate, I'm sure to rest easy tonight."

Count von Mariendorf thanked her and accepted the wineglass. He clinked glasses with his daughter, enjoying the crystalline tone, and took his time to savor the crimson nectar on his tongue.

"A fine vintage. From the year 410, I'd guess."

Hilda had little interest in such useless details and cut her father off before he started lecturing her on the merits of good wine. Hilda had always been indifferent to the cultural refinements about which a noble daughter was supposed to have knowledge—not only in regard to wine, but also gemstones and horse racing, flowers and haute couture. As far as she was concerned, knowing there were already experts on the subjects of wine and gemstones, she felt it better to leave such matters to those best qualified and to know which experts she could rely on when their knowledge was required. She'd known this ever since she was a little girl of not yet ten. Hilda was singled out for being a tomboy and was a social outcast among the other daughters of nobility with whom she sometimes interacted. In response to her father's worries, she declared with melodramatic elegance that she didn't care about being girlish, preferring instead to read books and take walks in the fields. One might have said that her present status of chief imperial secretary was the culmination of those childhood tendencies. Either way, she seemed born to occupy her current station.

"Which reminds me—about Heinrich. He's in bad health, as you know, and couldn't put in an appearance at the ceremony. But he was hoping His Majesty might honor him with a visit, if at all possible. How about it? Would you be willing to inquire of His Majesty on my behalf?"

Upon hearing the name of her feeble cousin, head of the Baron von Kümmel family, a gentle pall swept over Hilda's lively eyes. He'd once voiced his envy of Reinhard. But it wasn't Reinhard's abilities he so desperately wanted; it was his health. When she heard him say this, Hilda hesitated to chide him for such an immodest comment, as she normally would have done. She could understand the sentiments of Heinrich, whom she'd come to think of as a younger brother, but—and maybe it was cruel to say this—even if he'd been of sound health, he wouldn't necessarily have been able to accomplish as much as Reinhard. Heinrich had exceeded the limits of his abilities, and his body, long ago. And so, without a wick to burn, his inner flame had faded into a mere flicker over the years. It was only natural that he should curse his own infirmity and be jealous of the good health of others.

"Of course," answered Hilda. "I can't guarantee anything, but if it means that much to Heinrich, I'll see what I can do."

Both Hilda and her father knew Heinrich didn't have much longer to live. And even if it was somewhat selfish of him to make such a request, who were they do deny it?

And so, the seed was planted for the Kümmel Incident, which would capture widespread attention immediately following the new emperor's coronation.

II

Reinhard's coronation took place on June 22. At Hilda and her father's insistence, he paid a visit to the residence of Heinrich von Kümmel on July 6. During the interim, the young new emperor threw himself diligently into governmental affairs without rest, putting his administrative abilities to the ultimate test.

Reinhard's merits had often been compared favorably to those of Yang Wen-li on the military front, but he far surpassed the drive of his nemesis when it came to work ethic. With a decadence others might have poured into self-indulgences, and still without an heir, the golden-haired emperor followed his own honor code. And while his was an autocratic administration, his virtuousness, efficiency, and sense of justice set him apart from his Goldenbaum Dynasty predecessors. He had liberated the populace from the burden of having to pay exorbitant taxes to fund the extravagances of the nobility.

The following ten cabinet members were placed under Reinhard.

Secretary of State: Count von Mariendorf

Secretary of Defense: Marshal von Oberstein

Secretary of Finance: Richter

Secretary of the Interior: Osmayer

Secretary of Justice: Bruckdorf

Secretary of Civil Affairs: Bracke

Secretary of Works: von Silberberg

Secretary of Arts and Culture: Dr. Seefeld

Secretary of the Imperial Household: Baron Bernheim

Chief Cabinet Secretary: Meinhof

Without a prime minister in place, the emperor was the highest executive officer by default. This meant that, with Reinhard as emperor, the conquered universe was now under a system of direct imperial rule. Reinhard had abolished the former Ministry of Ceremonial Affairs—a government office that regulated the interests of the high nobles, investigated family backgrounds, and approved marriages and successions under the old empire—and established the Ministry of Civil Affairs and Ministry of Works in its place.

The Ministry of Works had its cogs in many machines, including interstellar transportation and communications, resource development, civilian spaceships and production of raw materials, as well as construction of cities, mining and manufacturing plants, transportation bases, and development bases. It also oversaw imperial economic reform and was granted the important function of maintaining social capital. A highly talented individual possessed of political acumen, managerial experience, and organizational skills was necessary to keep it all running smoothly. The thirty-three-year-old secretary of works, Bruno von Silberberg, was of the confident opinion that he possessed two of these qualities, but he had also been given another informal, yet no less important, title: Secretary of Imperial Capital Construction. In that capacity, he was to oversee Emperor Reinhard's secret plans to relocate the capital to the planet of Phezzan. In the future, he would annex all Free Planets Alliance territory and, once he'd doubled the empire's possessions, realize his plan of refashioning Phezzan as center stage of a new era of universal rule.

Compared to mobilizing grand armies across a vast ocean of stars and wielding his omnipotence to vanquish a formidable enemy, handling internal affairs was a set of simple, prosaic tasks. If foreign campaigns were Reinhard's privilege, then domestic matters were an uncreative duty. And yet, the young, elegant emperor never neglected the obligations incumbent in his position and authority. In Reinhard's estimation, even the smallest task was as important as the larger machinations that had brought him to this point.

According to one future historian, Reinhard's diligence as a politician arose from his guilty conscience as a usurper. Nothing could be further from the truth. Reinhard never felt that his usurpations constituted a lapse in his personal morality. He wasn't so deluded as to believe that the power and glory he'd hijacked from the Goldenbaum Dynasty were eternal. Neither had anyone ever guaranteed them to be. And while he'd never studied history with anything approaching the zeal of his rival Yang Wen-li, he knew that every dynasty ever birthed by human society had been conquered and overtaken, but that he was the atypical child who had destroyed the womb of order that predicated his existence. To be sure, he *had* hijacked the Goldenbaum Dynasty. But wasn't its very founder, Rudolf the Great, himself a deformed child who'd compromised the Galactic Federation of States, sucked millions dry of their blood, and forced his way to the top? Who had ever imagined that the intention of the emperor alone could produce an interstellar autocratic regime with enough military power to enforce it? Even Rudolf the Great, who'd walked his own path of self-deification, couldn't cheat death. The time had come for his magnum opus, the Goldenbaum Dynasty, to expire, and for a new volume to be written in its place.

Reinhard wasn't so immature as to ignore the gravity of his sinful deeds. Likewise, he could find no justification for the Goldenbaum Dynasty's actions. Others both living and dead had provoked in him an acute mixture of regret and self-admonishment.

On July 1, as early summer transitioned to the heights of the season, Secretary of State Franz von Mariendorf came to seek an audience with the young emperor. Count von Mariendorf thought himself unworthy of being a cabinet minister in the government of such a vast interstellar empire. Since the former dynasty, he'd never harbored a single political ambition. He reliably managed the estates of both the Mariendorf and Kümmel families, stayed clear of political strife and war, and tried his best to live a frugal life. He had no intentions of cozying up to power or status just to advance his reputation.

From where Reinhard stood, the new dynasty was under his direct rule. This meant that his cabinet ministers were no more than assistants, and so there was no need for someone so prodigious as a chief cabinet minister to aid him. Keeping as low a profile as he could, Count von Mariendorf devoted himself to coordinating the other cabinet ministers, while managing ceremonies and other organizational tasks at just the right level of involvement. Moreover, he was known as a man of honest virtue. As manager of the Kümmel family fortune, he could easily have embezzled those assets if he'd wanted to. Many such precedents filled the pages in the reference room of the old minister of ceremonies. Nevertheless, when Heinrich had inherited the family fortune at seventeen, it hadn't decreased one bit. In that same period, the Mariendorf family assets had in fact *decreased* slightly due to a heavy water mine accident. The count's impartiality was therefore never in doubt. As one fully aware of his daughter's abilities, he had developed her strong points. These were just some of the reasons that he'd been given the position he presently held.

What Count von Mariendorf had come to say caught Reinhard slightly off guard. After bowing deeply, the secretary of state asked the young emperor whether he had any intention of getting married.

"Married, you say?"

"Yes. Getting married, producing an heir, and with that heir determining the succession of your throne. It's your sovereign duty, after all."

Reinhard couldn't doubt it was a sound, if artless, argument. He preceded his response with a brief overture of silence.

"I don't intend to. At least not for now. I have too much else to do before I can even think of having a child."

His words were fall-off-the-bone tender, but the gristle of their rejection was ten thousand times tougher to chew. Count von Mariendorf bowed in silence. To him it was enough that he'd aroused discretion in the young emperor toward the social custom of marriage and that he'd affirmed its significance in securing the future of the throne. He knew better than to make too much of it, lest he incite the emperor's violent temper.

Count von Mariendorf changed the subject to his cousin Baron von Kümmel, a man without much time left to live—his health had been deteriorating for a long time—and who desired the once-in-a-lifetime honor of receiving an imperial visit at his home. With uncanny grace, Reinhard titled his golden head slightly, then nodded in assent.

Count von Mariendorf was pleased and took his leave to confront the next ordeal. Just before the regular cabinet meeting commenced at two o'clock, secretary of defense Marshal von Oberstein broached the subject with him.

"I understand you encouraged His Majesty to get married. If I might be so bold, what was your intention in doing so?"

The meek secretary of state could give no immediate reply. Count von Mariendorf knew the artificial-eyed secretary of defense wasn't a spiteful man, but he also knew that nothing escaped him and that it would be futile to hide anything from him. Von Mariendorf was still on his guard. He chose his words carefully and steeled his expression.

"His Majesty is only twenty-three years old. I know there's no need for someone so young to rush into marriage, but it's only natural that he should get married, if only to ensure the imperial line of succession. I thought it prudent to at least suggest a few potential candidates to be his empress."

Count von Mariendorf thought he noted a strange flicker in the secretary of defense's artificial eyes.

"I see. And would your daughter happen to be first on that list of candidates?"

Marshal von Oberstein's tone planted not a stinger but an icicle. Von Mariendorf felt the temperature around him lower to that of early spring. The secretary of defense's words were serious enough as a joke, but even more serious if meant in earnest. Gathering his wits, the count acted as if taking it in jest.

"No, my daughter is too strong-willed in her independence and self-sufficiency for a position like that. She's not one to put on the airs of a noblewoman, nor to seclude herself subserviently at court. My daughter is well-versed in many things, but I sometimes worry whether she's aware of even being a woman."

Von Oberstein didn't smile but nevertheless laid down his arms.

"Our secretary of state is a man of good sense."

Von Mariendorf breathed a sigh of relief.

Hilda recapped the situation when her father returned home.

"The secretary of defense is warning us not to deceive His Majesty or monopolize his political sovereignty. Whether his worries come from a place of genuine concern is of little consequence to me."

"The whole thing is absurd."

The count was discouraged. He had no intention of opposing the secretary of defense for the mere sake of gaining arbitrary political influence over the emperor. Furthermore, it was hard to imagine Reinhard as his daughter's husband, given the emperor's distant demeanor. In Franz von Mariendorf's reckoning, Emperor Reinhard was a great child prodigy, but being a genius didn't mean he had a higher capacity for emotion than everyday people. Of course, he possessed just such emotional energy, only it was unevenly distributed away from matters of love. As when tilting a water-filled cup, when one part reached the brim, the other receded from it. As in the famous anecdote of the ancient astronomer who accidentally fell down a well while looking up at the sky to study the movements of the stars, that receding end revealed itself on a daily level. And when it came to sexual love, Reinhard was at the very least an enigma.

As Viscount Albrecht von Bruckner, author of *The Galactic Empire: A Prehistory*, expressed it: "If you banished all the perverts and homosexuals from history and the arts, human culture would never have advanced to such a degree." But Reinhard simply lacked experience with intimacy, which was almost as worrisome to a sensible man like the count, who wanted nothing less for his daughter than a man who was ordinary, virtuous, and forthcoming. Then again, if Hilda wanted to get married…

"Anyway, Hilda, considering how blessed we've been by the emperor's good favor, we mustn't forget to keep our professional and personal lives separate. As the saying goes, there are as many seeds of misunderstanding as there are people."

Even to his intelligent and vivacious daughter, Count von Mariendorf was a typical father who knew she would do whatever she wanted regardless of what he said.

"Yes, I understand," said Hilda, if only to ease this confrontation with her mild-mannered father. In her mind, the conversation had already been over before it had even begun.

Her feelings for Reinhard and Reinhard's feelings for her were impossible to parse. For while certainly there was no hatred or disgust between them, there was a vast distance between "not hating" and "loving" someone, and there were limitless bands in the spectrum of good graces. Her weak point, and perhaps Reinhard's as well, was in trying to interpret through reason that which was based on anything but.

Hilda knew why Reinhard had agreed to pay a visit to the Kümmel household. Such a visit required careful political consideration. In the past, any emperor worth his crown would have thought twice before calling upon the residence of a rival minister for the first time, as many had before him. Such precedents were laughable to Reinhard. But the fact that Baron Heinrich von Kümmel was not one of Reinhard's meritorious, or even favored, retainers worked in the young emperor's favor. The golden-haired tyrant held the customs and propriety of the Goldenbaum Dynasty in utmost contempt, and so the idea of honoring an infirm member of the old nobility with an imperial visit intrigued him, if anything, as a way of rubbing the old system's nose in its own accident.

III

On that day, July 6, Emperor Reinhard visited the estate of Baron von Kümmel with sixteen attendants in tow. These included Hildegard von Mariendorf, Reinhard's private secretary and cousin to the Kümmel family patriarch; senior imperial aide Vice Admiral von Streit; secondary aide Lieutenant von Rücke; head of the imperial guard Commodore Kissling; and four chamberlains and bodyguards besides.

If you asked any of his subordinates, they would have told you that anyone ruling over the entire universe required a far stricter level of protection worthy of his status—an entourage of over one hundred, at least. When the old official responsible for court ceremonies, a man who'd served the Goldenbaum Dynasty for four decades, had suggested honoring that precedent, Reinhard's response had been curt:

"I have no intention of following any precedent established by the Goldenbaum Dynasty."

To Reinhard, even sixteen was going overboard. He preferred to be as casual as possible, on occasion even acting alone, inspiring one future historian to believe that Emperor Reinhard had a body double.

In truth, no one knew for sure, although one of his retainers did, in fact, once advise the use of a body double. As "Artist-Admiral" Mecklinger recorded it in a memo, Reinhard was none too happy with the suggestion:

"Is it not enough to look out for myself? Were I to come down with any serious illness, does that mean my double would be taken to the hospital instead of me? Don't ever suggest such a foolish thing to me again."

Miliary police commissioner Senior Admiral Kessler had left a like-minded memo, so it was assumed that either, if not both, of them had proposed the idea.

"To the emperor," noted Mecklinger, "the idea of going to any great lengths to ensure his personal safety is absurd. Whether out of confidence, overestimation of his own abilities, or philosophical resignation is anyone's guess."

Mecklinger knew when and where to draw the line between faith and respect. He admired Reinhard all the same and devoted himself fully to his cause, even as he kept a sharp eye on this once-in-a-generation character. Some part of his brain knew that at the head of the empire was someone who could conquer the universe as far as human hands could reach.

Baron von Kümmel's residence was unremarkable. His lineage boasted no outstanding rulers, idiosyncratic geniuses, or eccentric libertines and had hardly fluctuated in terms of status or assets since the reign of Rudolf the Great. And while the estate had been annexed and renovated numerous times over the past five centuries and was now nestled comfortably in a protective barrier of hedges and moats, no one had any interest in its avant-garde architecture now that old-fashioned conventions had made a comeback. That said, the property was grand enough to fit three hundred ordinary houses, and despite its lack of individuality, its modestly arranged greenery gave it a charm all its own.

Those who knew the head of the estate, however, could sense a certain vitality hidden behind it all. To all appearances, Master Heinrich, tenth-generation baron of the Kümmel family, was an even-keeled personality. This year he would turn nineteen. When he had been taken from his mother's womb after a difficult delivery, they had both been suffering from a congenital metabolic disorder. And so, even as he grew older, he was dying a slow death more than living. Had he been born to a common family, he wouldn't have made it past his first year. The procedure by which his inferior genes had been removed had rendered him a mere shell, but such drastic measure had been the only way to save his life.

Even had he been moderately healthy, it wasn't as if all the elegant young noblewomen would be lining up at his door, either. For while he was graceful enough in his features, Heinrich was of meager build and his blood was too thin. He ate not because he enjoyed it, but only to supply himself with enough energy to get through each day. As a result, he always weighed dietary considerations over taste. He existed only to prolong his life, like the watered-down gruel he often ate.

Despite enormous efforts, that diluted gruel had been reduced to little more than hot water. His personal mantra—"It won't be much longer"—seemed closer than ever to fulfilment. Knowing this, both Count von Mariendorf and Hilda had entreated the emperor to grant Heinrich's dying wish.

When the emperor's party passed through the gates of the Kümmel estate, the baron himself came out to greet him in his electric wheelchair, much to everyone's surprise. Heinrich's complexion was pallid, but his hair and clothing had been arranged to appear presentable. He locked eyes with Hilda, giving her the briefest of smiles, then bowed his head to Reinhard.

"I am moved beyond measure that Your Majesty graces my humble abode with his presence. Please consider this as much your home as it is mine. From this day forth, the Kümmel family name shall shine with unmerited glory."

Reinhard didn't care for excessive rhetoric but nodded coolly, saying only that he was glad to see Heinrich so happy and that his happiness was worth more than the most lavish welcome. Reinhard, too, could play the decorum game when he felt like it, and he was more than willing to oblige for Hilda's sake. In this case, a little mercy went a long way, and it was no skin off the back of his self-importance to give it. After his feeble greeting, Heinrich gave a short cough. Hilda bowed to the emperor and tended to her cousin.

"Don't overdo it, Heinrich, okay?"

Reinhard nodded with his natural grace.

"Fräulein von Mariendorf is right. I wouldn't want you to overextend yourself for my sake. Your health is paramount."

And yet, even as the young emperor offered these uncommon words of sympathy, a strange sensation ran through his veins. Was it just his guilty conscience as an able-bodied person? Or was it something more? It was the same feeling he got whenever he saw man-made points of light begin to fill the darkness of outer space on his battle screen. That feeling of going on the defensive. The calm before the storm.

Reinhard shook his head in imperceptible denial. There was no point in honoring intuition over reason here. His opponent was a half-dead invalid whose ambition and desire for power registered nowhere on destiny's radar.

"Please, do come inside. I've had a modest lunch prepared for us."

Riding his electric wheelchair, Heinrich showed his guests around the premises. A garden path of flagstones wound through a cypress forest. Although it was July, the imperial capital was spared the heat and humidity of the tropical zones, and so even Heinrich's modest landscaping gave the impression of being in another world. After walking some distance, a slight evaporation of sweat left their skin feeling pleasantly cooled.

They emerged from the forest at the rear of the estate, where the flagstones broadened into an open courtyard measuring twenty meters per side and nestled in the shade of two old elms. A meal was waiting for them on a marble table. The servants withdrew upon the party's arrival. Once everyone took their seats, the scene took on an unexpectedly different air as their humble young host stretched his back and flashed an ominous smile.

"A splendid courtyard, don't you think, Hilda?"

"That it is, Heinrich."

"Truth be told, Hilda has been here before. What she doesn't know is that there's an underground chamber right below us. It's filled with Seffl particles, ready at my command to welcome His Majesty into the underworld where he belongs."

And in that moment, everything went blank. Hearing the name of that extremely dangerous explosive chemical substance, Commodore Kissling's topaz eyes filled with dread as he reached for his holstered blaster. The other bodyguards followed suit.

"There, there, gentlemen. To Your Majesty, universal sovereign, unifier of all humanity. Born into a poor family, noble only in name, you who rose precipitously to the throne as the paragon of our age. And to you, his loyal subjects. I say this: unless you want this detonator switch to be pressed, I suggest you stay right where you are."

The young baron's tone was zealous yet lacking in strength, and so it took some a few moments to realize the gravity of what he'd just said. But the dangerousness of the situation was clear. They were all sitting over a bomb just waiting to go off. Hilda's voice shook off the silence, thick like molasses.

"Heinrich, you…"

"My dear Hilda. I never meant for you to get involved in this. Had it been possible, I wouldn't have wanted you to accompany the emperor. But now, even if I were to let you, and only you, get out of here alive, I don't think you'd comply, would you? My uncle will be much aggrieved, but it's too late to do anything about it now."

Heinrich's speech was interrupted several times by painful coughing fits. Commodore Kissling's team of bodyguards knew better than to try anything a second time, for the young baron's fist gripped the detonator switch as if it were an extension of his body, and they weren't about to lay down the emperor's life like a chip on a roulette table when the odds were stacked against them. Listening to the gasps of an invalid who they could probably kill with one pinkie, they stood stock-still in an invisible cage of helplessness, waiting to see what he would do next.

"I think the baron has something to say," whispered von Streit. "Let him speak all he wants. It'll buy us some time."

To this, Kissling and von Rücke nodded slightly, their expressions hard as rocks. Provoking this young man, who had every intention of assassinating the emperor, would only lead to the incineration of the Lohengramm Dynasty's figurehead, along with his attendants, in an instant. Heinrich held their lives in his hand, and it was all they could do to loosen his grip.

"What's on your mind, Your Majesty?"

Reinhard, who until then had been sitting without a word, lifted his shapely eyebrows in response to Heinrich's derisive smile.

"If I should die by your hand here, then that is a fate I shall have to accept. I regret nothing."

The young emperor, showing signs of heartfelt cynicism, curled his graceful lips into a glyph of self-derision.

"It's been only two weeks since my coronation. I doubt there has ever been a dynasty as short as mine. Not exactly what I'd hoped for, but your brazen act will immortalize my name in history. A disgraceful name, perhaps, but who am I to care about its future value? I don't even care to know your reasons for killing me."

A glint of enmity welled up in the invalid's eyes. Seeing the trembling in his almost colorless lips, Hilda withdrew into her shell. In that moment, she had accurately discerned her cousin's intent. Heinrich wanted Reinhard to beg for his life. If only the absolute ruler of the entire universe would kneel before him and appeal for clemency, then Heinrich could at last vent the humiliating powerlessness that had come to define him. And with that, he'd relinquish the detonator switch with blind satisfaction.

But in the same way that Heinrich could never be free from his frail body, neither could Reinhard be free from his fame and self-respect. As Reinhard had said when meeting face-to-face with Admiral Yang Wen-li of the Free Planets Alliance, he wanted the power to get on without following the orders of someone he despised. For Reinhard to regret his life and beg his intimidator for mercy now would negate every step he'd taken along the path to getting here. And when that happened, there were several people to whom he'd never be able to show his face again. People who'd protected his life at the expense of their own. People who'd loved him even when he lived in the depths of poverty.

"Heinrich, please. It's not too late. Just hand me the switch." Hilda demanded his concession, if only to buy some time, regardless of outcome.

"Ah, Hilda, even you get riled up now and then. To me, you were always so graceful under pressure, overflowing with radiant vitality. But now, seeing that darkened expression of yours, I must say I'm a little disappointed."

Heinrich laughed. Hilda keenly sensed that the pilot light barely keeping her cousin warm had been malice all along. There seemed to be no way out of this. Unable to look her cousin in his overzealous eyes, Hilda averted her own and held her breath. Commodore Kissling, whose topaz eyes and unusual gait had earned him nicknames such as "Cat" and "Panther," was slowly moving from his original position.

"I said, don't move!"

Heinrich's voice, expelled as if on cue, was neither loud nor forceful, but it exposed a vein of fury in the air all the same, and so its impact was enough to keep Kissling's daring spontaneity in check.

"Stay right where you are, for a few more minutes. Allow me the pleasure of holding the universe in my hands for just another moment or two."

Kissling implored Hilda with his eyes, but she ignored him.

"I've lived my whole life for these few minutes. Actually, that's not true. It's why I've held off death for so long. Let me keep it at bay just a little longer."

When Reinhard heard this, his ice-blue eyes glistened, filled with an emotion that was neither compassion nor anger.

Hilda noticed his fingers fondling the silver pendant hanging on his chest and found herself wondering, inappropriately enough under the circumstances, what was inside it. It had to be something of great importance.

IV

Senior Admiral Ulrich Kessler served as both commissioner of military police and commander of capital defenses. Either job was exhausting in and of itself. To take on both, even without the birth of the new dynasty, would have been nearly impossible for one man alone.

The fact that Kessler had enough presence of mind and body to withstand this double duty only confirmed his worth.

On the morning of July 6, in his office at headquarters, he met with a few guests, but it was the unexpected fourth who brought the most important business. Job Trünicht, a gentleman in the prime of his life who'd been the leader of the Free Planets Alliance until just last month, had sold his sovereignty to Reinhard and taken up residence within the empire as a means of ensuring his own safety. The information he brought was shocking.

"There's plot to assassinate His Majesty the Emperor being carried out as we speak."

The military police commissioner tried to keep calm, yet his eyes gleamed sharply, betraying their master's intentions. Even while commanding fleets in outer space, his eyes hadn't quivered in the slightest. But this was different, as every fiber of his being was loudly attesting.

"And how did you come by this knowledge?"

"Surely Your Excellency is aware of the religious organization known as the Church of Terra. I've dealt with them on occasion under the auspices of my former position. That's when I learned of a conspiracy being hatched within their ranks. They threatened to kill me if I informed anyone, but my loyalty to His Majesty—"

"I understand."

Kessler's reply was not at all polite. Like his admirals in arms, he cared little for the defeatist standing before him. Everything that came out of Trünicht's mouth reeked of a strong poison that made people hate him wherever he went.

"And the assassin's name?" the military police commissioner asked, to which the former Free Planets Alliance prime minister answered solemnly.

Trünicht made it a point to insist that he'd never once agreed with the tenets of the Church of Terra and that the one time he had cooperated with the church had been because the situation had forced his hand, not because he'd wished to. Kessler had heard all he needed to hear and barked an order to one of his men.

"Take Mr. Trünicht to conference room number two. He is not to leave that room until we get to the bottom of this. Do *not*, under any circumstances, let anyone near him."

Trünicht was placed under temporary house arrest under the pretense of his needing protection.

By the time Kessler acted, his informant no longer mattered. Kessler cared only about feeding himself, and there was no use for a dish once the meal was finished.

Kessler first rang the Kümmel residence on the visiphone, then Vice Admiral von Streit and Commodore Kissling, but couldn't get through to any of them. The reason was clear.

Even as the military police commissioner ground his teeth, he wasted no time in contacting his regiment nearest the Kümmel estate. The commanding officer was one Commodore Paumann, a former armed grenadier with plenty of battle experience for his young age. Kessler had more faith in those who fought bravely in battle than in trueborn military police. Although he himself fit the latter bill to a T, practically speaking, not even the finest police investigator or interrogator was going to help him in this case. What he needed was a battle commander.

Upon receiving his orders, Paumann was nervous but not upset. He jumped into action, ordering all 2,400 armed officers in his jurisdiction to the Kümmel estate at once. It was a textbook covert operation. He forbade the use of armored vehicles, knowing that the sound of their engines would give them away before they even arrived. The military policemen ran in their stocking feet to the Kümmel estate, carrying their laser rifles in one hand and their military boots in the other. Some would laugh back on it the next day, but in the heat of the moment their actions were anything but humorous as they surrounded the compound.

Kessler's plan didn't end there.

The 1,600-strong military police regiment under Commodore Raft raided the Church of Terra chantry house at 19 Cassel Street, rounding up all the believers they could find on-site. These weren't pacifists, however, and instead of surrendering, they immediately welcomed the military police who stormed their building by opening fire.

Commodore Raft ordered his men to return fire. Prismatic beams shot out in all directions. It was a brutal, if short-lived, shoot-out. Ten minutes later, Raft's men had made their way to the top floor, shooting anyone who stood in their way. At just past noon, they'd gained total control of the six-story building. Ninety-six believers were killed on the scene, fourteen died later of their injuries, twenty-eight committed suicide, and the fifty-two survivors, suffering from a variety of wounds, were arrested. No one escaped. On the military police side, eighteen were dead and forty-two wounded. Sect leader Archbishop Godwin had just been attempting to kill himself by drinking poison when a military police officer burst into the room and struck him with the butt of his gun. Godwin was placed in electromagnetic handcuffs and dragged unconscious from the scene, a failure at his own martyrdom.

The military police officers, still stoked by bloodlust, scoured the interior of the crimson-splattered building to gather any evidence that might prove the insurgents' complicity in plotting the emperor's assassination. They removed fragments of documents from the ashes of an incinerator, stripped corpses naked, pulled out pockets sticky with blood, kicked over altars, and tore up the floorboards, but turned up nothing. One of the wounded rebuked their blasphemous actions, only to be kicked to death by an officer in the back of the head where he'd been wounded.

As Commodore Raft's unit was performing its blood rite in one corner of the capital, the soldiers of Commodore Paumann's unit, having surrounded the Baron von Kümmel estate, put on their boots, awaiting their order to raid the compound. Those at the receiving end of that order could only comply, but the responsibility of the one giving it was immense. Their emperor's life was poised on the tip of Paumann's tongue.

Those whose lives hung in the balance of all this mobilization noticed a shift in their surroundings. A soundless stirring of the air brushed across their skin and stimulated their neural networks. After playing a quick game of catch with each other's gazes, they all shared the same thought—something that was impossible for someone like Heinrich, who'd never once experienced combat, to perceive. Help was on the way. Now all they needed to do was stall for time.

Heinrich's perception was focused on two things. First, the Seffl particle detonator switch in his hand, and second, the silver pendant that Reinhard kept fondling like a talisman.

Reinhard was moving his hand unconsciously. Or if it *was* conscious, then it was surely to provoke the needless caution of this would-be assassin. This made Heinrich even more interested in the pendant.

Hilda was also aware of this dangerous cycle but was helpless to do anything about it. Any interruption on her part might be impetus enough for Heinrich to put his sick curiosity into action.

Heinrich, after barely opening and closing his mouth a few times, broke the silence.

"Your Majesty, that pendant seems quite valuable to you. I would very much like to see it, and to touch it, if you would be so kind."

Reinhard's fingers froze. He fixed his gaze on Heinrich's face. Hilda trembled in fear, for she knew that her cousin had trodden his muddy feet into the emperor's inviolable sanctuary.

"Out of the question."

"I demand to see it."

"It's not yours to see."

"Just let him see it, Your Majesty," von Streit interjected.

"Your Majesty!" said Kissling simultaneously.

Both men knew their allies were closing in and saw no harm in buying themselves even a few more seconds by any means necessary. What was the point of angering Heinrich further with this childish resistance?

Reinhard clearly didn't share their views. The coolheaded, keen, and ambitious ruler his attendants all knew and served had disappeared, leaving in its place a man with the expression of a troubled boy. He was like a child desperately clinging to his toy box, which to the adults around him was filled with junk yet which he was convinced contained actual treasure.

In Hilda's eyes, Heinrich was now the real tyrant and would never tolerate this. Heinrich had crossed the line not only of her trust, but also of his own into boldest action.

"I'm the one holding the cards here. Or has His Majesty forgotten? Give it to me this instant. I will not ask you again."

"No."

Reinhard's obstinacy was hard to believe coming from a hero who'd crawled his way out of poverty as a young man with only a name to show for his nobility, only to become ruler of the greatest empire in history. Heinrich's irrational sentiments, it seemed, had been distorted and transferred over into Reinhard. Heinrich had a sudden fit, but his imbalanced passions erupted in an unexpected direction. His lifeless hand, which looked for all like a lab specimen fixed with formalin, reached out like a leaping snake and grabbed the emperor's pendant. Reinhard's graceful hand, which any artist would have desired as a model, struck the half-dead tyrant's cheek. Everyone's lungs and hearts ceased to function but went back online when the detonator switch flew from the Baron's hand and rolled across the flagstones. Kissling sprang at Heinrich, almost embarrassingly like a cat, and pinned him to the ground.

"Go easy on him!" Hilda shouted, by which time Kissling was already letting go of Heinrich's thin wrists. The baron's sickly frame had let out a crack that sent the topaz-eyed brave general into recoil. Feeling the aftertaste of having mustered far more violence than was necessary, Kissling left this traitor in the hands of his beautiful cousin. This was not Kissling's curtain call.

"Heinrich, you fool," whispered Hilda, cradling her cousin's weak body. It was all even someone of her intelligence and expressiveness could muster. Heinrich smiled. Not the malicious grin of moments before, but an almost pure smile, gilded by impending death.

"I wanted to do *something* before I died. No matter how evil or foolish it was. I wanted to do something before I died…that and nothing more."

Heinrich enunciated every word with strange clarity. He didn't ask for her forgiveness. Nor did Hilda demand that he beg for it.

"The von Kümmel barony dies with me. Not by infirmity, but because I acted so carelessly. My illness may soon be forgotten, but many will remember my foolishness."

After speaking his mind, the crater of Heinrich's life spewed its last glob of lava. His heart, abused by this one final act, was eternally released, and his veins changed from rivers of life to thin ponds.

Holding her dead cousin's face in her hands, Hilda shifted her gaze to Reinhard. The young emperor stood in silence, his luxurious golden locks fluttering in the summer breeze. His ice-blue eyes betrayed nothing of the raging sea within. He was still fingering the pendant with one hand.

Von Streit plucked the detonator switch from the stone, muttering something under his breath. Kissling shouted, announcing to their allies surrounding the mansion that the emperor was safe and sound. The silence was broken by a disturbance in the air as an unknown man jumped out in front of everyone—a straggler who'd fled from the Church of Terra raid and stolen into the compound. He locked his blaster on Reinhard, letting out a hostile roar. But von Rücke was one step ahead of him, shooting out a ray of light from his blaster. The man turned around as if his survival instinct had suddenly kicked in. Von Rücke pulled the trigger again, hitting the center of the man's back. The man threw up his arms like a sprinter leaping across the finish line, did a half turn, and fell headfirst into a thicket of common broom.

Three of von Rücke's personal bodyguards carefully dragged out the body. That's when von Rücke noticed the distinct embroidery on his clothing that would confirm his suspicions. He silently mouthed the words: *Terra is my home, Terra in my hand.*

"So he's one of those Church of Terra cultists?" whispered Vice Admiral von Streit from over his shoulder.

He of course knew the name of the religious organization that had somehow expanded its influence throughout both the empire and the alliance in recent years. There were also those who'd heard of Terra yet knew little of Earth.

Everyone was at least aware of Earth as the birthplace of all humankind and understood that it had once been the center of the known universe. It continued to revolve around its sun, but the meaning of its existence had been lost to a distant past. Hardly anyone mourned its loss. It was nothing more than a modest planet, forgotten—if not compelled to be vanquished from memory—in the frontier.

Soon enough, however, the name "Earth" would ring in people's ears to the accompaniment of an ominous elegy, as it was revealed to be a strategic base for an outrageous conspiracy to assassinate the emperor.

V

Upon returning to Neue Sans Souci, Emperor Reinhard had reverted to his usual dictatorial self, as if his life hadn't just been hanging in the balance of an invalid's hands. But because he never explained how his silver pendant had incited a most unforeseen turn of events, both Vice Admiral von Streit and Commodore Kissling felt a lack of closure. Hilda, at any rate, being related to a criminal who had engaged in a wanton act of high treason, was placed under house arrest.

Senior Admiral Kessler, who held concurrent posts as military police commissioner and commander of capital defenses, flagged Reinhard down in the corridors. Suppressing the surge of emotions swelling inside him, he formally congratulated Reinhard on his safe return and apologized for not knowing of Heinrich's intentions beforehand.

"Not at all. You did well. Did you not suppress the Church of Terra's headquarters where the plot was hatched? You've nothing to blame yourself for."

"Your magnanimity knows no bounds. Incidentally, Your Majesty, Baron von Kümmel may be dead, but he's still a criminal of the highest order and must be dealt with accordingly. How do you suggest we proceed from here?"

Reinhard shook his head slowly, causing his luxurious golden hair to sway attractively.

"Kessler, imagine you've just apprehended someone who put your life in danger. Do you punish the weapon he used to do it?"

It took a few moments for the military police commissioner to grasp what the young emperor had left unsaid. Namely, that no one was to charge Baron von Kümmel with a crime. Which meant, of course, that Hilda and Count von Mariendorf were to be exonerated. If anyone needed to be blamed and punished, it was the religious fanatics pulling strings from the shadows.

"I will interrogate the Church of Terra believers immediately, bring out the truth, and punish them as you see fit."

The young emperor nodded silently and turned away, looking through the reinforced window at the long-neglected garden. A feeling of disgust roared like a distant ocean deep inside him. Although he'd found great fulfillment in fighting to gain power for himself, there was no joy in continuing to fight to keep the power he already had. He spoke telepathically to his silver pendant: *How I enjoyed battling at your side against a worthy enemy! But now that I've become the mightiest ruler of all, I sometimes wish I could defeat myself. If only there were more great enemies. If only you'd lived just a little longer, then I might've satisfied my heart's desire. Isn't that right, Kircheis?*

The emperor's intentions were conveyed to the military police through Kessler. The fifty-two Church of Terra survivors were brought before military police, who were seething with loyalty to their emperor and a desire to avenge the attempt that had been made on his life. Kessler proceeded to dole out punishments so cruel that the surviving Terraists envied the dead. Kessler and his men could have gotten all the information they needed without resorting to a truth serum, but they wasted no time in using the strongest drugs at their disposal. One reason was that they were capital offenders, and the necessity of getting confessions was far more important than any concern for the well-being of those giving them. The other reason had to do with the tenacity of the Terra believers. It was as though they *craved* martyrdom, which only fueled the animosity of their interrogators. Such fanaticism provoked only revulsion in those outside their faith.

During one such interrogation session, a doctor was hesitant to administer the full dose and cowered at the officers' harsh words.

"You're worried they'll go crazy? It's a little late for that, don't you think? This lot has been crazy from the beginning. These drugs might just bring them back to normal."

In the interrogation room, five levels below military police headquarters, the amount of blood spilled far exceeded the amount of information retrieved to show for it. The Church of Terra sect established on the planet Odin had only carried out the plot, and had neither given nor drafted the order.

The chief offender, Archbishop Godwin, after failing to bite off his own tongue, was injected with a copious amount of truth serum. He gave up nothing at first, much to the doctor's amazement. After the second injection, cracks appeared in his mental levees, and little by little information began trickling out. Still, even he could only guess as to why he'd been ordered to assassinate the emperor at this point in time.

"As time goes by, the foundation of that golden brat's power will only grow stronger. He may reject his ostentation as supreme ruler, value simplicity, and try to take down the barrier between subjects and citizens, but he will eventually brandish his power and make lavish use of his entourage, of that you can be sure. We'll never get a chance like this again."

"Blond brat" was a term only Emperor Reinhard's opponents used to curse him. Those words alone were enough to convict Archbishop Godwin of lèse-majesté. In the end, however, he wasn't judged in a courtroom. After receiving his sixth injection of truth serum, he bashed his head against the ceiling and walls of the interrogation room, muttering incoherently, until he died, bleeding from every orifice.

The severity of this interrogation left no doubt about the truth. The Church of Terra had committed high treason. The only option was to make the church acutely aware of the nature of its offense.

"But where's the Church of Terra's motive? I'm still baffled as to why they would aim to murder Your Majesty."

This was a doubt felt not only by Kessler, but by all chief statesmen who knew of the incident. For all their discernment, the dreams of fanatics were impossible to divine with only limited truths as their dowsing rods.

Until now, Emperor Reinhard had always had more apathy than tolerance for religion. Naturally, he could no longer remain indifferent about the Odin sect, which, regardless of goals or methods, had a mind to disavow his very existence. He'd never failed to reward his enemies with more retribution than they deserved. The only reason he'd been so generous this time around was another matter altogether—one left for his private consideration only.

Among Reinhard's subordinates, anger and hatred toward the Church of Terra was much more violent among civil officials than soldiers. Foreign campaigns had come to a standstill because of his control of Phezzan and the Free Planets Alliance's surrender. And while the age of civil officials had arrived and that of the military had been eclipsed, if the new emperor were to be overthrown by terrorism now, the entire universe would spiral into conflict and chaos, and the guardian of universal order would be lost to them forever.

And so, on July 10, an imperial council was convened, even as the fate of Earth, or at least that of the church, was losing its grip on the future.

CHAPTER 2:
PORTRAIT OF A CERTAIN PENSIONER

I

WHILE THIS BLOODY INTERMEZZO was reverberating around Emperor Reinhard's person, in the Free Planets Alliance capital of Heinessen, now a protectorate of the Galactic Empire, "Miracle" Yang Wen-li was living out the pensioner's lifestyle he'd always wanted. Or so it seemed.

Even though he was exalted as Emperor Reinhard's most worthy opponent, Yang had never once, from the beginning of his life, desired to be a military man. He'd only enrolled in the Officers' Academy in the first place because the tuition had been free and it had offered courses in his true interest, history. Since the moment he'd first put on his uniform, he'd been pining for a chance to take it off. After pulling off the unthinkable El Facil Evacuation eleven years back, one medal and promotion after another had made the uniform heavier. And now, at the age of thirty-two, he had finally been able to retire.

Yang's pension, as befitting his status, was an atonement for the many allies and many more enemies whose blood had been shed under his watch. The very notion pierced his soul, and it was all he could do to put himself at ease now that his desire from twelve years ago had been granted at last. Yang brazenly left behind memos to that effect: *The thought of getting paid for nothing is almost shameful. On the other hand, getting paid for not killing people seems like a more proper way to live, or at least a happier one.* But any historians biased against him ignored these sentiments.

Commodore at twenty-eight, admiral at twenty-nine, and now marshal at thirty-two. Under more peaceful conditions, these achievements would have seemed like the daydream of a mental patient. To him, being called the alliance's greatest, most resourceful general alive was nothing short of history's greatest misappropriation of adjectives. Nearly all the alliance's military successes over the past three years had been pulled from his black beret like the magician's proverbial rabbit. That the alliance itself had bowed to the empire didn't necessarily work to his advantage, and so he couldn't help but fret over this historic turn of events.

Immediately after his retirement, Yang got married and set up house on June 10 of that year. His bride was twenty-five-year-old Frederica Greenhill, who'd worked as Yang's aide while on active duty, ranked lieutenant commander. She was a beautiful woman with golden-brown hair and hazel eyes and had been only fourteen years old during the escape from El Facil. She had never forgotten that seemingly inept black-haired sublieutenant, now an intergral part of her reality. Yang had known how she felt about him but only this year had felt emboldened to reciprocate. Even then, their signals had gotten crossed more than Frederica would've liked.

The wedding was a modest affair. The main reason behind this choice was that Yang hated lavish ceremonies. He was also worried that an extravagant wedding would appear to be an ideal pretext for former alliance leaders to congregate and hatch some dire plot. Arousing the Imperial Navy's suspicion at this point would be extremely unwise.

Any big to-do would also necessitate inviting domestic and foreign bigwigs, which meant that Yang would need to endure drawn-out speeches from people whose company he didn't particularly enjoy. Worst of all, he would have to invite the galactic imperial commissioners and others who now held high positions in the alliance government. All of this was more trouble than it was worth.

As a result, among Yang's old subordinates, of those still on active duty, he invited only Vice Admiral Alex Caselnes. The rest were all retired and in hiding on Yang's orders.

On the day of the ceremony, his bride looked unbelievably beautiful. Yang, as ever, looked like an immature scholar, despite the great pains he'd taken with his uniform, and his closest allies took every opportunity to remind him of that.

"A regular princess and the pauper," chided Caselnes in response to Yang's grumbling over his tuxedo. "If only you'd bitten the bullet sooner, you might've gotten by just fine with your military uniform, like me. Looking at you now, I'd say the uniform suits you better after all."

Even in uniform, Yang somehow looked more like a boy than a soldier, and so he didn't think it made any difference in the end.

Vice Admiral Walter von Schönkopf, former commander of the Rosen Ritter fleet and commander of fortress defenses at Iserlohn under Yang, mixed his own verbal cocktail of cynicism and regret: "You've escaped a military prison, only to march yourself into the cell block of marriage. You're an odd duck, Mr. Yang."

To which Caselnes responded, "Odd isn't the word. One week of married life has enlightened him to something he never learned in ten years of bachelorhood. I suspect he'll sire a great philosopher one day."

Yang's Officers' Academy lowerclassman, the retired Dusty Attenborough, agreed and threw his own meat into this roasting. "The way I see it, Yang got the best of the spoils of war in his new bride. Fitting for our 'Miracle Yang,' seeing as she lowered herself to his level and all."

Yang's ward, the seventeen-year-old Julian Mintz, shook his flaxen, longish-haired head to this round of criticism.

"Admiral, it amazes me that you could lead such people to victory. They're all backstabbers, if you ask me."

"How do you think I got to be this way in the first place?" quipped Yang, as only a person of character would do. "Resolve has to come from somewhere."

Those in attendance demanded that Yang and his bride kiss, and he approached her like a man on drunken legs. For just a moment, Julian flashed a pained expression at Frederica's vivacious, beautiful face. First, because he'd held a vague longing for her for quite some time. Second, because he would be leaving the planet Heinessen that very night to embark on his own new journey. And while the latter was by his own choice, it was only natural that his emotions should run rampant in his young heart once he was ten thousand light-years away from the people he loved. Any loneliness he'd ever felt before would now be magnified to cosmic levels.

Yang's interlocutors left after the wedding. Julian, too, bid his farewells to the newlyweds and took his leave of the young bride and groom before they set out for the lakes and marshes of their mountain honeymoon. After ten days in a secluded villa, they returned to begin their new life in a rented house on Fremont Street. Because Yang's prior residence, the house on Silverbridge Street, had been official military housing, naturally he'd had to move out when he'd retired.

Thus, Yang seemed to have turned the first page of his ideal life. But the reality of it was not as sweet as he'd imagined, for reasons of both his own and others' making.

Combining the pensions of Marshal Yang and Lieutenant Commander Frederica, although less than what would have been given to royalty and titled nobility, was enough to guarantee them more freedom of activity and material surplus than they knew what to do with. Even so, pensions were provided only when the government finances existed to do so, and in that regard the state of things was deteriorating beyond their control.

The alliance's new administration, of which João Lebello was prime minister, had been bankrupted by the war. Because of a security tax being loaned to the empire in accordance with the peace treaty, they needed to improve their financial situation toward funding the rebuilding effort. There was much to be done, but for now they were focusing on the short term. The administration expressed its determination for financial reform by restructuring the power system as follows:

Those holding public office faced average pay cuts of 12.5 percent, and Lebello himself relinquished 25 percent of his salary. Whereas before there'd been nothing but wind and rain outside Yang's window, now that the alliance had taken the scalpel of reduction to soldiers' pensions as well, that damp wind had crashed through the glass and chilled him to the bone.

A former marshal's pension cut was 22.5 percent, that of a former lieutenant commander 15 percent. Yang understood that this disparity reflected their ranks, but that did nothing to stop him from feeling that his ideal of getting paid without having to wage war had already been trampled on. He wasn't dead to money, but he'd never had the experience of having more money than he knew what to do with. Either way, he knew its worth well enough. Yang had never been one to work harder just to increase his earnings, and future historians were right in at least one respect when they described him as "someone who had no interest in making money."

Even so, putting their pensions together didn't guarantee the most comfortable life after all. But the fact that Yang's retirement had become oppressive had nothing to do with money, but rather with a certain unease lingering just beyond the surface of his new life.

The first signs were already appearing during their brief time in the mountains. Every time Yang went fishing for trout in the lake, threw wood into the fireplace to stave off the chill of high-elevation nights, or bought fresh milk from the local farmstead, he couldn't shake the feeling that someone was watching their every move.

II

In May of SE 799, year 490 of the old Imperial Calendar and year one of the New Imperial Calendar, the Bharat Peace Treaty was put into effect. In accordance with Article 7, the imperial high commissioner was to be stationed in the alliance capital. His duties were to negotiate and consult with the alliance government as proxy for the emperor, but his carrying out of inspections in accordance with the treaty gave him the power to interfere with domestic affairs, making him closer to a governor-general.

Helmut Lennenkamp's appointment to this important office was evaluated thusly by the man known as the "Artist-Admiral," Ernest Mecklinger.

"At the time of appointment, he was far from the worst choice. But over time, he has *become* the worst. Now everyone will suffer the consequences of this decision."

Helmut Lennenkamp was a sullen middle-aged man, his dignified mustache rather out of place among the rest of his features. But he was a sound tactician who'd racked up medals in all types of battles, and by all accounts lacked nothing when it came to organizing troops. He was, for a time, Reinhard's superior when Reinhard was lieutenant commander, and had an especial dislike for "that golden brat." Aware of this critique, Reinhard was magnanimous enough to make sure that Lennenkamp was treated fairly, to the extent that no one talked about him behind his back. His name was therefore included in the list of candidates drawn up by the Lohengramm Dynasty's founder, much to no one's surprise.

Lennenkamp was blessed with many virtues—among them loyalty, a sense of duty, diligence, impartiality, and discipline—and his subordinates relied on him with appropriate respect and trust. As the subject of a volume in a series of imperial commissioner biographies, he would've received much praise. But from anything other than a military perspective, his lack of Oskar von Reuentahl's flexibility and Wolfgang Mittermeier's open-mindedness, his tendency to chase helplessly after both his own virtues and the virtues of others, and the incompatibility of his temperament as a superior military man and a human being—all of this would need to be recorded as well.

Lennenkamp was backed by four battalions of armed grenadiers and twelve battalions of light infantry when he commandeered the high-class Hotel Shangri-La in the center of Heinessenpolis to set up his executive office. Although Admiral Steinmetz's grand fleet was holding down the Gandharva star system, being stationed in what had been enemy territory until just yesterday with that much military force was unimaginable for a coward.

"If those alliance bastards want to kill me, let them try," he'd said of the situation, raising his shoulders defiantly. "I'm not immortal, but in the unlikely event that I should die, then the alliance dies with me."

A "great military" was Lennenkamp's ideal, and for him it wasn't so far-fetched to think he might achieve it. He believed in superiors who had affection for their men, men who in turn respected their superiors, and comrades who trusted and helped one another without resorting to injustice or insubordination. Order, harmony, and discipline were his most cherished values. In a sense, he was an extreme militarist, one who would surely have counted himself a loyal follower of the Goldenbaum Dynasty's founder Rudolf the Great, had he been born in that time. Of course, he didn't have the inflated ego of a Rudolf von Goldenbaum, but Lennenkamp didn't use his lord as a mirror to see himself from an objective point of view.

On Lennenkamp's orders, Yang Wen-li was being surveilled by the Imperial Navy as a potential threat to national security.

Yang was increasingly irritated at having to report his destination and planned time of return every time they went out. Whether on active duty or retired, the government kept tabs on its highest-level officers. This was to be expected. And yet, the Imperial Navy had never given him any indication of being prison wardens. Rather, their surveillance was something the alliance government had suggested to the Imperial Navy. And while it was understandable that the alliance government would go to great lengths to keep such a close eye on Yang without giving the Imperial Navy any excuse for its interference, Yang wanted nothing more than for them to get it over with.

Yang complained to his new wife, wanting to know what pleasure they got out of tormenting a peaceful, harmless man like him, although anyone who knew the full score would never have bought into his claims of innocence. He'd supported Julian Mintz's trip to Earth, planned the escape of Admiral Merkatz and others banished from the empire, and had carried out not exactly *anti*-imperial but certainly *un*-imperial activities, and so it was bold of him to play the role of hapless prisoner.

On that point, Frederica kept silent. In her opinion, it was in his favor that he'd earned the suspicions of the Imperial Navy and compromised the position of the alliance government.

"In that case, go ahead and be as lazy as you want."

Yang nodded happily at his wife's advice. Living peacefully, quietly, and idly suited him just fine. Yang had every reason to enjoy his indolence.

And so, he began to spend each day lazily, even carelessly, quietly disregarding even the most obvious signs of surveillance.

One day, Captain Ratzel, in charge of monitoring Yang, gave a report to his superior.

"Marshal Yang lives a quiet life. I see no reason to believe he's stirring up anti-imperial sentiment of any kind."

Lennenkamp's response was cynical, to say the least:

"He has a beautiful bride and food on his table. I can't say I'm not jealous. An ideal life, wouldn't you say?"

Lennenkamp put a high value on hard work and serving one's country, and saw no merit in someone who'd once held important military office throwing the responsibility of defeat into a closet of forgetfulness and living out the rest of his life on a comfortable pension without a care in the world. A man of Lennenkamp's common sense and values couldn't wrap his head around Yang Wen-li. Something just didn't add up, and he was determined to get to the bottom of what he saw to be mysterious behavior.

Yang had forced Lennenkamp to swallow the bitter medicine of defeat on two occasions. If Yang had been a man possessed of any militaristic virtue, then Lennenkamp's chagrin might have been balanced by his respect for a superior enemy. But unfortunately for both parties, they were all too often opposite sides of the same coin, and so duty compelled Lennenkamp to keep one eye over his shoulder at all times.

To Lennenkamp, it was all camouflage. Yang Wen-li didn't seem the type to be content in living out the life of an idle pensioner until he was old and decrepit. Surely, in his heart, he was harboring a long-term plan to restore the alliance and overthrow the empire. His normal daily life was nothing more than a ruse to gloss over that fact.

Lennenkamp's opinions toward Yang were myopic, the viewpoints of a quintessential patriot soldier. Paradoxically enough, Lennenkamp had forced his way through the marshlands of his prejudice and the dense forest of his misunderstanding to reach the gates of truth, before which he now stood, his hands itching to push them open.

But his subordinate lacked his level of conviction. Either that, or he wasn't nearly as jaded. If Reinhard had made a mistake in choosing Lennenkamp, then Lennenkamp had made a mistake in choosing Ratzel. As the captain was monitoring Yang, he courteously delivered the following message:

"To Your Excellency, Marshal, this must come as an inconvenient and irritating development. But I am at the whim of my superior and, as a petty official, am obliged to obey. Please accept my sincerest apologies."

Yang waved his hand slightly.

"Oh, please, think nothing of it. We're all slaves to our paycheck. Isn't that right, Captain? I was the same way. It's more than a piece of paper; it's a chain that binds."

Captain Ratzel needed a few seconds to grin, partly because of Yang's poorly constructed joke and partly because Ratzel's sense of humor wasn't all that developed to begin with.

It was under these circumstances that Yang permitted himself to be observed by Ratzel. Even in a democratic regime like the Alliance Armed Forces, let alone the Imperial Navy, commands from on high could be unfairly harsh. Of course, Yang couldn't help but feel a certain level of discomfort with Ratzel's boss.

"Lennenkamp holds rules and regulations to be self-evident. Even if going against them were justified, I doubt he'd even consider it. He'd do his worst, so long as it meant following the rules."

Even if Yang was right, he didn't care about rules. He simply hadn't revealed how he felt, because he knew when and where to shout, "The king has donkey ears!" In any case, he'd somehow carved out a status for himself worthy of a pension. Then again, he'd also been denounced in a pointless court hearing like a meek lamb in a round of rulers and their lapdogs, as Caselnes and friends watched critically from the sidelines. But so long as the Galactic Empire existed, Yang's military genius was indispensable. Removing him from the equation over questionable behavior was unthinkable. Despite being taunted mercilessly in court, he'd emerged from the discomfort of that memory having come to grips with Lennenkamp's way of doing things.

"Then you don't like Lennenkamp?"

To his wife's intentionally reductive question, Yang answered:

"It's not that I don't like him. He just gets on my nerves is all."

That was more than enough for Yang.

Yang wasn't fond of scheming. He hated to look at himself when working out a plot to deceive others. But if Lennenkamp crossed the line and meddled in Yang's personal affairs, he would resort to underhanded methods to drive him away. Yang's nerves were still on edge. If push came to shove, he'd retaliate with another shove for good measure. He was fully prepared to meet any consequence of his return head-on.

Nevertheless, even if Yang outwitted Lennenkamp's fastidiousness, it wasn't likely that anyone more tolerant would be appointed in his place. He couldn't afford the mistake of driving out a dog, only to then invite in a wolf. If someone like the coolheaded, astute Marshal von Oberstein, for example, were to come into the picture, Yang would feel mentally suffocated.

"That bastard Lennenkamp! I could…"

Realizing the indecency of what he was about to say, Yang acted the gentleman and redressed himself.

"Sure, it'd be ideal if Mr. Lennenkamp left us alone, but the problem is who would replace him. I'd gladly take advantage of a traitorous type who took pleasure in doing as he pleased behind the emperor's back. But Emperor Reinhard has yet to appoint someone like that."

"We can assume Emperor Reinhard would only appoint such a person if he himself were a corrupt ruler, right?"

"Ah, you've hit the mark there. That's it exactly." Yang exhaled through a bitter expression. "It behooves us not only to welcome the enemy's corruption, but also to encourage it. Isn't this a depressing topic? Whether in politics or the military, I know very well under whose jurisdiction evil lies. I bet God is enjoying every moment of this."

Meanwhile, in the high commissioner's office, Senior Admiral Lennenkamp was again giving orders to Captain Ratzel.

"Stay vigilant in your surveillance. That man is up to something—I can feel it. We must eliminate anything that could bring harm to the empire or His Majesty the Emperor before it becomes a reality."

Ratzel was silent.

"Have you nothing to say?!"

"Yes. As you command, from now on I'll keep an extra-close eye on Marshal Yang." It was the answer of a talentless actor.

Seeing the way Lennenkamp's mustache quivered, Ratzel knew his behavior was not at all to his superior's liking.

"Captain," said Lennenkamp, raising his voice. "Let me ask you something. Do we need to be obeyed, or do we need to be welcomed?"

Ratzel knew what his superior wanted to hear but hesitated to answer right away. He looked away again, his tone passionless.

"To be obeyed, of course, Your Excellency."

"Exactly."

Nodding gravely, Lennenkamp continued his tirade.

"We're both victors *and* rulers. Building a new order is *our* responsibility. At this point, I no longer care about being ostracized by the losers. If we're ever going to fulfill our grander duty here, then we must be steadfast in our determination and faith."

Ernest Mecklinger likewise took down the following memo:

Most likely, the emperor will take the heat for this personnel selection failure. I don't agree with that. The only reason the emperor hasn't noticed Lennenkamp's fixation with Yang Wen-li is because the emperor himself has none. Fixation with someone who has defeated oneself towers over the mind like an enormous mountain range. And while it's possible for a bird with strong wings to fly over those mountains, to a bird who can't, they are the very essence of hardship. In my opinion, Lennenkamp needs to strengthen his wings a bit more. The emperor didn't appoint him to be Yang Wen-li's jailor. Certainly, the emperor isn't omnipotent. But it's unacceptable to blame an astronomical telescope for not also functioning as a microscope.

III

Yang Wen-li wasn't the only one under imperial surveillance. Most other high-level officers, at least those whose whereabouts were known, were being subjected to the same treatment. The Free Planets Alliance, after barely avoiding total domination by the Imperial Navy, was like a criminal on death row, waiting for the inevitable while authority figures rattled the cage with their sticks.

As an authorized staff member of the alliance government, Commissioner Lennenkamp was allowed the privilege of attending all official meetings. His presence was somewhere between nuisance and token member. Although barred from giving orders and expressing opinions, neither could the alliance debate freely for fear of what he might think.

João Lebello, who was both the alliance's prime minister and chief executive officer as chairman of the High Council, had succeeded Job Trünicht after the latter had relinquished his political authority. Since nibbling on the sweet fruit of power, he'd been cultivating a withered orchard.

Lebello was determined not to give the empire any excuses. He would maintain the independence, if only nominally, of the Free Planets Alliance, which had two and a half centuries of history to show for itself. Sooner or later, the Free Planets Alliance would need to restore total independence. The Galactic Empire had enough military power to annex the Free Planets Alliance at any time it wished. That it hadn't already done so didn't mean it wouldn't in the future. Emperor Reinhard was just waiting for a more opportune moment to fit that last piece into the puzzle of his rule.

The Bharat Peace Treaty was an invisible chain holding down the Free Planets Alliance's limbs. Under Article 4, the alliance was required to pay an annual security tax of one trillion five hundred billion imperial reichsmark to the empire, thereby putting enormous financial pressure on the alliance. In accordance with Article 6, the Free Planets Alliance had dutifully enacted a national law against any activities that would hinder friendship with the empire. Lebello, along with proposing this Insurrection Act to congress, had to ban Article 7 of the Charter of the Alliance, which guaranteed freedom of speech and assembly, to which the principlists cried foul over this self-denial of a democratic government.

Lebello knew as much. But the world was in crisis mode, and wasn't it worth amputating its necrosis-ridden arms to save the entire organism? In addition, Lebello was worried about the alliance's greatest military hero,

Yang Wen-li. Lebello had been deceived by the conservatives and could only shudder at the image of revolutionary banners unfurling on both the imperial and alliance sides.

Lebello knew full well that Yang Wen-li wasn't the type of person to gain power by brute military force, as the last three years could attest. But just because Yang had acted one way in the past didn't guarantee he would act predictably in the future. Former admiral Dwight Greenhill, the father of Yang's new bride, had been a man of good sense, but had not political and diplomatic pressures compelled even him to side with the die-hards, driving him to instigate a coup d'état? And when Yang had suppressed the coup and rescued the democratic government, he had briefly been in a position to become a dictator himself. But immediately after liberating the occupied capital, he'd returned to the front lines, content in his position as commander of frontier defenses. Although Lebello thought that a praiseworthy action, people were malleable creatures. If a man like Yang, no longer able to withstand the monotonous life of retirement, were to have his dormant ambitions awakened, there was no telling what he might be capable of and to what lengths he'd be willing to go to protect the integrity of his ideals.

And so, the very government from which Yang Wen-li was receiving his pension was also keeping a close eye on him. The reality of the situation might go over Yang's head, but it was only a matter of time before he connected all the dots. For all Lebello knew, maybe Yang already had. Yang was no masochist, and found no joy whatsoever in being the target of constant surveillance. Still, he had no desire to make a show of his objections, if only because he knew that the present government was in a tough spot. He couldn't help but sympathize, to a point. Besides, no manner of protest would stop visitors from showing up at his door unannounced. For now, he could only play things by ear and see where it led him.

Whatever others expected of him, however they presumed to interfere, Yang intended to enjoy the rest of his life, relaxed and paid for. That is, until something unexpected took place the next day that changed his mind forever.

His new wife, Frederica, like her slothful husband, did little else other than eat and sleep. Aside from scribbling down his randomly dictated flashes of historical insight, she spent her time relaxing. That didn't mean, however, that she enjoyed this unproductive, ordinary life. Had she followed her husband's example, the home she'd just made would have become a weed-infested garden soon enough. At the very least, she wanted to maintain it as their sanctuary.

Their newlywed home had become a training ground for her role as housewife, and she took to it with wavering commitment. As a girl, she'd managed the house in place of her ailing mother, but in retrospect, her father had done much to ease her burdens until she'd entered the Officers' Academy and left the house at sixteen. Food was rarely a focus of curriculum at the academy, where she learned which plants were okay to eat should she ever find herself lost in the wilderness, but never how to make a home-cooked meal. Although she'd planned to teach herself one day, and despite a superior memory that had earned her the nickname of "Walking Computer" at the academy, she felt inadequate when it came to domestic life. Maybe she just needed practice.

In the file of her memory, five thousand years' worth of human history and the exploits of Yang's combat experience and commendations had been perfectly catalogued, yet no amount of scholarship or lofty philosophy came in handy when brewing her husband's favorite black tea or planning a menu that would stimulate his appetite in the summer months.

Yang had never once complained about the meals Frederica prepared. Whether because he truly liked her cooking, because he didn't like it but was being considerate of her feelings, or because he just didn't even care, was beyond her. Whatever the reason, it wasn't long before she'd exhausted her culinary repertoire and found herself wanting to learn more.

"Darling," she asked timidly, "are you at all dissatisfied with my cooking or the way I keep house?"

"Not at all. Especially that thing you made…Well, whatever it was called, it was delicious."

Frederica hardly felt comforted by this enthusiastic yet vague response.

"I just wish I could give you more variety. Cooking has never been my strong suit."

"Your cooking is fine, honest. Oh yes, remember that sandwich you made for me when we were fleeing El Facil? That was really tasty."

Even Yang wasn't sure whether he was telling the truth or just paying lip service. After all, that was eleven years ago. Frederica appreciated that he was trying to put his wife at ease, but she hoped he would be more forthcoming about these things without her having to ask.

"Sandwiches are all I'm good at making. Actually, that's not true. I can also make crepes, hamburgers…"

"So, basically, you're an expert when it comes to anything with layers, right?"

But Yang's attempts at being impressed, whether generous or thick-headed, made Frederica call her abilities into question. Was "Breakfast: Egg Sandwich, Lunch: Ham Sandwich, Dinner: Sardine Sandwich" the only kind of menu she knew how to devise? Did the full extent of her abilities in the kitchen fit only between two layers of dough?

Four years of dorm life at the Officers' Academy and five years of military life had left her ill prepared for her new role as housewife.

Julian Mintz, before leaving for Earth, had given her instruction on brewing a strong black tea to Yang's liking. With masterful care, he'd demonstrated the perfect temperature of the water and the exact timing involved, but when he'd complimented Frederica's attempts to replicate the process, she'd wondered if he was being genuine, because it never came out the same whenever she tried making it for Yang. Clearly, her husband looked at the world very differently than she did. She wanted them to be on the same page, but it seemed Yang was already skipping ahead to the end without caring much for the events leading them there.

IƲ

Alex Caselnes, known as the cubicle king of the Alliance Armed Forces for aiding Yang with countless administrative tasks, also couldn't shake the uncomfortable feeling that he was being watched by the Imperial Navy. Convinced his house had been bugged, he avoided speaking with Yang on the visiphone. One day, while sipping coffee next to his knitting wife, he tutted at the five surveillance guards outside his window.

"Look at them, working so hard day after day. And for what?"

"At least we don't need to worry about getting robbed, dear. Public funds are paying for our protection. Shouldn't we be grateful for that? Maybe I could offer them some tea or dessert?"

"Have it your way," her husband said, only half-listening.

Mrs. Caselnes made coffee for five, then told their daughter, Charlotte Phyllis, to call in the most arrogant-looking guard she could find. Soon after, the nine-year-old led a young, freckled noncommissioned officer inside, his arm linked doubtfully with hers. The officer was visibly uncomfortable and regretfully declined the coffee offered to him, saying he wasn't allowed to engage in any activities that might distract him from his work while on duty. After the officer apologized and returned to his watch, it fell upon Caselnes to figure out how to conserve those five cups of coffee. But his wife's gesture had its desired effect, as from that point on the guards softened up whenever they saw the couple's two children running about.

A few days later, Mrs. Caselnes made a raspberry pie and told her daughters to bring it to the Yang house. Charlotte Phyllis held the pie box in one hand and her younger sister's hand in the other, prompting forced smiles from the imperial surveillance team as they approached the door and rang the intercom.

"Hello, Uncle Yang, Big Sister Frederica."

To these innocent, if unwittingly demeaning, forms of address, the master of the Yang household felt a twinge of wounded pride, but his new wife cordially invited the two small messengers inside all the same and rewarded them, as Julian Mintz once had, for their labor with a honeyed milkshake. To soothe her deflated husband, Frederica cheerfully cut the pie, only to discover a water-resistant bag inside containing several carefully folded clandestine messages.

Thus, Marshal Yang and Vice Admiral Caselnes hit upon an underhanded, if pedestrian, way to communicate with each other. And while the sheer audacity of it was enough to fly under the surveillance guards' radar, they were careful not to abuse it. In any event, it didn't take long before Frederica had exhausted her repertoire of cakes and pies, which were already hard enough to make. This gave her the perfect excuse to visit Mrs. Caselnes on a more regular basis in order to learn more recipes. It wasn't a total lie, because she did want a reliable teacher to school her in not only the ways of the kitchen, but also domestic life in general.

It was on this pretext that the young couple brought a gift to the Caselnes household. When she went out onto the street, Frederica was met with scornful glares from the locals. This was more than understandable, given that the cause of their oppression was standing right before them. It was in moments like these that, despite her best efforts to ignore the surveillance guards, Frederica was glad for their presence.

Two fully armed imperial soldiers turned idly in her direction. That they shed not a single bead of sweat, despite being drenched in the summer sun, was just one of many indications of their rigorous training and combat experience. Such burliness lent them a rather inorganic, unworldly countenance that was at once comforting and unsettling. Still, they trembled once they locked Yang in their sights. They all knew his face from their solivisions, but to them a marshal wasn't supposed to lead so simple a life as to walk around unguarded in broad daylight in a faded cotton shirt. Clearly, he'd lost his mind, and it was the first time they'd seen an expression that was even remotely human on his face.

Seeing that the young newlyweds were standing outside their gate on the monitor, Caselnes called out to his wife.

"Hey, Mrs. Yang is here."

"Really? By herself?"

"No, hubby's with her, too. Although if you ask me, I'm not sure a commander and his aide make for the most compatible match."

"I don't see why they wouldn't," said Mrs. Caselnes, offering her calm assessment. "They're much too big for the civilian life. I think settling down would be a mistake for them. I'm sure they'll take off to wherever it is they belong soon enough. Their destiny is out there somewhere."

"I didn't realize I'd married a fortune-teller."

"I'm no fortune-teller. Call it a woman's intuition."

Watching his wife saunter off into the kitchen, Caselnes muttered something under his breath and made for the foyer to greet their guests. His two daughters skipped along behind him.

When he opened the door, the Yangs were speaking with some of the imperial soldiers assigned to the Caselnes household. To their haughty interrogation about the purpose of their visit and the contents of their bags, Yang replied sincerely and with great patience. As the two Caselnes girls pushed their father lightly aside, the soldiers saluted and backed down. Yang handed Charlotte Phyllis a present.

"Give this to your mom. It's Bavarian cream."

Now it was Yang who was on the receiving end of Caselnes's reprimands when he entered the living room.

"So, I can't help but notice that you don't come around here much anymore."

"What's eating you, oh great husband of Madam Caselnes?"

"Would it kill you to bring over a bottle of cognac from time to time? What's with all the girly dishes?"

"Well, if I'm going to kiss up to someone, it'd better be the one who wears the pants in this family. Last time I checked, wasn't it your wife who's going to all the trouble to make dinner for us?"

"Man, you're whipped. Who do you think paid for those ingredients? Food doesn't just fall from the sky. No matter how you slice it, the one who wears the *real* pants around here—"

"Is your wife, like I said."

While the active vice admiral and the retired marshal were engaged in their light verbal sparring match, Mrs. Caselnes briskly doled out table-setting instructions to Frederica and the girls. As Yang watched them with a sidelong glance, he couldn't help but think that, in Mrs. Caselnes's eyes, Frederica and her two daughters were on the same level of domesticity.

"I would love to learn more about cooking. You could start me off with a few basic meat dishes, some seafood dishes, and then some egg dishes. I was hoping you might show me the ropes—that is, if it's not too much trouble."

Nodding to Frederica's enthusiastic words, Mrs. Caselnes answered with a somewhat ambiguous expression on her face.

"You're certainly raring to go, Frederica. But there's no need to be so systematic about it. Things like cooking should happen organically. Besides, more important than providing for your husband is learning how to discipline him. He'll walk all over you if you go too soft on him."

After the Yangs left, Mrs. Caselnes praised Frederica's bravery in the strongest possible terms.

"I thought she looked rather composed under the circumstances. Healthy, too." Caselnes paused to stroke his chin, his expression serious. "But if Julian doesn't come home soon, he'll be welcomed back by the corpses of a young couple who died of malnutrition."

"Don't say things like that. It's bad luck."

"I was only joking."

"Jokes are like chili peppers: best used in moderation. You don't exactly have the most balanced sense of humor. Sometimes, you're not careful and you cross the line. Do it too much, and others might start taking it the wrong way."

Alex Caselnes, not yet forty, worked as acting general manager of rear services, where he was consistently praised for his competence as a military bureaucrat. But at home, he was just another wrinkled shirt in need of ironing. Knowing he was defeated, he lifted his younger daughter onto his knee, then whispered into the little ear nestled in her brown hair: "Daddy didn't lose that one. Knowing when to back down and make one's wife look good is the key to keeping the family peace. You'll both understand soon enough."

He suddenly recalled his wife's prediction. If Yang took off into the universe, he would have to think about his own course of action. His daughter looked curiously at her father's face, the calmness of which was now disturbed.

V

Helmut Lennenkamp's prejudice against Yang Wen-li would also make a big impression on future historians seduced into thinking of Yang as a "hero for democracy" and an "extraordinarily resourceful general." They would interpret Yang's actions more as worshippers than as researchers, as if his actions were predestined to put him on the path to greatness. Even his seemingly mediocre retirement, they concluded, was a farsighted and deeply laid stalling tactic in anticipation of his ultimate goal to overthrow the empire. To Yang, it would've been an annoying overstatement. Getting paid even at his young age to live an ordinary life without having to work was nothing to be praised for. That was provocation enough to get him back in the game.

Yang did, in fact, have a deeply laid plan. Maybe it was just a way for him to pass the time, but the details, as conveyed after the fact by witnesses, went down something like this:

The primary objective of his plan was to rebuild a republican system of government, unsullied by the inevitable dangers of a military dictatorship. In the best-case scenario, he would escape from the Galactic Empire's clutches and restore total independence to the Free Planets Alliance. At the very least, he could aim for a democratic republic, no matter how large or small in scale. A nation was the *methodological embodiment* of the welfare and republican principles of its people. But it was also more than that. From time immemorial, those who would deify a nation parasitized its citizens, and it was pointless to shed new blood trying to save them. Yang would need to be more resourceful if he was going to affect lasting change.

With a suitable political system in place, the reconstruction was to be divided into four parts: A. Fundamental principles; B. Government; C. Economy; and D. Military.

The entire plan hinged on the integrity of A. A sound philosophical foundation would determine how much enthusiasm could be harvested toward rebuilding a republican government and restoring the people's political authority. If the people saw no significance in such a project, then no amount of planning or scheming would bear fruit on their already weary limbs. To kick-start the process, Yang needed either the tyrannical rule of a despotic government or a charismatic sacrifice. Emotional and physiological reinforcement would be necessary to handle the trauma that would result from either scenario. Were this to be attempted by a purely republican faction, the situation would more than likely degenerate into conspiracy. Yang had never subscribed to the constant mantras around notions of effort. Without patience and sober action, no amount of even the best-meaning effort would bring about true and lasting change.

Although B was the direct outcome of A, not only would the alliance retain autonomy in domestic affairs, but it would also be possible to organize an anti-imperial faction at the highest level of administration. Placing someone on the front lines with experience in both taxation and public order was preferable to the alternative. In addition, Yang and his cohort would need to position cooperative workers both within the empire and the Phezzan Dominion under direct imperial control. Said workers, especially those who were intimately linked to the center of the enemy's authority, didn't even need to be aware of their complicity. In fact, it was better that they weren't. These were extremely underhanded tactics, to be sure, but so were bribery, terrorism, and any number of other methods used by the most power-hungry players. The only logical outcomes from such actions were jealousy, animosity, and betrayal.

In the case of C, more so than in B, cooperation of Phezzan's independent merchants was essential. Given that the alliance was required to pay the empire an annual security tax of one trillion five hundred billion imperial reichsmark, there was no hope of finances changing for the better anytime in the near future. One idea was to loan money to Phezzanese merchants at high interest rates, thereby granting mining development privileges and route priority, but guaranteeing indefinite expansion was no easy sell. The important thing was to make those merchants understand it was in their best interest to cooperate with the republican faction more than with the empire. So long as they had a stake in industrial nationalization and monopolization of material-goods-related policies, asking independent Phezzanese merchants for their cooperation would be a cakewalk. One reason why great empires of the ancient world faced uprisings from their own people was because authorities coveted unjust profits, enforcing monopolies on the salt necessary for human existence. Considering this lesson of the past, they would need to give Phezzan's merchants appropriate benefits, although this wasn't so much of a worry since the rebuilding of a republic concerned both Phezzan and the alliance.

Only after A through C were completed could D taste the sweet flavors of reality. At the present stage, there was no need for a tactical plan. Military rebuilding would yield an organization responsible for staunching anti-imperial activities. For this, a core unit would be necessary. And while the infrastructure was already in place, they still needed the benefit of military reinforcement. There was also the matter of who would lead. The self-respecting Admiral Merkatz had enough character and ability to do just that, but given his former allegiance to, and recent defection from, the empire, he couldn't be trusted to lead a republican regiment. Admiral Bucock was another possibility. In either case, further deliberation on the matter was a tall order.

Underlying all of these was an implicit golden rule: diminish the enemy and increase the enemies of the enemy, even if they aren't allies. Everything was relative.

These were the cornerstones of Yang's plan, but he had yet to fit them into a grander scheme on paper. He couldn't afford to neglect the competence of High Commissioner Lennenkamp when it came to maintaining public order, nor could he leave behind any evidence that would deem him a traitor under the new dynastic terms.

From first to final movement, the whole notes of this "Insurrection Symphony" were ordered on the sheet music of Yang's brain. Only their composer knew where to pencil in every tie, slur, and rest. But if Yang was ever asked why his name didn't come up in the affairs of military leaders, he had an answer prepared: "I'm through working. My mind is spent. At this point, I can only sell the rest of me to a greater cause. Let them do with me what they will."

Yang's plan came down to the all-important task of what he called "restoring the clan." As far as he was concerned, the nation was nothing more than a tool, the purpose of which depended on the intentions of those wielding it. He'd said as much to others repeatedly and had even jotted it down for his own amusement.

Above all, however, he'd managed never to incur the hatred of Reinhard von Lohengramm. On the contrary, one might say no one else regarded Yang so highly as his archnemesis. From Yang's perspective, Reinhard was a military genius without equal, an absolute monarch of great discernment and little self-interest. His government was impartial, virtuous, and immune to criticism. It wasn't far-fetched to think that most people were rather happy with the prospect of his long reign.

But even as Reinhard brought about universal peace and prosperity by force of political suggestion, people were getting used to relinquishing their own political power to others. Yang couldn't abide by this. Perhaps it was idealistic of him, but there had to be a way to broker peace among the different galactic factions without blindly supporting even the most well-meaning regime of despotism.

Yang wondered if the good government of a tyrant wasn't the sweetest drug when it came to one's awareness as a citizen. If people could enjoy peace and prosperity, knowing that politics were being justly managed without them having to participate, express themselves, or even think, who would ever want to get involved with something as bothersome as politics to begin with? The obvious downside to such a system was that people grew complacent. No one ever seemed to exercise their imagination. If the people were troubled by politics, then so was their ruler. What happened, for instance, when he lost interest in politics and began to abuse his limitless power to satisfy his own ego? By then, it would be too late for anyone to devise a suitable counterstrategy, for their ingenuity would have already atrophied beyond the point of no return. A democratic government was therefore essentially just compared to an autocratic one.

That said, Yang's own stake in democratic principles wasn't entirely immovable. Yang sometimes found himself musing that, if change for the better were possible, and humanity could enjoy the fruits of peace and prosperity indefinitely, then was there really any use in getting so caught up in the minutiae of politics? He felt embarrassed thinking back on his own shameful abstention from voting, when he would drink himself unconscious on the eve of an election day and wake up the next night, long after the polls had been closed. Those were hardly the actions of an honorable man.

Such self-assessment was necessary when embarking on something as grand as universal reformation. Most people would have called this commitment to change nothing less than "faith." And while it wasn't the word Yang would have used, he would never be able to accomplish anything so monumental if it required him to see his enemies as inherently bad people.

Even among future historians were those who thought that all faith was pardonable. Those same historians would invariably criticize Yang Wen-li for so often expressing his contempt for faith:

"Faith is nothing more than a cosmetic used to cover up the blemishes of indiscretion and folly. The thicker the cosmetics, the more difficult it is to see the face underneath."

"Killing someone in the name of faith is more vulgar than killing someone for money, for while money has common value to most people, the value of faith goes no further than those it concerns."

As Yang would've argued, one needed only to look at Rudolf the Great, whose faith had destroyed a republican government and left millions dead, to realize that faith could be a dangerous virtue. Anytime someone used the word "faith," Yang's respect for that person dropped by 10 percent.

In fact, Yang told his wife, downing his "tea-spiked brandy," as someone who was attempting nothing less than destroying the new order, he was likely to go down as one of history's most abhorrent criminals, and Reinhard as history's legitimate poster child for greatness.

"No matter how you slice it, the very anticipation of corruption is reprehensible, because you're ultimately taking advantage of other people's misfortune in order to tear it down."

"But aren't we just waiting it out at this point?" prompted Frederica.

She calmly reached for the brandy bottle, but Yang beat her by a hair.

"Your timing needs work, Lieutenant Commander."

Yang began pouring more brandy into his tea but, seeing his wife's expression, poured only two-thirds of what he'd intended and capped the bottle, saying apologetically:

"We only desire what the body demands. Eating and drinking whatever we feel like is best for our health."

Yang's point of view may have been broader, and the range of his sight longer, than most people's, but he couldn't possibly grasp every phenomenon in the universe. For just as he was settling down into married life, ten thousand light-years away from home, on the Galactic Imperial capital planet of Odin, a deployment of punitive forces was being readied at Reinhard's command.

CHAPTER 3:

I

WHENEVER LIVES WERE irrevocably changed by circumstances beyond their control, people often dug up the term "fate" from the graveyards of their memories to reassure themselves that everything was meant to be. Julian Mintz, who had yet to turn eighteen, wasn't old enough to fully exhume fate from his own mental graveyard, and he resorted to sleeping in a fetal position under his bed, waiting for something, *anything*, to happen.

According to Yang Wen-li, his legal guardian of five years, fate had "the face of a gnarled old witch"—a natural sentiment for someone who'd spent eleven years in a profession he'd never wanted.

Five years ago, Julian had been sent to then-Captain Yang Wen-li's house under Travers's Law, which placed war orphans in the homes of other soldiers. And when, after dragging along a trunk that was bigger than he was, he'd come face-to-face with a black-haired, dark-eyed man who looked neither like a soldier nor a hero, Julian thought he'd glimpsed the profile of fate, which in his eyes was fair complexioned. He never could have imagined how that fate would change on his trip to Earth.

The cradle of human civilization, which he was seeing for the first time in his life, emerged on the main screen of the starship *Unfaithful* as a dimly colored mass. Of all the planets Julian had ever seen, he wouldn't have counted Earth among the more beautiful. Maybe it was just his preconception, but the cloudy globe practically broadcast itself as a planet laid to barren waste.

Over one month since departing from Heinessen, Julian found himself in the innermost frontier star zone of imperial territory.

On the occasion of his departure, it was decided that, between Phezzan and Iserlohn, they would take the former route. Until just a few days ago, this very sector had been embroiled in a bloody conflict between the Imperial Navy and the Alliance Armed Forces. Its militarily strategic position had played a central part in Iserlohn Fortress falling into the hands of the Imperial Navy for the first time in two and a half years. It was currently closed to civilian vessels.

Every time Julian thought of Iserlohn Fortress, a disturbance rippled outward along the watery surface of his emotions. It had been the year SE 796 when his guardian, Admiral Yang Wen-li, had surrendered Iserlohn, once believed impregnable, without shedding a single drop of the blood of his allies. After the alliance's crushing defeat at the Battle of Amritsar, Yang had served as commander of both Iserlohn Fortress and its patrol fleet, and continued to stand on the front lines of national defense. Julian had stayed by his side, repairing to Iserlohn. He'd spent two years on that giant artificial planet, itself sixty kilometers in diameter and, if you counted both soldiers and civilians, boasting a population of five million. It was then that he'd officially become a soldier. It was also where he'd experienced his first battle. He'd gotten to know many people, some of whom he'd found himself forever parting from.

In the hourglass of his life, the most sparkling among those grains of sand had been plucked from Iserlohn. That this place, which had brought about qualitatively richer memories than any other in his mere seventeen years of existence, had fallen under imperial control was indeed regrettable. When Iserlohn Fortress had been rendered powerless by the Imperial Navy's magnificent strategic planning, Yang Wen-li had abandoned it without hesitation, opting instead to guarantee the mobility of his fleet. Yang had known he'd made the right decision, and even if he hadn't,

Julian would've supported him anyway. Still, Julian had been astonished at Yang's audacity, and not for the first time. Yang's actions were always surprising in Julian's eyes.

Unfaithful's captain, Boris Konev, walked up and stood next to Julian. "A pretty gloomy planet, don't you think?" he said with a wink.

Konev had transported Julian not merely in his role as captain. He was a proud former independent merchant of Phezzan, a childhood playmate of Yang Wen-li, and the cousin of the Alliance Armed Forces' ace pilot Ivan Konev, killed in action. His investment in Julian's safety was therefore of multifaceted and utmost priority. *Unfaithful* had been originally built as a military transport for the alliance and had become his property through Caselnes's arrangements by way of Yang. He'd wanted to name it after his beloved *Beryozka*. Unfortunately, that name came with far too much baggage to pass through imperial territory without raising a red flag. Because the ship was illegality incarnate, they had to keep up appearances as much as possible. *Unfaithful*, then, seemed like a worthy compromise. To Konev, it was a declaration of truth so obvious that it might just go unnoticed.

Julian felt a tap on his shoulder and turned to see Commander Olivier Poplin, who'd linked up with them midway through the journey. The young ace smiled at Julian with his green eyes before turning to the screen.

"So that's where it all began—the mother planet of the entire human race, huh?"

An unoriginal thing to say, to be sure, but the ring of nostalgia in Poplin's voice wasn't all that genuine to begin with. Nearly thirty centuries had passed since Earth had lost its status as the center of human civilization, and ten centuries more since the young ace's ancestors had taken flight from its surface. The well of sentimentality for Earth had run dry a long time ago, and far be it from Poplin to waste any tears in refilling it.

In any case, Poplin hadn't reunited with Julian out of any attachment to Earth. He couldn't care less about an outdated frontier planet.

"I've no interest in seeing a feeble old mother," he said, with usual bluntness.

Konev, who'd been consulting with his astrogator, Wilock, came back to rejoin the conversation.

"We'll be landing in the northern Himalayas, the usual drop-off point for pilgrims. You'll find the Church of Terra's headquarters nearby."

"The Himalayas?"

"Earth's largest orogenic zone. I know of no safer place for us to land."

Konev explained that it had once been an energy supply center during Earth's golden age. Establishment of hydroelectric power from the thaw of alpine snow, solar power, and geothermal energy sources had been carefully arrayed so as not to interfere with the natural beauty, all while supplying light and heat to ten billion people. More relevantly, shelters for the Global Government's top brass had been carved out deep underground.

When the United Anti-Earth Front's grand forces, blind with revenge, had plowed their way into the solar system and assaulted this "proud planet" with everything they had, the Himalayas, along with military bases and major cities, had been an epicenter of attack. The flames of a giant volcanic eruption nine hundred years earlier had increased their height. Soil, rock, and glaciers had formed a moving wall, taking down everything man-made in their path. The Himalayan mountains were a point of Earthly pride, sometimes even objects of religious worship, but to those still being abused and rejected in the colonies, they were nothing but a towering symbol of oppression.

Global Government representatives requested a meeting with the United Anti-Earth Front's commander in chief, Joliot Francoeur, to broker peace. But Francoeur hadn't come to beg for mercy. With a pride befitting any legitimate leader of the entire human race, he explained that protecting Earth's honor was the responsibility of *every* human being. If they lost sight of that now, then there was no hope left.

Francoeur's answer was coldhearted:

"My mother lived in luxury by the fruits of her own labor. And now, what rights can she claim? The way I see it, you have two alternatives. To ruin, or to be ruined. The choice is yours."

Francoeur told them of his former lover who killed herself after being raped by an Earth Force soldier. The Global Government's representatives were overwhelmed by the raging violence in his eyes, at a loss for words. Over the past several centuries, Earthers had planted seeds of hatred in the hearts of the colonized and by their actions accelerated the growth of that hatred. Never once had Earthers showed compassion, let alone entertained the possibility of compromise.

Dejected, those same representatives committed mass suicide while on their way home. Beyond having to bear the responsibility of their failed negotiations, it was the inevitable banquet of destruction waiting for them back on Earth that drove them to such extreme measures.

Said banquet lasted for three days. Only after strict orders came down from United Anti-Earth Front leaders did Francoeur put an end to the slaughter. Amid whipping winds and roaring thunder, his youthful face came to resemble a waterfall as rain and tears of violent emotion flowed down his cheeks.

Thinking about the amount of blood shed on this small planet's surface and the weight of its maledictions sent an electric current of tension through Julian's body. Whereas before he'd always been confronted with questions of an uncertain future, this time he stood face-to-face with the undeniably horrific past that was the legacy of everyone aboard the ship.

II

Julian Mintz's travel itinerary to Earth was far from linear. Heading straight for the forsaken planet from Heinessen was illegal.

Despite having submitted his letter of resignation, as someone who'd been an officer of the Alliance Armed Forces until just a few days before, his status as Yang Wen-li's dependent was still rather vague from the viewpoint of the Imperial Navy and alliance government surveilling him. The fact that Julian and his security guard, Ensign Louis Machungo, had gotten away safely did little to assuage his worries about the pressures his escape might've placed on Yang and Frederica.

Yang had risked a lot for Julian's sake. He'd worked everything out with the aid of Caselnes and Boris Konev, procuring a ship and formally registering Julian and Machungo as crew. And all of this without raising so much as an eyebrow at either the Imperial Navy or alliance government. All the while, he would mutter under his breath things like, "A real father would hardly do as much for his runaway son."

Once they'd left Heinessen's gravitational field, Julian and the rest of the crew were on their own. The outcome of their journey hung solely on his discretion and Boris Konev's resourcefulness as they ventured into the Church of Terra's dark side. If they returned safely, it would be the first time anyone had succeeded in doing so.

And yet, even with all these meticulous arrangements, the first hurdle impeding their course appeared before the first day had even ended when an unexpected signal stopped everyone aboard *Unfaithful* in their tracks:

"Halt your ship, or we will open fire."

The Imperial Navy was possessed of an overwhelming military power that resonated with the worst of human instincts. They couldn't be sure the Imperial Navy wouldn't destroy a compliant civilian ship and pass it off as self-defense.

When Konev was asked if he had any intention of making a break for it, Julian shook his flaxen-haired head. Who knew how many inspections they would undergo on their way to Earth? It was in their best interests to treat each imperial encounter as the first.

But when Konev did as instructed, the young sublieutenant who transferred onto their ship to conduct a spontaneous inspection only asked if they had any young women on board. When he was met with an unequivocal no, his expression was that of a child desperate to get his homework over with.

"I don't suppose you're carrying any weapons, habit-forming substances, or human contraband, either?"

"Of course not," said Konev. "We're just humble, fate- and law-fearing merchants. Feel free to search to your heart's content."

Julian felt as though he'd just witnessed a textbook illustration of the saying, "Civility is second nature to the Phezzanese." Boris Konev was living proof of both its truth and effectiveness.

Seeing it was useless to make something out of nothing, the imperial destroyer captain let them off the hook. Free as he now was to navigate deep into Free Planets Alliance territory and inspect all vessels registered with the alliance, he'd only been confirming that fact as a subtle reminder of his authority to do so. Beginning in the Gandharva star system, now imperially supervised by terms of the Bharat Treaty, the destroyer captain and his crew had been under the command of Senior Admiral Karl Robert Steinmetz. Steinmetz, as was rare for an imperial admiral at the time, was concerned for the alliance and was strict about his subordinates not inflicting unnecessary cruelty upon civilians under martial law. The inspection came and went as nothing more than a formality. Nevertheless, Julian Mintz's journey was getting off to a rocky start.

Julian reunited with old friends in the Porisoun star zone. Merkatz's fleet had been hiding in the half-destroyed, abandoned supply base of Dayan Khan. Although this reunion had been planned, any communications regarding it had been scrambled via cryptocomm waves, allowing *Unfaithful* to make a successful approach to Dayan Khan. Julian cried out with surprise to see a familiar face the moment he stepped off the ship.

"Commander Poplin!"

"Yo, how's it hanging, boy? You must have, what, a dozen girlfriends by now?"

His dark-brown hair and shining green eyes were a welcome sight. Olivier Poplin, the 28-year-old ace pilot, was a master of air combat techniques on par with the late Ivan Konev, and Julian's single-seat spartanian fighter craft instructor. He'd followed Admiral Merkatz and the others in abandoning the alliance, which in their minds had become a vassal nation under the empire's terms of peace, and had been lying low ever since.

"There's time for that yet, Poplin. But for now, that position has yet to be filled."

"I'll say." Poplin winked, but got no response. "Man, you're no fun. Anyway, how'd everything go back on the home front? Did our esteemed marshal and Princess Frederica have their wedding?"

"Yes, a modest one, as you can well imagine."

Poplin whistled with admiration.

"Our esteemed marshal may have pulled off many miracles, but none of them compare to shooting an arrow through Princess Frederica's heart. Then again, knowing the strangeness of her proclivities, I bet she stepped right up to the target."

Julian was about to ask what all those other lady-killers at Iserlohn had been doing with themselves, when Admiral Merkatz and his aide, von Schneider, appeared. Julian took his leave of Poplin and approached the exiled guest admiral.

After exchanging salutes, Merkatz welcomed the boy with a warm, if slightly weary, smile. Now over sixty, he was the very picture of a dignified military man. Although he'd worked as Yang's advisor at Iserlohn Fortress, he carried himself like Yang's superior.

"Glad to see you made it one piece, Sublieutenant Mintz. And how is Marshal Yang?"

Julian was out of uniform while Poplin was in his, replete with black beret. Merkatz and the others wore the silver-trimmed black of the Imperial Navy. It was a dreary setting, but at least the officers' mess was clean and had coffee in ample supply. After the usual greetings were dispensed with, von Schneider sat upright.

"For the moment, we have sixty ships. Not nearly enough for a fleet, and far from war ready." Von Schneider's expression was stern. "It was the most Admiral Yang could arrange for us and still evade imperial detection. We're truly grateful, of course, but numbers equal power. Given the present circumstances, we have the resources to mobilize a patrol fleet of one hundred ships at most. The fact that Admiral Yang sent you here can only mean one thing: he has something up his sleeve that he's not telling us."

Von Schneider stopped there, looking at Merkatz and Julian.

"About that," said Julian, "I have a verbal message from Admiral Yang, so I will convey it to you in kind."

Julian cleared his throat and righted his posture, taking care to relay the message verbatim.

"According to Article 5 of the Bharat Treaty, the Alliance Armed Forces are required to dispose of any and all remaining battleships and carriers. Accordingly, 1,820 ships are slated to be decommissioned on July 16 in the Lesavik sector."

Julian repeated the date and the location before concluding:

"I trust that Merkatz's independent fleet will make the best of the situation. End of message."

"I see. Make the best of the situation? Say no more."

A broad smile came to Merkatz's lips. Von Schneider looked at him with interest because the officer he deeply respected seemed to have gotten more in touch with his sense of humor since the exile.

"Very well, then," concluded von Schneider. "But does Admiral Yang have any insights as to how the situation might change after this?"

"Admiral Yang didn't tell me what was on his mind, but you can be sure he doesn't want to be a hermit all his life," answered Julian.

Or does he? Julian thought.

"I think Yang is waiting it out. He once said something to me: 'There's no point in setting fire to the fields during the rainy season, when the dry season is sure to come.'"

Had the imperial high commissioner, Senior Admiral Lennenkamp, been privy to this information, his suspicions would've hit their expected target. Either way, Yang was a dangerous character, and Lennenkamp most certainly had the foresight to know that.

Next to a nodding Merkatz, von Schneider remembered something.

"Julian, I heard Lennenkamp has been dispatched from the empire as commissioner."

"You heard correctly. I take it you're familiar with the man, Commander von Schneider?"

"His Excellency Merkatz knows more about him than I do. Isn't that right, Your Excellency?"

Merkatz put a hand to his chin, choosing his words carefully.

"An excellent military man, make no doubt about it. Loyal to his superiors, fair to his men. But if he takes even one step outside his uniform, he might not be able to see the forest for the trees."

Julian understood this to mean he was shortsighted, but he nonetheless felt a shadow of uneasiness stretching toward Yang and his new bride. Yang wasn't exactly popular among military supremacist types.

"Julian, did Admiral Yang give you any indication of how long we are to wait?"

"Yes, he said about five or six years."

"Five or six years? Come to think of it, I guess we *will* need that much time. At the very least, it should be enough to make a dent in the Lohengramm Dynasty."

Merkatz gave a deep nod.

"Can't we expect something unusual to happen in the interim, though?"

Julian's question made Merkatz think as he'd intended it to. Over time, the former imperial veteran had come to hold Julian's strategic awareness in high regard.

"I predict—let's say, hope—that nothing happens. Too much has gone down to bring us to this point. There are still many preparations to be made. If we're too careless in flying a flag against the empire, one impatient step forward could set us two back."

Merkatz's words made an indelible impression in the clay of Julian's memory.

"Memos and such are entirely unnecessary," Yang once told Julian. "Anything you've ever forgotten wasn't all that important to begin with. In this world, there are only those things we remember, which are sometimes the worst, and those things we forget, which don't matter to us at all. That's why memos are unnecessary."

And yet, Yang never went anywhere without his notebook.

Seeing as they had ten hours until departure, Julian was encouraged to take a nap in Poplin's room, which looked like a burglar had just ransacked it. Its tenant was busy packing, whistling to himself all the while.

When Julian asked what he was doing, the young ace winked at him.

"I'm going with you."

"You are?!"

"Don't worry. Admiral Merkatz gave me the go-ahead." His green eyes glittered jovially. "You know, I wonder if there'll be any women on Earth."

"I should think so."

"Duh, I'm not talking mere biological females, but good, mature women who understand a man's worth."

"Well, I can't make any promises there," said Julian with natural prudence.

"Hmm, oh well. Honestly, I'm so far gone that I'd settle for any biological female right now. Have you noticed there are hardly *any* women around here? I never thought that far ahead when I signed up for this hitch. Joke's on me, I guess."

"I feel your pain."

"Not cute, man. Every word you say rubs more salt into the wound. When you first came to Iserlohn Fortress, you were like a porcelain doll."

"But if you come with me to Earth, Commander, what will all those pilots do without you?" With nonchalant high-handedness, Julian had tilted the conversational mirror back in Poplin's direction.

"I'll leave them all to Lieutenant Caldwell. It's about time he stood on his own as a commander. The way he relies on me for everything, he'll never grow up otherwise."

It was a sound argument, but Julian thought that relying on the one expressing it was more problematic than the argument itself. By the same token, Julian wasn't so emotionally obtuse as to downplay Poplin's concerns, which he concealed with good humor.

"Just don't blame me if we don't find any beautiful women on Earth."

"Then you'd better pray there are scores of man-starved beauties waiting with bated breath for our arrival."

Just then, Poplin's eyes widened. He clapped Julian on the shoulder and brought him to the spartanian loading zone.

"Corporal von Kreutzer!"

In response to Poplin's voice, a fully suited pilot came running over. The pilot, who was of small frame, had a face that was hard to make out from all the backlight.

"This one could very well be the next Ivan Konev, if not the next Olivier Poplin. Hey, why don't you take off your helmet and greet our guest. This here's Sublieutenant Mintz, the one I've been telling you about."

The helmet came off to reveal a full head of luxurious black tea–colored hair. A pair of indigo eyes looked directly into Julian's own.

"Corporal Katerose von Kreutzer, at your service. I've heard a lot about you from Commander Poplin, Sublieutenant Mintz."

"Pleased to meet you," answered Julian, but only after Poplin nudged him with an elbow. He was dumbstruck, for this teenage pilot, beyond the measure of Poplin's praise, had done something wholly unexpected.

With one flick of her indigo eyes, Katerose looked away from Julian at the ace pilot.

"I need to have a word with the mechanics. If you'll excuse me?"

Poplin nodded. The girl vigorously saluted and turned on a heel. Her actions were brisk and rhythmical.

"I know, she's quite a knockout. But I'll tell you straight, I've never laid a hand on her. I draw the line at fifteen-year-olds."

"I wasn't asking."

"Women are like wine. They need time to mature to their fullest-bodied flavor. If only Karin were two years older."

"Karin?"

"That's my little pet name for Katerose. How about it? You're both at that cheeky age. I think you should go for it. Talk to her."

With a bitter smile, Julian shook his flaxen-haired head.

"She didn't seem to notice me at all. Anyway, there's no time for that."

"Then *make* her notice you. And make the time to do so. You were born with that baby face, so use it. Yang is that one-in-a-million exception who can just laze around and have a beautiful woman throw herself into his lap."

"I'll keep that in mind. By the way, from her name, I take it she's an imperial refugee?"

"You may be right, but she rarely talks about her family. There must be something going on there. Why not ask her yourself if you want to know so badly? Lesson one, my unworthy disciple."

Poplin clapped Julian on the shoulder and smiled. Julian tilted his head to the side. Hundreds, if not thousands, of portraits hung in the corridors of his memory, but in Katerose he'd sensed a perfect match. For reasons he couldn't explain, seeing that girl's face had struck him with déjà vu.

Admiral Merkatz and his aide, von Schneider, as well as the commander of the notorious Rosen Ritter regiment, Captain Rinz, watched from the control room as *Unfaithful* made its departure. It was a sober parting, with no guarantee of a return.

"Before July rolls around, we must finalize plans for reclaiming our battleships."

"Yes, I agree."

But Merkatz was focusing on something deeper within.

"Von Schneider, my role in all of this is to preserve our military strength in preparation for the future. Most likely, the sun of that future will rise not for me, but for someone younger who doesn't drag the heavy shadow of the past behind him."

"You mean Admiral Yang Wen-li?" asked von Schneider.

Merkatz didn't answer, and neither did von Schneider expect him to. Both knew better than to speak in hypotheticals.

They returned their attention to the screen as the independent merchant ship *Unfaithful* disappeared silently into a high tide of stars. They continued to stand before the screen long after the ship was impossible to distinguish from the innumerable points of light surrounding it.

III

Boris Konev, captain of *Unfaithful*, would turn thirty that year. His legal status was secretary of the Free Planets Alliance commissioner's office occupied by the Phezzan Dominion, but that status had been in limbo ever since the autonomy of Phezzan had been compromised. Under any other circumstance, he might've been overcome with uneasiness.

But Konev wasn't in the least bit discouraged or embarrassed. For one thing, he was still alive, and the laws he was subject to were just the shading of a line drawing.

"We'll be entering Earth's atmosphere in one hour," he announced to his modest crew. "Once we land, my work will be half-finished. While on Earth, be sure to stay clear of danger and misfortune. Transporting dead bodies is miserable work, and I'm in no mood for it."

Konev let out an incongruous laugh.

"You'll be posing as Church of Terra pilgrims. You'll likely feel out of place, but only because it's extremely unnatural for anyone other than pilgrims to come all this way."

Julian voiced his assent, while Poplin only laughed, saying he was more than aware of that fact. During their journey, he and the ship's captain often looked at each other askance, exchanging cynical bons mots before and after meals. The young ace went so far as to say he had a natural aversion to anyone with the last name Konev.

"What's the current population of Earth?"

"Approximately ten million, according to Phezzan's trade bureau data. Not even 0.1 percent of the total population during its golden age."

"And are they all Church of Terra followers?"

"Hard to say."

Regardless of scale, the fact that one denomination had managed to seize full planetary control and bring about a unity of church and state didn't leave much room for religious freedom. Otherwise, nonbelievers would have set up their own social systems. Such was Konev's supposition.

"Religion is a convenient tool for those in power and ensures that all hardships are rooted not in politics or flawed authority, but in unbelief. Revolution is furthest from the mind of anyone who buys into that ideology." Boris Konev spat out those words with overt malice. Although he'd managed to avoid selling his ship through the income he made transporting Church of Terra believers to the holy land, he'd had his fair share of disagreeable passengers. He sensed a certain naïveté in radical believers but had zero sympathy for the religious leaders who exploited those believers for personal gain.

"I hear that the Church of Terra's leader is an old man known as the Grand Bishop," said Julian, "but have you ever met him?"

"I'm not so important as to get inside access. Even given the chance, I'd have no interest in meeting him. Maybe it's pride talking, but I've never found pleasure in listening to the preaching of old men."

"The Grand Bishop or whatever that old man's called," Poplin interjected, "must have some beautiful daughters or granddaughters."

"You think so?"

"I'm sure of it. And they're bound to fall head over heels for the young rebel hero."

Now it was Boris Konev's turn to laugh with scorn.

"I think our Commander Poplin should be a teleplay writer for children's solivision dramas. Then again, children are growing up faster than ever these days and might not be all that impressed by something so formulaic."

"But don't you know that formulaic stories deal with eternal truths?"

Julian's guard, the dark giant Ensign Louis Machungo, offered his own opinion with a smile:

"But if such an austere religious leader were to get married and have daughters, how could that religious organization exist in the first place, I wonder?"

Poplin knitted his eyebrows, and Konev nodded with satisfaction.

"Be that as it may…"

Poplin folded his arms, his eyebrows still knitted.

"The way I see it, whatever those Church of Terra folks profess to love isn't Earth itself." ·

The legacy of Earth entailed controlling those living on other planets by monopolizing political and military influence, and by the fruits of its own labors. That's what the Church of Terra loved.

"They're only using Earth as a pretext for what they really want, which is to restore the privileges once enjoyed by their ancestors. If they really loved their planet, then why involve themselves in wars and power struggles at all?"

Maybe Poplin was right, thought Julian. Although he wasn't trying to disavow religion, there was something immoral about any religious organization desirous of political authority. Controlling people not only on the outside but also on the inside was the worst totalitarianism imaginable, and the Church of Terra had done its utmost to achieve its current monopoly in both realms. All too often, people accepted a completely uniform existence by overcoming diversity of value systems and individual tastes. Those who professed to be God or divine representatives wielded the power to kill those who didn't believe. They couldn't just sit around and wait for such an age to come.

On July 10, Julian set foot on Earth's soil. No one could have predicted that it would be the same day on which the galactic imperial council would decide to take Earth by force.

CHAPTER 4:
PAST, PRESENT, AND FUTURE

I

AS THE ATTEMPTED ASSASSINATION OF Emperor Reinhard was unfolding on Odin, the Twin Ramparts of the Imperial Navy, marshals Oskar von Reuentahl and Wolfgang Mittermeier, were away from the imperial capital on their own respective missions. The former, as secretary-general of Supreme Command Headquarters, was conducting a domestic fortress inspection, while the latter, as commander in chief of the Imperial Space Armada, was overseeing the military exercises of newly built ships and fresh recruits in the Jötunheimr star system.

An urgent message prompted both men to return to the capital at once. They were beyond surprised, livid over the fact that the emperor's life had fallen prey to such a cunning scheme. That an imperial council was convened only after they'd returned showed just how highly the emperor held them in his esteem.

Meanwhile, the Ministry of Defense was busy reorganizing all military districts under its jurisdiction. The solar system that included Earth was set to be assigned to the ninth military district, which for the moment existed only on paper, having neither headquarters nor commander to its name. The Galactic Empire was notorious for having an uneven distribution of military power at its center, the fleets it normally used for foreign campaigns setting out in grand formations from the capital of Odin. Reinhard had ordered their reorganization to free himself of excess authoritarianism.

Once the recalibration of military districts was complete, it would become the responsibility of the secretary-general of Supreme Command Headquarters to oversee them. The secretary-general would also be taking on the job of commander in chief of domestic forces. Von Reuentahl's responsibilities were enormous, to be sure, if only on paper.

The relationship between secretary of defense Marshal von Oberstein and secretary-general of Supreme Command Headquarters Marshal von Reuentahl was far from honey-sweet. They politely avoided making eye contact with one another, speaking and listening only as they felt was necessary. Sometimes emotions got the better of them, and their exchanges of cynicism and blame became as heated as physical altercations, despite the fact that the secretary of defense was technically the secretary-general's superior. As much as they hated each other, however, neither von Oberstein nor von Reuentahl could deny the other's strengths. Von Reuentahl was renowned as a general of both wisdom and courage who always preferred reason over sentiment in formal settings. Von Oberstein, on the other hand, a man so sharp and coolheaded that he was said to be "sculpted out of dry ice," was thought of as an empty shell devoid of emotion. And while he was clearly prejudiced, he never made any effort to dispel his prejudices. On that front, at least, no one could blame him for wearing his heart on his sleeve.

Von Reuentahl had become close friends with the Gale Wolf after sharing so much in the way of death with him in the battlespace and saving each other's lives. Not even an elevation in rank had any adverse effect on their tight connection. About von Oberstein, Mittermeier avoided the usual slander—"that cold-blooded son of a bitch von Oberstein," "that merciless von Oberstein," and the like—but said quite simply, and in a tone which, like his swift and determined tactics, no one could imitate, "That damned von Oberstein."

Aside from these three, others who attended the July 10 imperial council were Secretary of the Interior Osmayer, chief of the Domestic Safety Security Bureau Lang, military police commissioner Senior Admiral Kessler, and Chief Cabinet Secretary Meinhof, along with Senior Admirals Müller, Mecklinger, Wahlen, Fahrenheit, Wittenfeld, and von Eisenach, as well as senior imperial aide von Streit and secondary aide von Rücke. Including the emperor himself, that made for a total of sixteen. Secretary of state Count von Mariendorf, father to chief imperial secretary Hilda, was still under house arrest, and so the chief cabinet secretary was serving as his proxy.

Reinhard would never be happy without his two most trusted men at the imperial council. Despite being a monarch in the absolute sense, there were times when he had to hide his discomfort. Hilda's absence bothered him above all. Although he'd had other private secretaries before her, some lacked follow-through despite their loyalty, while others had blatantly sucked up to him as a means of furthering their own plans for success.

A dispatch to Earth was unanimously approved by the council, although individual differences arose regarding the pros and cons of the deployment. This wasn't a matter to be taken lightly, and so Lang, chief of the Domestic Safety Security Bureau, requested a short recess to consider the matter further. Since the Church of Terra's true motives were still unclear, Lang expected a dispatch of troops to be successful only after a detailed investigation and private inquiry were conducted. The emperor laughed at the mere suggestion.

"Stop skirting around the issue. The Church of Terra's rancor is already obvious, so what possible need could there be for any further investigation and inquiry?"

"I see your point, but—"

"And are you so sure you've made no slipups in your own investigations of those cultists so far?"

"Again, I see your point."

Lang robotically blurted out his artless answers.

"Which means they will recognize no authority other than that of their God. Rather, any investigation will tell us the same thing: namely, that the church wouldn't so much as hesitate to violently eliminate anyone standing in their way. If they have no interest in coexisting inside the new system, then I see no reason not to let them martyr themselves for their beliefs. I could show them no greater mercy."

Lang blushed and bowed to the emperor's decision, which superseded his meager bureaucratic judgment.

Whenever Emperor Reinhard stirred in his seat, his lion's mane of golden hair bobbed magnificently. With every flick, some would write, it was as if a plume of gold dust were being scattered in the air. But to his attendant, Emil von Selle, sitting patiently against the wall behind him, such descriptions were no exaggeration. The fourteen-year-old now lived at court and had been given all he needed to study medicine while seeing to the young emperor's needs. No one saw anything wrong in granting him this privilege. Emil knew better than to let his ardently revered lord down.

"As His Majesty has rightfully stated, we cannot expect to coexist with the Church of Terra's followers," said the orange-haired Senior Admiral Wittenfeld. "It's about time we gave those insurgents the punishment they deserve, if only to demonstrate the extent of our will and might."

"Shall we go ahead and demonstrate that to its fullest extent, then?"

"Yes, let's do just that. And I would be honored if Your Majesty would grant me the honor of doing so."

But the emperor shook his head and laughed slightly.

"Deploying the Schwarz Lanzenreiter to take over a single frontier planet would be overkill. I would have you stand down this time, Wittenfeld."

After silencing the reluctant general, Reinhard cast his gaze to another. "Wahlen!"

"Yes, Your Majesty."

"Your orders are as follows: Take your fleet and head for the Terran solar system. There, you will suppress the Church of Terra's headquarters."

"Understood!"

"You are to apprehend their founder and any other religious leaders you can find. You will then escort them back to the capital. As for the rest, kill them for all I care. Whatever you do, do *not* lay a hand on those unaffiliated with the church. Not that I would expect any nonbelievers to be hanging around on Earth."

Had Boris Konev been in attendance in the imperial council's lowest seat, he would have applauded the emperor's insightful plan.

Wahlen stood up from his seat and bowed reverently to the emperor.

"I am beyond honored to have been given this great responsibility. Rest assured, I will destroy those Church of Terra insurgents, arrest their leaders, and make them realize the true meaning of Your Majesty's sanctity and lawful providence."

The golden-haired emperor nodded, lightly lifting a hand to signal adjournment. The dispatch to Earth was now in the hands of those doing the actual grunt work.

No organization exists without inconsistencies and internal strife, and even the newly birthed Lohengramm Dynasty had a run in its stocking when it came to spearheading domestic safety in the wake of the Kümmel Incident.

Between the military police force and the Domestic Safety Security Bureau, a dangerous antagonism had been making waves. Military police commissioner Senior Admiral Kessler and chief of the Domestic Safety Security Bureau Lang were too different in temperament to achieve any sort of accord. The former was a military leader, the latter a newcomer with no achievements to speak of. But Lang had been chief of secret police since the former dynasty had been in power, and as such had earned his position as one of secretary of defense Marshal von Oberstein's closest confidants. Moreover, the organization known as the Domestic Safety Security Bureau was itself part of the Bureau of Internal Affairs. There was no way that Secretary of the Interior Osmayer, whose job it was to oversee domestic safety, was going to watch his own authority being infringed upon and the established bureaucracy thrown into disorder.

Thus, Secretary of the Interior Osmayer and military police commissioner Kessler maintained a tacit connection, deepening covert opposition between Secretary of Defense von Oberstein and chief of the Domestic Safety Security Bureau Lang.

After young Emil brought in coffee and withdrew, Secretary of Defense von Oberstein sought an immediate audience with the emperor. Although that in and of itself wasn't a rare thing, von Oberstein took Reinhard by surprise when he asked his sovereign to give the matter of marriage some serious thought. For a moment, Reinhard's expression waxed boyish, and then a bitter smile played across his graceful face.

"Count von Mariendorf said the same thing. Is my not having a spouse really that unusual? You're fifteen years older than me. Aren't *you* the one who should be settling down?"

"No one will mourn the loss of the Oberstein name. But not so with the Lohengramm royal line. So long as the dynasty continues to uphold justice and stability, its people will pay for its continuation with their own blood if they have to, and it would bring them much joy should Your Majesty marry and produce an heir."

These terms, laid out for the emperor's sake, had real worth for von Oberstein as well. He went on:

"But once the empress's father and older brothers—which is to say, the heir's maternal relatives—boast vainly of your honor by association, wielding your authority as if it were their own, it will bring great harm to the nation. Throughout ancient history, there have been many cases of an emperor doing in the entire family of his new bride upon marrying her, to strike at the root of evil before it sprouts. I only ask that you please bear that in mind."

Reinhard's eyes were filled with ice-blue brilliance. Had any subordinate other than the secretary of defense said what von Oberstein just had, no doubt lightning would have struck that person down. But the trust between them was such that von Oberstein would be taken as seriously as he spoke freely.

"If I'm not mistaken, it would seem you're opposed to one person in particular wearing the empress's tiara. But don't you think it's an inappropriate subject to bring up before a single candidate for empress has yet to be decided?"

"I know it's premature."

"So, it would be extremely awkward if the empress were to become second to the emperor, politically speaking? Is that what you're thinking?"

Had von Reuentahl or Mittermeier been there to witness this conversation, they would surely have been on the edges of their seats. They knew firsthand what it felt like to be a target of Reinhard's scathing criticism.

Von Oberstein, for his part, was unfazed.

"Your Majesty discerns well."

"But if I marry, a child will be born."

"That's a good thing, of course, because it will systematically guarantee the continuation of the dynasty."

Reinhard clicked his tongue sharply and stroked his youthful face. This gave him an idea, prompting him to change the subject.

"Count von Mariendorf and his daughter are still under house arrest?"

"Seeing as they're directly related to that traitor von Kümmel, it's only a matter of course. Were we living under the Goldenbaum Dynasty, the entire family would've been executed or banished by now."

Reinhard wound a finger around the pendant hanging from his neck.

"In other words, not only does the Church of Terra have aims on my life, but it also wants to take away my indispensable secretary of state and chief imperial secretary?" Reinhard's private emotions and public authority had been wounded enough. "I see no further point in keeping them under house arrest! As of tomorrow, father and daughter von Mariendorf are to be released and reinstated to their full official capacities."

"Understood."

"One more thing. I forbid anyone to blame the von Mariendorfs for this foolish incident. Anyone who purposefully goes against my prohibition on this matter must prepare to be punished for insubordination."

The absolute monarch's intentions towered over national law and people's emotions alike. Von Oberstein bowed his head deeply and accepted the young emperor's incontrovertible will. Reinhard locked his ice-blue gaze on von Oberstein, and turned his tall, elegant figure around, his voice and expression extinguished.

By the time von Oberstein returned to his office at the defense ministry, a report, sent directly from the resident high commissioner's office without going through Lennenkamp, was waiting for him:

"The commissioner has ordered an intensification of surveillance of Marshal Yang Wen-li. There is reason to believe Yang has close connections with antigovernment movements within the alliance."

Upon receiving the report from the defense ministry's Bureau of Investigations director, Commodore Anton Ferner, secretary of defense Marshal von Oberstein narrowed his artificial eyes.

"The masses need a hero to unify them. It's only natural that the alliance's extremists and fundamentalists would idolize Yang Wen-li. Without him, they have no rallying point."

"Lennenkamp? I wonder…"

"Do you think we should let this slide? Even if Marshal Yang has no intention of rebelling at present, so long as he has primary color paints at his disposal, at some point he will make a mess of the canvas."

Even though Ferner had found von Oberstein in a heartless mood, he saw the secretary of defense as an invaluable asset who'd exhibited no signs of erosion from the recent tide of events. The secretary of defense turned to his subordinate with indifference, showing no malice.

"Let's stay out of it for now. Lennenkamp especially hates it when people intrude on his authority."

"Yes, but, Your Excellency Secretary, if Commissioner Lennenkamp is too careless in dealing with the alliance's golden boy, Marshal Yang, the grassroots alliance resistance against the empire might just get out of hand. The bigger a fire gets, the more difficult it is to put it out."

Commodore Ferner's voice had the slightest affectation of an actor reciting his lines. This time, there was something other than indifference in von Oberstein's discernment.

"I've exceeded my brief. Please, strike what I just said."

Now that Ferner had recognized his mistake, von Oberstein dismissed him with a wave of his bony hand.

Ferner left with a bow. He couldn't help but guess the defense secretary's innermost thoughts.

Did von Oberstein have something planned for Marshal Yang? Like burying a magnet in the sand and coming up with small bits of metal, he was covertly rallying the alliance's anti-imperial diehards and democratic fundamentalists around Yang. And what then? What was the pretext behind executing Yang? Was it to eradicate distress from the empire's future? Or was it to expand the influence of fanatical Yang supporters to bring about a rift in the anti-imperial forces? If he managed to encourage internal conflict and mutually destroy both sides from within, the empire's hands would remain clean in their grab for alliance territory.

But will things really develop as the defense secretary expects them to? Ferner thought to himself.

In the realm of the battlespace, Yang Wen-li excelled at playing the resourceful general who could drive even a military genius like Emperor Reinhard into a corner. With neither fleet nor soldiers, was Yang Wen-li in fact resigned to being an ingredient in Marshal von Oberstein's dish? Didn't cornered rats always throw themselves upon the cats chasing them? If so, then Lennenkamp was sure to get bitten first. A trivial pity.

"In any case, this will be something to watch. Whether the defense secretary's will will be done, whether the current peace will come to define an age, or whether this is just the eye of the storm, history is at a crossroads. Every decision from this point forward will have dramatic ramifications."

Ferner curled the corners of his mouth into a cynical smile. As a staff officer of the former high noble army, he'd plotted to assassinate

Reinhard. Not out of animosity, but out of faith to his position. That fateful night, Reinhard had allowed him to act as his subordinate and under von Oberstein primarily marked achievements in strategic planning and office management. He wasn't a person of lawless ambition, but as a spectator, he clearly enjoyed unrest over peace, for he was possessed of a strange confidence that, by his own ability and dynamism, he could survive any situation.

Von Oberstein turned toward his empty office with an inorganic glint in his eye.

Whatever a lord lacked, his retainers had to make up for. To von Oberstein, the Lohengramm Dynasty and Emperor Reinhard constituted an opus worth betting one's life on. It was incomparable in rapidity and in the beauty of its theme, but von Oberstein took issue with its durability, or lack thereof.

In a salon of the Mariendorf residence, the count and his daughter were sitting on sofas, watching the languid dance of time go by.

"I don't feel any pity for Heinrich," said Hilda to her father. "For a few minutes, he stood proudly on that stage as the lead actor in a production of his own making. I have a feeling that he purposefully chose that location to pour his life into one final performance…"

"Performance, you say?"

Her father's voice was intelligent, if devoid of vitality.

"I don't believe that Heinrich had any intention of assassinating His Majesty. Leaving aside why the Church of Terra convinced him to attempt such a heinous act, he took on the dishonor of being called an assassin just to have those last few minutes of his life."

Thinking about it in such a way only somewhat placated her father's grief. Hilda knew that her father, who'd never sired a son, had always felt a certain affection for his feeble nephew. But now Hilda wondered if her own thoughts hadn't caught the sleeve of truth. Baron Heinrich von Kümmel had refused a gradual death and had chosen to gather his meager life savings and burn the powder of his short existence in a flash of radiance. Hilda couldn't bring herself to see this as a great act. Then again, there was probably no other way for Heinrich to have purified the violent envy and jealousy he felt toward Reinhard.

Hilda reached out her hand and picked up the bell on the table, intending to ask her butler Hans for some coffee. But the fair-complexioned and broad-shouldered Hans appeared before the bell had even made a sound.

"My lady," the butler announced in a high voice. "There's a visiphone call for you directly from the imperial palace. The man on the screen has introduced himself as von Streit, and he would like to share some good news. Please come to the visiphone room at once."

As Hilda returned the unrung bell to the table, she stood up with the sprightly movement of a boy. Hilda had been expecting good news. The young golden-haired emperor couldn't very well banish Count von Mariendorf and his daughter from the court forever. Neither could she help but predict that the imperial court would show one side of its thorny crown sooner or later.

Hilda had to protect her father and herself so as not to give secretary of defense Marshal von Oberstein's hunting dogs a scent trail to follow.

"Did they really think I'd give in so easily?" she muttered while making her way down the hallway.

Hans looked over his shoulder with a dubious glance.

"Is something the matter, my lady?"

"Oh, it's nothing. Just talking to myself."

Even as she said these words, Hilda caught herself wondering whether the typical noblewoman would've kept her mouth shut. She hit her head of short, dull-blond hair lightly with her fist. Why should she care at all about how other women carried themselves at court? It was unlike her to think of such things.

II

Happiest of all about Count Franz von Mariendorf and Hilda having their house arrest lifted was Marshal Wolfgang Mittermeier.

"Who does that damned von Oberstein think he is anyway?" he said to his wife, Evangeline. "Entire families pleading guilty to treasonous crimes, regardless of complicity, is an outdated custom that ended the moment this dynasty began. I can think of no better candidate for empress than Hilda. If the two of them produced an heir, you can be sure he'd grow up to be one sagacious prince. Wouldn't that be something?"

"I suppose, but all that matters in the end is how they feel about each other."

Evangeline kept her husband's impertinence in check, turning her head to the side in that birdlike way he loved. At twenty-six, she had no children, the innocence she had when they were first married almost entirely untarnished. As ever, the way she managed the household had a musical rhythm to it that pleased Mittermeier to no end.

"I didn't take your hand in marriage because you were a capable military officer with a promising future. It was for who you were, and still are, my dear."

"If I'd known that, I might've been more suave when I proposed. I didn't know much back then…"

The chime on their home computer indicated a visitor. Evangeline left the salon with that cadence in her step he so adored and soon came back to announce that Admiral von Reuentahl had come to see him.

Oskar von Reuentahl had visited the Mittermeier residence much less often than Mittermeier had visited his, and so his presence told him something serious was going on. Although he saw families and marriage through the dark lenses of extreme prejudice, he always adhered to etiquette when stepping foot inside a friend's home. He also presented a bouquet of flowers to the woman of the house out of sheer politeness.

As Evangeline Mittermeier put that evening's jonquils into a vase and brought in a plate of homemade sausage and cottage cheese to her husband's guest, the Twin Ramparts of the Imperial Navy were already watering their own flowers of conversation with wine.

Having no interest in being privy to this male bonding session, Mrs. Mittermeier put down the dish and left with the name "Trünicht" riding her ear.

"A man like Job Trünicht is sure to go down in history as an extraordinary salesman," said von Reuentahl with disdain.

"Salesman, you say?"

"Yes. First, he sold the Free Planets Alliance and his democracy over to the empire. And now, the Church of Terra. Every time he rolls out a new product, history changes. He's right up there with the Phezzanese merchants."

"I suppose you're right. He is a top-notch salesman. But as a buyer, he leaves a lot to be desired. He buys only contempt and vigilance. Who would respect him? All he does is sell off his own character by the piece."

The secretary-general of Supreme Command Headquarters gave an unpleasant smile.

"You speak correctly, Mittermeier. He doesn't need the respect or love of others to live. His stalks may be thick, but his roots run deep. He's like a parasitic plant."

"A parasite indeed."

The two famed generals fell into silence for no apparent reason.

Onetime commander of the Alliance Armed Forces' Iserlohn Fortress, Admiral Yang Wen-li, had been keenly aware of Trünicht's enslavement to a fear and hatred that went beyond the limits of common sense. Although not quite so serious, von Reuentahl and Mittermeier came to the same conclusion.

"We can't just write him off as a mean bastard, either. He's far from a common man, in the worst sense. We'll just have to keep an eye on him, either way."

At this point, while making not insignificant contributions to the development of the Lohengramm Dynasty, when it came to lack of respect and goodwill, there was no one quite like Trünicht. Even Marshal von Oberstein, although not particularly well liked, had at least become an object of reverence. But Trünicht was utterly lacking in popularity. Echoes of his tainted legacy were still being felt throughout the Free Planets Alliance, and likely would be for a long time to come.

After suppressing the alliance capital of Heinessen and facing Trünicht for the first time, Oskar von Reuentahl's attitude was one of extreme indifference, while Wolfgang Mittermeier's eyes danced with conspicuous animosity. Of course, Hilda had no choice but to deal with Trünicht in the two admirals' stead, but it was entirely impossible to look with favor upon any politician who would sell his own country and people in exchange for something so petty and fleeting as personal security.

Evangeline brought in some of her homemade chicken aspic, announcing that Mittermeier's subordinate Karl Eduard Bayerlein had come to visit. The brave young general appeared in the doorway, his usual enthusiastic self.

"Your Excellency, I had some business nearby, so I hope you don't mind my stopping by. Plus, I caught wind of an odd rumor."

Bayerlein had one foot in the room, which now hovered five centimeters above the floor. He hadn't expected von Reuentahl to be there. Flustered, he cobbled together a formal salute.

"What kind of rumor?"

"It's nothing, really, only…There's no proof, so I can't say for sure whether it's even true."

Von Reuentahl's presence weighed heavily on the young Bayerlein's heart. Mittermeier urged him with a seemingly bitter smile.

"No matter. Just tell me."

"Yes, Your Excellency. It's something I heard from the alliance prisoners of war."

"Oh?"

"They're saying Admiral Merkatz is still alive."

Before Bayerlein closed his mouth, silence stepped in and took a lap around the room. Mittermeier and von Reuentahl looked away from Bayerlein and at each other, sharing the same strong feelings. Mittermeier verified with his subordinate.

"*That* Merkatz? Are you saying Wiliabard Joachim Merkatz didn't die after all?"

His use of the demonstrative "that" of course had a very different ring to it than when he was applying it to von Oberstein. Bayerlein shrugged.

"I can only tell you that's what I heard."

"But I thought Merkatz was killed in action during the Vermillion War. Who would be so irresponsible as to spit on his grave by spreading misinformation about him?"

"Like I said, it's only a rumor."

The young general lowered his voice. Waves of regret were springing up around him.

"It's not outside the realm of possibility," muttered von Reuentahl, as if releasing himself from the grip of a fixed stereotype. "We know the remains were never identified. I wouldn't put it past him to fake his own death."

Mittermeier groaned.

If Merkatz had survived the Vermillion War, the Galactic Empire would demand his death. As former commander in chief of the Coalition of Lords, Merkatz had antagonized Reinhard. After that, he'd defected and had since denied any involvement with the young golden-haired sovereign.

"But it's only a rumor."

To these words, Mittermeier nodded.

"You're right. It would be foolish to go around pointing fingers at this point. Let's leave it to the Domestic Safety Security Bureau to uncover the truth."

"If there's nothing else, then, I guess I'll be going…"

Bayerlein had surely wanted to use the rumor as a pretext for enjoying a drinking bout with the superior he so admired. Von Reuentahl's being there had upset that plan. Sensing as much, Mittermeier made no effort to detain him further. He filled their glasses and changed the subject.

"By the way, I hear you've changed women yet again."

Holding his glass, the secretary-general of Supreme Command Head-quarters curved his lips into a slight smile.

"If only that were just a rumor as well, but it's true."

"Get wooed by another vixen, did we?"

That such instances had become increasingly frequent was one reason why Mittermeier couldn't bring himself to criticize his friend's philan-dering ways too strongly.

"You're way off. It was *I* who was on the prowl."

A mixed light swayed in his heterochromatic eyes.

"I made her mine through my own authority and violence. I've become more and more vicious. If I don't repent, I won't hear the end of it from von Oberstein and Lang."

"Don't talk like that. It's not like you."

There was bitterness in Mittermeier's voice.

"Sure…"

Von Reuentahl beamed at his friend. He nodded as if taking advice, then topped off his glass with more wine.

"So, what really went down?"

"To tell you the truth, she nearly killed me."

"What?!"

"I'd just gotten home and was walking through the door when she came at me with a knife. Apparently, she'd been waiting several hours for my arrival. Normally, I welcome a beautiful woman waiting for my return." The reflections of undulating wine flickered in his mismatched eyes. "She introduced herself as Elfriede von Kohlrausch, adding that her own mother was the niece of Duke Lichtenlade."

"A relative of Duke Lichtenlade?!"

The young heterochromatic admiral nodded.

"Hearing that, even I was convinced. She had every reason to hate me. In her mind, I'm her granduncle's sworn enemy."

Two years prior, in SE 797, year 488 of the former Imperial Calendar, the Galactic Empire had experienced the upheaval known as the Lippstadt War, when political and military leaders had been divided into two factions. A confederation led by Duke von Braunschweig and Marquis von Littenheim had sought to overthrow the axis represented by prime minister Duke Lichtenlade and supreme commander of the Imperial Navy Duke Reinhard von Lohengramm. This axis, having set up the old authoritarians and younger men of ambition not as friends but as a foundation for its plans, enraged the high nobles by monopolizing their authority.

While Admiral Merkatz, a veteran commander of the Coalition of Lords, came to be defeated not only by the wits of his enemies but also by the indifference of his comrades, Reinhard returned with victory in his hand. His victory, however, would be accompanied by tragedy. When an assassin's gun aimed at him was blocked by Siegfried Kircheis's body, the golden-haired youth lost more than a friend, but also his better half, and for a while it crippled him. Had he known that, Duke Lichtenlade would likely have purged the young alliance men in one stroke and tried to capitalize on his full authority. Reinhard's subordinates beat him to the punch, burying Duke Lichtenlade and his clique, thus securing Reinhard's authority.

Mittermeier shook his head.

"As far as enemies go, you and I are no different."

"No, we *are* different," said von Reuentahl. "At that time, you rushed to parliament to steal the seal of state. And what did I do? I showed up at Duke Lichtenlade's private residence to restrain that old man. I'm more the enemy for being directly involved."

Von Reuentahl vividly recalled that night from two years ago. When he'd kicked down Lichtenlade's door with a group of trained soldiers, the old authority figure had been reading on his elegant bed. The old man had dropped his book to the floor, knowing he was defeated. After he'd been apprehended by the soldiers, von Reuentahl had turned the book over with the heel of his military shoe and read the words on the front cover: *Ideal Politics.*

"Incidentally, I was the one who ordered the execution of that old man and his entire family. All the more reason for her to resent me."

"Did she always know what had happened?"

"Not at first. She does now."

"You didn't…"

"Yes. I told her."

Mittermeier heaved a sigh with the entire upper half of his body as he ruffled his honey-colored hair with one hand. "What was the point in doing that? Why did you tell her such things? Do you hate yourself that much?"

"I told myself the same thing. Even I knew it was useless. It only hit me after the fact."

Von Reuentahl poured a small waterfall of wine down his throat. "It's tearing me up inside, I know it."

III

Elfriede stirred on the sofa. The evergreen oak door opened, and the master of the von Reuentahl residence cast his tall shadow across the floor. With his mismatched eyes, the man who'd taken Elfriede's virginity admired her cream-colored hair and fresh limbs.

"I'm touched. It seems you haven't run away after all."

"It's not as if I've done anything wrong. Why would I need to run away?"

"You're a criminal who tried to kill the secretary-general of the Imperial Navy's Supreme Command Headquarters. I could have you executed on the spot. The fact that I haven't put you in chains should tell you what a forgiving man I can be."

"I'm not a habitual criminal like all of you."

One couldn't wound the pride of a veteran hero with such cynicism and get away with it. The young admiral with the heterochromatic eyes let out a short, derisive laugh. He closed the door behind him and made his slow approach. His ferocity and grace were in perfect harmony. Ignoring his intention, the woman's eyes were drawn to him. When she came to her senses, her right wrist was firmly in his grasp.

"Such a beautiful hand," he said, his breath reeking of alcohol. "I've been told my mother's hands were also beautiful, as if carved from the finest ivory. She never once used those hands for anyone but herself. The first time she picked up her own son, she tried to stab him in the eye with a knife. That was the last time she ever touched me."

Caught in von Reuentahl's attractive gaze of gold and silver, Elfriede held her breath for a moment.

"Such a pity! Even your own mother knew her son would one day commit treason. She threw her feelings aside and took matters into her own hands. If only I had an ounce of her bravery. That such a splendid mother could give birth to such an unworthy son!"

"With a little adjustment, we could use that as your epitaph."

Von Reuentahl released Elfriede's white hand and brushed back the dark-brown hair hanging over his forehead. The sensation of his hand remained as a hot ring on the woman's wrist. Von Reuentahl leaned his tall frame against a wall tapestry, deep in thought.

"I just don't get it. Is it so terrible losing the privileges you had until your father's generation? It's not like your father or grandfather worked to earn those privileges. All they did was run around like children."

Elfriede swallowed her response.

"Where's the justice in that lifestyle? Noblemen are institutionalized thieves. Haven't you ever noticed that? If taking something by force is evil, then how is taking something by one's inherited authority any different?"

Von Reuentahl stood upright from the wall, his expression deflated.

"I thought you were better than that. What a turnoff. Get out, right now, and find yourself a man more 'worthy' of you. Some dimwit who clings to a bygone era in which his comfortable little life would've been guaranteed by authority and law. But before that, I have one thing to say."

The heterochromatic admiral banged the wall with his fist, enunciating every word.

"There's nothing uglier or lowlier in this world than gaining political authority regardless of ability or talent. Even an act of usurpation is infinitely better. In that case, at least one makes a real effort to gain that authority, because he knows it wasn't his to begin with."

Elfriede remained on the sofa, a seated tempest.

"I get it," she spat out, her voice filled with heat lightning. "You're just a regular rebel to the bone, aren't you?! If you think you have so much ability and talent, then why not have a go at it yourself? Sooner or later, your conceit will compel you to go against your present lord."

Elfriede ran out of breath and sank into silence. Von Reuentahl changed his expression. With renewed interest, he gazed at this woman who'd tried to kill him. A few seconds of silence passed before he spoke.

"The emperor is nine years younger than I am, and yet he holds the entire universe in his own hands. I may harbor animosity toward the Goldenbaum royal family and the noble elite, but I lack the backbone to overthrow the dynasty itself. There's no way I could ever be a match for him."

As he turned his back on the woman struggling to find her retort, von Reuentahl left the salon in stride. Elfriede watched as his broad-shouldered silhouette receded, but she suddenly turned away, having caught herself waiting for this abominable man to look back over his shoulder. Her gaze was fixed on an unremarkable oil painting and stayed that way for ten seconds. When she finally looked back, the master of the house was gone. Elfriede had no idea whether von Reuentahl had indeed looked back at her.

IV

The military's VIPs were actively mobilizing their Earth dispatch. No one in the imperial government had gotten any sleep.

In the Ministry of Arts and Culture, under Dr. Seefeld's direct command, compilation of *The Goldenbaum Dynasty: A Complete History* was under way. The Goldenbaum line had been effectively destroyed, but not without leaving behind a vast amount of data hoarded under the name of state secrets. The arduous task of sifting through it all was sure to throw light on various pieces of information hitherto considered to be off-the-record or the stuff of rumors, and the ministry's task was to ensure that every last incriminating detail would be preserved for all posterity.

The Alliance Armed Forces' retired marshal Yang Wen-li had the will of a historian, but since the age of fifteen, when his father's death had plunged the Yang family into economic hardship, he'd gone through life stumbling along the edge of reality. If he could have seen the research-ers of the imperial Ministry of Arts and Culture combing daily through mountains of undisclosed data, he would have been salivating with envy.

Emperor Reinhard made no indication that the Ministry of Arts and Culture was to dig up especially damning evidence about the Goldenbaum Dynasty. There was no need. No matter the dynasty or system of author-ity, good deeds were valorized and propagandized, while foul deeds were concealed. Undisclosed information was therefore guaranteed to contain evidence of wrongdoing and misconduct. The researchers kept silent throughout the process, but surely struck gold everywhere they dug as they unearthed load after load of the Goldenbaum Dynasty's misdeeds and scandals.

Rudolf von Goldenbaum, who'd founded the Goldenbaum Dynasty five centuries before, was as far from Reinhard as a ruler could be. He was a hulking mound of self-serving justice, invisible to the eyes of faith. He achieved success as a military man first, as a politician second. His physical and mental aptitude were immense, but like a middle school math teacher recycling the same old rudimentary equations, he never evolved beyond the template to which he'd grown accustomed. To those who didn't share his thoughts or values, he responded at first with an iron fist, and later with the many deaths brought about by its impact. How many historians had been killed in order to maintain his just and righteous image?

Reinhard had no interest in such methods.

Rudolf the Great had been a literal giant, one who ruled over all by his incomparably intimidating air. His more civilized successor, Sigismund I, was a most capable tyrant. He unilaterally suppressed the republican insurrection, at the same time maintaining a relatively fair governmental administration for those "good citizens" who followed along. He deftly used a carrot-and-stick policy to reinforce the cornerstone of the empire laid by his grandfather. And while the third-generation emperor, Richard I, who followed him loved beautiful women, hunting, and music more than government, he never once overstepped his bounds as sovereign. He lived a guarded life, walking a delicate tightrope between his headstrong empress and sixty concubines, never once tumbling to the ground.

The fourth emperor, Ottfried I, was more resolute than his father but was of sound health, austere and prosaic. To anyone who knew him, he was a total bore. It seemed his only objective in life was to digest a precise daily schedule with as little variation as possible. His utter lack of interest in music, fine art, or literature had earned him the nickname "Earl Gray," for his life was indeed dull and colorless. It is said the only books he voluntarily read were the memoirs of founding father Rudolf the Great, along with a few random volumes on home medicine. He was a solemn conservative who abhorred any kind of change or reform like a virus and clung to the precedents set before him by Rudolf the Great, whom he so admired.

One day, on orders from his doctor and nutritionist, Ottfried had finished his lunch of vegetables, dairy products, and seaweed. He was just heading out for his fifteen-minute constitutional, right on schedule, when an urgent message informed him that a giant explosion on a military base had left more than ten thousand soldiers dead.

The emperor seemed unimpressed by the news.

"This report wasn't on today's agenda."

For him, the almighty schedule was an inviolable entity—this despite the fact that he lacked both the creativity and planning ability to set one up himself. Such duties he left to the imperial private secretary, Viscount Eckhart, whose responsibility and authority mounted like sand in an hourglass. Before anyone knew it, Eckhart came to hold double posts of privy councillor and secretary-general of the imperial palace, where he served also as secretary for the imperial council. As even those of little insight could see, the ashen emperor had become nothing more than a cheap automaton dancing to whatever tune Viscount Eckhart played for him. When the emperor died, no one cared enough to commemorate his life in any meaningful way.

Ottfried's son Kaspar was set to become fifth emperor of the Galactic Empire. As the imperial prince, he showed above-average intelligence, but those colors faded as he matured. It's likely he hid his wisdom as a way of rebelling against Eckhart's despotic tendencies. "If the late emperor was dull prose," whispered his senior ministers, "then our current sovereign is equally dull poetry." Indeed, he was much more like his grandfather than his father, prizing the arts and beauty above all things. Only he was less skillful at walking the tightrope his grandfather had left unfrayed.

What raised the eyebrows of the empress dowager and senior ministers was the crown prince's apparent lack of interest in the opposite sex. He particularly favored a castrato of the imperial choir. Castrated at a young age, the castrati had long preserved the boy-soprano tradition and remained an integral part of imperial and church choirs.

Even after Kaspar's coronation, he fell in love with an elegant fourteen-year-old singer named Florian, lending no ear to any of the marriage proposals the empress dowager brought before him, no matter how attractive the prospect.

Rudolf the Great, who'd slaughtered homosexuals en masse as pollutants that would otherwise infect the future, had now produced a homosexual among his descendants. Listen closely enough, and one could almost hear his cries of outrage from the beyond the grave.

Meanwhile, the real political power remained firmly in Eckhart's grasp. Having risen to the rank of count, he was now a man of unrivaled influence, half-jokingly referred to as the "mooching emperor." He made the national treasury his personal playground, where he threw around the weight of a corpulent body devoid of its virility. As he wore down his sense of responsibility and ability as a political administrator, his power sickness continued to afflict him. He tried offering his own daughter as the new empress, but she resembled her father now more than ever.

Eckhart approached the emperor in the hopes of taking his lord's eyes off Florian, but while the emperor had always followed his counsel on other matters, he couldn't be persuaded or coerced on this one. The moment Eckhart walked into the Rose Room, he was shot and killed by a gang under command of one Baron Risner. Risner, who'd always detested Eckhart's tyranny, had received the emperor's consent to execute this "disloyal retainer." That was all well and good, but in the wake of this disturbance, the emperor left a written declaration of abdication on his throne and absconded with Florian and a handful of jewels to boot. This was exactly one year after he'd taken the throne.

Following 140 days of vacancy, the younger brother of former emperor Ottfried, Archduke Julius, picked up the abandoned crown. The senior imperial ministers, however, had their eyes on his more popular son, Franz Otto.

At the time of his coronation, Emperor Julius was already seventy-six years old yet was in extremely good health for his age. Five days after his enthronement, he'd set up a harem of twenty beautiful concubines, and a month later added twenty more.

It fell to the middle-aged crown prince, Archduke Franz Otto, to satisfy the needs of national politics while the emperor satisfied those of his still-virile flesh. Franz Otto corrected much of the corruption left over from the Eckhart era, enforced the law, and reduced taxes slightly for common citizens. The senior ministers were confident they'd made the right choice. But Julius I, whom they expected to expire sooner rather than later, held firm to the throne into his eighties, then his nineties.

In the end, by a strange twist of fate, when Emperor Julius was ninety-five, the "oldest crown prince in human history," His Highness Archduke Franz Otto, died of illness at seventy-four. And because the archduke's sons had all died young, his grandson Karl became "great-grand heir to the imperial throne" at twenty-four.

Karl had only a few years to wait before donning the imperial crown, although to him it seemed the emperor might live on forever. Julius had been an old man for as long as Karl could remember. He was still an old man and would continue to be for years to come. Would this "immortal bag of bones," he mused, continue to suck the life force out of future generations, carrying on even as he continued to wither in that jewel-encrusted coffin he called a throne?

Karl wasn't a particularly superstitious young man, but superstition had made him see the emperor through faintly colored lenses of fear and hatred. Consequently, his malice toward the old emperor was, outside of his own ambitions, at the very least cultivated in the fertilizer of self-preservation. All of this speculation and impatience led to the first parricide in the entire history of the Galactic Empire.

On April 6, year 144 of the old Imperial Calendar, a 96-year-old Julius I was having dinner with five of his concubines, whose combined age still fell short of the emperor's single life span. After wolfing down his venison with the appetite of a teenager, he was finishing off the meal with some chilled white wine when he started gasping for air. He vomited up his meal and, moments later, died in a spasm of agony, white silk tablecloth still clutched in his hand.

The old emperor's sudden death shocked his senior ministers, less out of suspicion than by their own relief that the old man had finally perished. In truth, his ministers, almost without exception, were bored with him. Archduke Karl presided over a grand, if emotionless, funeral. The senior ministers all expected the young new emperor to implement fresh administration after a requisite period of mourning. The people expected nothing. Lacking any political authority whatsoever, they did the best they could, living lives of hard labor and simple pleasures. But on May 1, coronation day, the public was just as amazed as the senior ministers when not Archduke Karl but former archduke Franz Otto's second son and Karl's cousin, Marquis Sigismund von Brauner, solemnly accepted the imperial crown.

The reasons behind the enthronement of Sigismund II were, of course, never made public. Now, more than three thousand years later, the archives at last revealed the truth behind this last-minute switch. Upon the old emperor's sudden death, the five concubines who'd been seated at his table were forced by Archduke Karl to follow their master to the grave. Having served the old emperor as faithfully as they had, in this time of crisis they panicked, refusing to carry their duties over to the next reign. For that crime, they were sentenced to take their own lives.

The five concubines were confined to a room nestled in the rear palace, where they were forced to drink poison. Just before taking that fatal dose, one of the concubines wrote the truth in lipstick on the inside of her bracelet and had it sent to her older brother, an officer in the imperial brigade. Upon reading her message, her brother learned that Archduke Karl had coated the inside of Julius's wineglass with a poison that, once absorbed into his stomach lining, rapidly diminished the ability of his red blood cells to absorb oxygen. His younger sister, the concubine, had been bribed by Karl into being an accomplice. The brother decided then and there to exact revenge for his sister's death. He brought the evidence before Sigismund, second in line for the throne. Sigismund was pleasantly surprised at having just cause to oust Karl, and after shuffling things around within the palace, succeeded in forcing Karl to give up his succession to the imperial throne. He was unable to make known the fact that the emperor had been poisoned by his own great-grandson, and so he carried out his own little coup d'état behind closed doors.

After being confined to the palace, Karl was transferred to a mental institution on the outskirts of the imperial capital. There, behind thick walls, he was treated well enough to live a long life, eclipsing his great-grandfather by expiring at the age of ninety-seven. By the time of his death, the reigns of Sigismund II and Ottfried II had passed into the age of Otto Heinz I. There was no longer anyone at court who remembered the name of the old man who'd failed to take the throne more than seventy years before. Between Karl's death in year 217 of the Imperial Calendar and the Battle of Dagon that the Free Planets Alliance took in 331, the Goldenbaum Dynasty would see eight more emperors, giving rise to their own stories across a spectrum of good and evil.

As he ran his eyes over this unofficial interim report presented to him by the Ministry of Arts and Culture, Reinhard found himself at times smiling derisively, at others pausing to go deep into thought. Though he lacked Yang Wen-li's passion for history, those with designs on the future couldn't get there without knowing the blueprints of the past.

Not that every indicator was to be found in what had already come to pass. Reinhard wasn't one to follow someone else's path.

Because now, everyone was following his.

CHAPTER 5:
CHAOS, DISORDER, AND CONFUSION

I

IN THE LATTER HALF OF SE 799, in the first year of the New Imperial Calendar, a change that no one could have accurately predicted came to pass. The enactment of the Bharat Treaty in May of that year, in conjunction with Reinhard von Lohengramm's coronation the following June, was supposed to have put an end to two and a half centuries of war and implemented a new universal order in its place. And while it was too optimistic to think this might go on forever, common sense dictated that the new dynasty would at the very least devote itself to the establishment of a new system, that the alliance would be bereft of vengeful power, and that the next few years would be relatively peaceful ones. Even Emperor Reinhard and Yang Wen-li couldn't escape the gravity of common sense between their own plans and the universes of which they dreamed.

In response to Commodore Ferner's doubts, secretary of defense of the Imperial Navy Marshal von Oberstein claimed he'd done nothing more than read into these sudden developments and use them to his advantage, as anyone in his position might have done.

"It's your choice whether you want to believe me," von Oberstein had said.

Of special mention about the chaos that ensued in the latter half of SE

799 was that those only tangentially involved wanted to claim themselves as instigators, while those who'd been more proactive in their involvement, despite recognizing themselves as actors on an intergalactic stage, denied their roles as producers and playwrights.

Those who believed unconditionally in a higher power called it "God's will" or "a twist of fate" and threw themselves like stones in a glass house of blind following. But cursing unbelievers like Yang Wen-li—"If my pension suddenly increased tenfold, I might believe in God, too!"—made things harder for themselves by looking for answers within the range of human reason. Whenever Yang spoke of God, Frederica unconsciously looked at her husband differently, unable to suppress a certain uneasiness over putting God in the same category as inflation. Yang's conclusion was that everything was a coproduction between a dead playwright and living actors. But if asked who that playwright was, he would have been hard-pressed to come up with an answer. If anything, he might have said it was "an actor who believes himself to be a playwright." In other words, Helmut Lennenkamp, the Galactic Empire's high commissioner and senior admiral.

Although it was Reinhard who'd put Lennenkamp in that position, that didn't mean he'd surveyed the play's story in its entirety and decided on its cast. Lennenkamp was thirty-six, just four years Yang's senior, but by all outward appearances he appeared no older than twenty.

Yang wasn't the type to let on about the hardships of the battlespace and had always been indifferent to the fortitude so giddily ascribed to him by war correspondents. Admiral Steinmetz, who'd once suffered defeat because of him, took one look at Yang, who seemed nothing more than a lanky, boyish student, and muttered with disappointment.

"I lost to *him*?"

Then again, Steinmetz knew full well the folly of judging a book by its cover and blamed such thinking on his own part for leading to his defeat in the first place.

Lennenkamp couldn't let go of this fixation. According to Artist-Admiral Mecklinger, Walter von Schönkopf had some choice words about Lennenkamp:

"So, he's that much of a big shot, is he?"

Whether Lennenkamp was indeed a big shot remained to be seen.

This was how a modest, irresponsible rumor grew into a tide that changed history.

Attaching the phrase "or so I hear" to the statement "Merkatz is still alive" started it all by clouding the memories of a nervous population. Von Reuentahl and Mittermeier laughed off the very notion of Merkatz's survival for the same reason.

As Ernest Mecklinger recorded it:

It didn't take us long to confirm the truth of that rumor. Nevertheless, a second truth remains to be verified. Namely, who circulated that rumor in the first place, and why.

While concluding it was just one form of never-ending groupthink, the manifestation of delusional hero worship, Mecklinger was almost tempted to think that this was all meant to be. He therefore saw no reason to deny the veracity of its effect, even if the cause was born in deception:

The rumor has created the reality. Either that, or an unwitting public has interfered with the passage of time by digging its heels into a past it just can't let go of.

Mecklinger was exercising self-restraint in putting it the way he did.

In any event, this rumor, which since June had hovered around countless lips like dark matter, crystallized into something even darker on July 16 when, in the Lesavik sector, the more than five hundred alliance ships supposedly being decommissioned and dismantled were hijacked.

The man responsible for carrying out this operation was Admiral Mascagni, who might have feigned ignorance had only the ships been seized.

But the fact that four thousand of his men had vanished along with the hijackers wasn't something he could chalk up to illusion.

During a hearing at Joint Operational Headquarters, his entire being oozed with sweat and excuses.

"In full compliance with the Bharat Treaty, we were in the middle of demolishing our relinquished warships and carriers, when suddenly, upwards of five hundred ships of unknown affiliation showed up…"

This number was, of course, an exaggeration, although there were some among his men who inflated that number to five *thousand* ships, and so Mascagni's testimony was deemed relatively objective. Continuing with his "objective" testimony, Mascagni said the intruders, after making a grand entrance, had sent a seemingly credible transmission offering their assistance. With the war now over, he saw no reason to fear enemy deception, and the ships, he now saw, were undoubtedly of Alliance Armed Forces make, and so he welcomed them with full assurance that nothing would go wrong. But the moment he did welcome them aboard, the warships were taken from them at gunpoint. The working flagship—which is to say, Admiral Mascagni himself—was taken hostage, while the other ships were helpless to do anything. Moreover, this "band of thieves" announced themselves as a group of freedom fighters opposed to the imperial autocracy. They claimed a common goal and bid anyone who would join their cause to lay down their arms and follow them, upon which four thousand of Mascagni's men, fed up with their lot, ended up doing just that.

Naturally, people were interested in who was behind all this. Several groundless theories suggested Admiral Merkatz as the culprit.

If true, then Merkatz's disappearance following the Vermillion War had surely been orchestrated under Yang Wen-li's baton.

Only this part of the rumor was more correct in practice than in theory. Yang saw the value in it the moment he heard it.

II

Had Yang Wen-li not anticipated the ripple effect of circulating such a dangerous rumor? Not that he could have stopped it even if he *had* anticipated it. Yang had never considered drawing out the Imperial Navy using

Merkatz as a scapegoat, as such a strategy would have been too risky for everyone involved. That said, neither could he assume a lack of affiliation once he set Merkatz free. It was, perhaps, naive on his part to deny the potential of a single rumor. In any case, he was neither almighty nor omnipotent, and it was all he could do to follow the trail of events in the hopes of one day carving out a significant detour of his own.

As Mrs. Caselnes put it to Frederica:

"Yang is so young to have risen to such a high rank in such a short amount of time, but it's all because of the war. Now that we're in a time of peace, he's got nothing to do. You've got to admit, Yang has never looked more content than he does now."

Frederica agreed. Surely, Yang had never considered himself to be one of the elite, and neither did the elite consider Yang to be one of them. And yet, despite his lack of political clout and authoritarian intentions, Yang had earned his position through an uncanny aptitude in the heat of battle and the string of commendations born of that aptitude.

The elite were an exclusive group of people who shared such profound awareness of themselves as self-righteous leaders and an implacability toward distribution of privilege that, even had their door been open to him, Yang wouldn't have cared to step through it. What would be the point of walking into a den of wolves who saw him as nothing more than a meddlesome sheep?

Yang had always been a heretic. Whether at the Officers' Academy, in the military, or in the national pantheon of authority, he preferred to sit in the corner, sticking his nose in a favorite book while letting the just cause of an arrogant orthodoxy at the core of the alliance's center of power waft in one ear and out the other. And when that aloof heretic outshone them all by his grand achievements, the orthodoxy praised him even as they cursed themselves for having to treat him so politely.

One can only imagine how much this incurred the elite's anger and animosity. Yang was more than vaguely aware of their frustrations. He also knew how ridiculous it was to waste his consideration, and he put it out of his mind.

The orthodoxy spoke of barring Yang from their ranks more out of instinct than intellect. Although he was a military man, Yang rejected the significance of all wars, even—if not especially—those in which he'd been involved. He also denied the majesty of the nation and saw the military's raison d'être not as protecting citizens but as protecting the special rights of the very authority figures who'd parasitized the nation. There was no way they were going to let a natural-born provocateur such as Yang Wen-li into their innermost circle. They had even tried subjecting Yang to a political thrashing in an above-the-law hearing, but in a panic had ended up having to dispatch Yang directly from the courtroom into the battlespace to fight the Imperial Navy's massive invasion of the Iserlohn Corridor. As it turned out, the one man they detested above all was the only one who could save them.

They conferred upon him the rank of marshal, making him the youngest to bear that insignia in the history of the Alliance Armed Forces, and awarded him enough medals to weigh by the kilo. And still, that insolent heretic had the gall to give them not so much as a thank-you for all the praise they openly bestowed upon him. Anyone else in his position would have bowed his head in deference, groveled, and begged to be allowed into their ranks, but Yang crammed their hallowed medals into a wooden crate and tossed them into the basement, out of sight and out of mind. He also skipped out on important functions, preferring to go fishing instead of debating the allotment of privileges he saw to be arbitrary at best. To them, the most precious things in this world were forcing others into submission, openly appropriating taxes from the population, and creating laws that guaranteed personal profit. Yang, on the other hand, kicked aside those things as casually as he might pebbles on the side of the road. An intolerable heretic, indeed.

Yang's lack of interest in trying to seize power by military force was ultimately due to the fact that he placed no value whatsoever on authority. It was his contempt for those who desired power—for their sense of values, their way of life, their very existence—that made him smile with scorn.

People in high positions of power couldn't help but despise Yang Wen-li, for to affirm Yang's way of life was to deny their own. One can only imagine the depths of their indignation over their paradoxical relationship to Yang.

They'd been waiting for an opportunity to tear him down from his national hero's seat and throw him into a bottomless pit. But not even that was an option so long as the Galactic Empire posed a threat to their own ascendency. The Galactic Empire continued to thrive, even if its significance had changed. What was once an enemy nation had now become a sovereign ruler. Had not the elite's shining star, Job Trünicht, given himself over to the empire in exchange for a comfortable life? Were they, perhaps, resentful that he'd taken the easy way out, leaving them to cough at the dust he'd left in his wake? Although his firebrand speech had saved millions of soldiers from certain death, one of the joys of his power was expending the lives of his citizens like cheap commodities. Anyone deceived by such cajolery as Trünicht's was a fool. He'd sold the alliance's independence and democratic principles to the empire for the pocket change of personal safety. But had they not also sold Yang Wen-li, who'd made the Imperial Navy eat its own foot on numerous occasions, in exchange for their own safety? In any case, the alliance was no longer. Seeing the nation as indestructible was an ideal that only mindless patriots believed in. They, however, knew the truth, and it was all they could do to cling to their assets, waiting for a chance to jump ship onto another that wasn't sinking.

Thus, a few shameless "merchants" had a mind to sell the commodity known as Yang Wen-li to the empire. Several pieces of anonymous intel to that effect had been sent to the imperial high commissioner, Senior Admiral Helmut Lennenkamp. Their content was virtually identical.

"Yang Wen-li lied about Admiral Merkatz's death and helped him escape in preparation for a future revolt against the empire, at which time Yang himself will rally his soldiers together to rise again."

"Yang plans to mobilize the anti-imperialists and extremists within the alliance under the banner of revolution."

"Yang is an enemy of the empire, a destroyer of peace and order. He will lord over the alliance as a tyrant, invade the empire, and try to crush the entire universe under his military boot."

Captain Ratzel, who oversaw surveillance of Yang, presented Lennenkamp with this anonymous intel inside the building that was a hotel turned commissioner's office. The commissioner watched calmly as Ratzel's expression changed from astonishment to anger while he read over the intel.

"If this information is correct, Captain, then I must say the mesh of your surveillance network isn't nearly tight enough."

"But, Your Excellency," said Captain Ratzel, mustering fortitude against the former enemy general, "you can't possibly take any of this seriously. If Admiral Yang had any inclinations toward being a dictator, why would he wait until such a difficult time as this when he had plenty of opportunities to seize that power before?"

Lennenkamp gave no response.

"To begin with, you can be sure these informants have been rescued from danger by Admiral Yang. And however much the political situation has changed, those who would turn their backs on the ones to whom they're most indebted aren't to be trusted. If and when, as they themselves claim, Admiral Yang does monopolize power as dictator, you can be sure they'll change the colors of their flag at once and prostrate themselves at his feet. Are you really going to lend credence to such shameless slander, Your Excellency?"

As Lennenkamp listened, an unpleasant expression arose on his otherwise-blank face. He nodded silently and dismissed the captain.

Ratzel had never understood his superior's state of mind.

It wasn't that Lennenkamp believed this anonymous intel. It was that he *wanted* to believe it. Rejecting Ratzel's admonition, he advised the alliance government to have retired marshal Yang Wen-li arrested on charges of violating the Insurrection Act. On July 20, a simultaneous order was given to the armed grenadiers unit affiliated with the commissioner's office to be on standby. Chaos, Part the Second, had begun.

An invisible noose had been placed around Yang's neck. The frenzied thinking of alliance leaders and Lennenkamp would never compare to Yang's stable foresight and precaution. In the end, so long as Yang was breathing, he would always be an obstacle they would need to avoid. In order to prevent that, Yang would need to bow to the authorities or lose to Lennenkamp in the battlespace. The former wasn't something of which Yang was incapable, while the latter wasn't something that could be dragged upstream from the past and corrected.

Udo Dieter Hummel was chief of staff of the imperial high commissioner. What Hummel lacked in creative thinking he made up for with his penchant for dealing with the law and administrative subjects efficiently and in good order. Because of his diligence, to Lennenkamp he was a most satisfactory assistant and, in any case, overly creative types with less than half a heart for anything other than their own creations were an unnecessary hazard in a militarily occupied administration.

Nevertheless, there were such things as formalities in this world, and the Free Planets Alliance was an independent nation founded on those formalities. Lennenkamp was no colonial governor-general. His jurisdiction went only as far as the Bharat Treaty specified. Hummel's assistance was indispensable in allowing him to make the most of his power within the scope allotted to him.

Hummel had also been carrying out a more important duty behind the scenes: namely, reporting Lennenkamp's every word and deed to Secretary of Defense von Oberstein.

On the night of the twentieth, Lennenkamp called Hummel into his office for one of their regular debriefings.

"Seeing as Marshal Yang isn't a subject of the empire, he will be punished in accordance with alliance laws."

"I know, the Insurrection Act."

"But that'll never fly. Yang helped Admiral Merkatz escape before the Bharat Treaty and the Insurrection Act were even put into effect. We can't just apply the law retroactively. What I was going to suggest is the alliance's National Defense Base Act."

As soon as he'd taken up his new post, Hummel had brushed up on the alliance government's various laws and ordinances in the hope of finding a legal loophole to nail Yang once and for all.

"When Marshal Yang helped Admiral Merkatz escape," Hummel

continued, "his furnishing of military ships was tantamount to an abuse of his authority over national resources. Under normal law, it would be possible to charge him with malfeasance. He's guilty of a far greater crime than violation of the Insurrection Act."

"I see."

Lennenkamp grinned, his mouth stiffening under his splendid mustache. He wanted any possible excuse to execute Yang Wen-li only because he was regarded by the new dynasty and its emperor as public enemy number one, not because he wanted to dispel some personal grudge of defeat. He wanted to make that clear, so as not to be misunderstood.

Yang Wen-li was renowned for his invincibility, his youth, and his seemingly inherent virtue. If accused of malfeasance simply for treading on Article 3, Yang's renown would also be tarnished.

Lennenkamp's private secretary appeared and saluted.

"Your Excellency Commissioner, there's an FTL incoming from the secretary of defense."

"The secretary of defense? Ah, von Oberstein, you mean," said Lennenkamp, somewhat forced, and with a joyless cadence in his step made his way to the special comm room.

The image was slightly blurred, being transmitted from ten thousand light-years away. Not that Lennenkamp cared. Von Oberstein's pale face and oddly glinting artificial eyes aroused no fascination in those disinclined to aesthetics.

The secretary of defense got right to the point.

"From what I hear, you've ordered the alliance government to execute Yang Wen-li. Is this your way of seeking vengeance for losing to him in battle?"

Lennenkamp went white with anger and humiliation. The blow to his heart was so deep he didn't bother to ask if that's what everyone had been told.

"I can assure you this is *not* a personal matter. My recommendation to the alliance government to execute Yang Wen-li is nothing more than an attempt to clear a path toward a better future for the sake of the empire and His Majesty the Emperor. To say that I'm trying to resolve a grudge would be a gross misinterpretation."

"Just making sure we're on the same page. There's no need to get all worked up."

There was no mockery in von Oberstein's businesslike tone. Lennenkamp nevertheless picked up on negative vibes behind it. The secretary of defense's mouth slowly opened and closed on-screen.

"Allow me to tell you how to get rid of both Yang Wen-li and Merkatz at once. If, by your own hand, you do manage to, as you put it, clear a path toward a better future for the empire, your achievement will surpass those of marshals von Reuentahl and Mittermeier."

Lennenkamp was displeased. He didn't like that von Oberstein was stirring up his competitive spirit, or that he couldn't help but approve of its outcome.

"By all means, then, give me your instructions."

After a short yet deep psychological civil war, Lennenkamp had given in.

"There's no need for any complex maneuvers," said the secretary of defense, with no sense of triumph. "Even knowing you have no such privilege, you will demand that the alliance hand Admiral Yang over to you. You will then officially announce that you are taking him away to the imperial mainland. Once you've done so, Merkatz and his clique are sure to come out of hiding to rescue the hero to whom they're so indebted. That's when you strike."

"Do you really think it'll be that easy?"

"There's only one way to find out. Even if Merkatz doesn't show himself, Admiral Yang will still be under our control. It'll be up to us whether he lives or dies."

Lennenkamp was silent.

"If we're going to incite the anti-imperialists within the alliance, the first thing we need to do is to arrest Yang Wen-li despite his perceived innocence. That will be enough to send his sympathizers on a rampage. Sometimes one needs to fight fire with fire."

"If I could just ask you one thing, Secretary. Does His Majesty Emperor Reinhard know of this?"

A questionable expression flickered across von Oberstein's pale face.

"I wonder. If it concerns you so much, why not ask him yourself? See what His Majesty thinks of your intentions to kill Yang Wen-li."

Of course, Lennenkamp couldn't speak of such things to Emperor Reinhard. Something he struggled to understand was how the young emperor could hold Yang Wen-li in such high regard. Or maybe the emperor just hated Lennenkamp more.

But it was too late for Lennenkamp to jump out of the race now. If he stopped swimming, he would sink to the bottom. Sooner or later, the alliance would need to be completely subjugated. Safeguarding universal order as soon as possible was therefore of paramount importance. Because Yang was such a dangerous character, he had to be eliminated at all costs. And if Lennenkamp could pull off such a grand achievement, he could have any position he wanted, superseding the limited positions that von Reuentahl and Mittermeier had held for most of their careers. Imperial marshal, director of the Imperial Navy, and who knew what else…?

After ending the transmission, von Oberstein looked blankly at the opaque screen.

"One must bait a dog with dog food, a cat with cat food."

Commodore Ferner cleared his throat nearby.

"But Commissioner Lennenkamp may not succeed. If he fails, the entire alliance government will side with Admiral Yang and unite as a show of resistance against the empire. Is that what you want?"

Von Oberstein was unfazed by Ferner's misgivings.

"If Lennenkamp doesn't follow through, so be it. Someone else will just have to carry out that duty in his place. The one who clears the road and the one who paves it needn't be one and the same."

I see, thought Ferner. *Any harm that comes to an imperial representative will be a clear violation of the treaty and will serve as an excuse to mobilize his troops once again in all-out conquest.* Did the secretary of defense intend to conquer the alliance once and for all, scapegoating not only Admiral Yang but Lennenkamp as well?

"But, Your Excellency Secretary, don't you think it's too early to be taking over the alliance?"

"If we're just going to back down from our objective and do nothing, then we'd better come up with a better backup plan."

"Certainly."

"We cannot allow Lennenkamp to become marshal while he lives. It is, however, an honor for which he is posthumously qualified. Being alive isn't the only way to serve one's nation."

Ferner wasn't surprised to be privy to such sentiments. Perhaps von Oberstein was correct in his estimation of Lennenkamp. Not only in this case, but in overwhelmingly most others, von Oberstein spoke soundly. Then again, Ferner was opposed to thinking of human beings as mere variables in the equations of others. And what would happen if von Oberstein found himself in Lennenkamp's position? Had the secretary of defense never considered that possibility? But Ferner wasn't bound by duty to voice such concerns.

III

Upon receiving Lennenkamp's "counsel," the alliance's High Council chairman João Lebello found himself in a predicament. It went without saying this was a grand imperial pretext, and he couldn't just ignore the fact that Yang was the cause of it.

"Yang fancies himself a national hero. Wouldn't letting down our guard now make light of the existence of our nation?"

Lebello was suspicious. If only Yang had listened, no doubt he would have grown bored and lost the will to rebel. But, seen only from the outer circumference of the situation, such suspicions as Lebello's weren't surprising. From the perspective of society at large, any man naive enough to throw away a seat of highest authority at such a young age for a pensioner's life was nothing more than a degenerate. It was more compelling to assume that he was hidden away in some obscure corner of society, working on something bigger than anyone could fathom.

Yang had underestimated his own false image. Those bitten by the hero-worship bug were prone to hyperbole, going so far as to believe that Yang was laying down a millennium's worth of future plans for the nation and humanity at large in his sleep. Even Yang, depending on his mood, was prone to such rhetoric:

"There are farsighted warriors in the world. I know that for a fact. I don't sleep neglectfully, but am thinking deeply about the future of humankind."

And because he was known to spout such things, those who didn't get the sarcasm out of context polished Yang's false image even more. Anytime Julian Mintz heard Yang talking like that, however, he would just brush it off:

"Then allow me to make a prediction about the admiral's future. At seven o'clock tonight, you will have a bottle of wine for dinner."

As Lebello saw things, he was forced to choose between incurring the wrath of the empire by protecting Yang, thus risking the very existence of the alliance, or sacrificing Yang alone to save the alliance. Had he been a more audacious man, he might have appealed to Lennenkamp's coercions, if only to buy himself more time. Lebello had convinced himself that the commissioner's intentions were the emperor's intentions. And while he usually voiced his conclusions after much mental turmoil, he decided to invite his friend Huang Rui, who'd left government service, to share that turmoil in progress.

"Arrest Admiral Yang? You're serious?"

Huang Rui almost asked Lebello if he was insane.

"Understand me. No, you must understand. We mustn't give the Imperial Navy any excuse. Even if Yang is a national hero, if he endangers the peace of our good nation, I'll be forced to execute him."

"But that goes against all reason. While it may be true that Marshal Yang aided in Admiral Merkatz's escape, the Bharat Treaty and Insurrection Act had yet to be put into effect. Any retroactive application of the law is forbidden under the alliance constitution."

"Not if Yang encouraged Merkatz to hijack those ships, in which case that would've been *after* the treaty was put into effect. There's no need whatsoever to apply to law retroactively."

"But where's the proof? Let's just say Yang went along with it. I doubt his subordinates would do the same. They might even take matters into their own hands in rescuing Marshal Yang by force. No, that's precisely what would happen. And what do you plan on doing when infighting breaks out within the Alliance Armed Forces as it did two years ago?"

"In that case, I'll just have to execute them as well. It's not as if they're beholden to Marshal Yang in any way. Their place is to protect the fate of the nation at all costs, not Yang alone."

"I wonder if they'd agree with that. I know I wouldn't. And another thing, Lebello—it makes me uneasy to think what the Imperial Navy's intentions really are and what they might be planning. Maybe they're waiting for us to rouse Admiral Yang's subordinates and bring about civil unrest. That would give them every excuse to intervene. Not that they ever do as they're told anyway."

Lebello nodded but could think of no better plan to rescue their nation from danger.

If asked to personify the questionable existence of fate, Lebello was convinced its limbs would flail around as its central nervous system struggled to control itself. In any case, the situation was quickly escalating.

The next day, on the twenty-first, the chairman was paid a visit by Enrique Martino Borges de Arantes e Oliveira, who oversaw the central think tank of the alliance government as president of Central Autonomous Governance University, a training school for government bureaucrats. They met for three hours for a closed-door discussion. When they came out of the chairman's office, several guards observed that Lebello's lips were pursed in an expression of defeat, while Oliveira wore a thin, insincere smile. In that meeting, a proposition was made that was even more radical than Lebello's original decision.

On the following day, the twenty-second, morning dawned peacefully on the Yang household. Frederica's hard work and effort had paid off. Her cheese omelets were now to both of their liking, and her black tea–brewing skills were improving. Although it was summer, Heinessenpolis was spared the heat and humidity of the tropical zones. The wind passing through the trees layered their skin with the fragrances of chlorophyll and sunlight. Yang had carried his desk and chair to the terrace so that he could try his hand at writing out some of his thoughts, basking in the waltz of light and wind composed by summer. He had a distinct feeling that he was setting down what would one day become a famous literary composition. Or maybe he was just deluded.

Ninety percent of the reasons for war will be shocking to posterity. As for the other 10 percent, how much more shocking to those of us in the here and now…

When he'd written that far, rustic sounds echoed from all directions, and the pleasant summer waltz faded in a flourishing cadence. Yang looked toward the entranceway and knitted his brow when he saw a tense Frederica leading half a dozen men in dark suits toward the terrace. The men introduced themselves gruffly. Their leader shot a glance at Yang.

"Your Excellency Marshal Yang, by authority of the Central Public Prosecutor's Office, you are hereby detained on charges of violating the Insurrection Act. You will come with me at once, unless you'd like to contact your lawyer first?"

"Sadly, I don't know any lawyers," said Yang, discouraged. He then politely asked to see some identification.

Frederica examined it for him. After determining its veracity, she visi-phoned the Public Prosecutor's Office to confirm. Frederica's uneasiness was palpable. The nation and government weren't always right, as she well knew, and Yang knew better than to resist arrest.

"Don't you worry," he said to his wife. "I'm not sure what crime I've committed, but there's no way they'll execute me without a trial. This is still a democracy. Or so our politicians say."

He was, of course, speaking also to his uninvited messengers. Yang gave Frederica a kiss, a skill in which he'd made no improvement since getting married. With that, the youngest marshal in the history of the Alliance Armed Forces, in his off-white safari jacket and T-shirt, was forced to bid farewell to his beautiful wife.

After watching her husband go, Frederica rushed back into the house. She threw her apron onto the sofa, opened a drawer in her computer desk, and took out a blaster. Grabbing half a dozen energy capsules in her palm, she walked upstairs to the bedroom.

She came back down ten minutes later, clad in her active-duty uniform. Her beret, jumper, and half boots were all black, the scarf and slacks ivory white. In mind, body, and attire, Frederica was armed to the teeth.

She stood before the body-length mirror at the bottom of the stairs, adjusted the beret sitting on her golden-brown hair, and checked the position of the holster at her hip. Unlike her husband, she'd graduated from Officers' Academy with full honors and was an excellent marks-woman. Even when devoting herself to desk work as Yang's aide at HQ, she never parted with her blaster and wore the same uniform as her male counterparts, always prepared to fight back in the unlikely event that enemy soldiers ever stormed the premises.

With everything in order, she spoke to her reflection in the mirror.

"If you think for one second we're going to let you run our lives, you're sorely mistaken. The more you beat us, the more your hands will hurt. Just you wait and see."

This was Frederica's declaration of war.

IV

Despite not being handcuffed, Yang Wen-li was dragged into one of the low-rise buildings of the Central Public Prosecutor's Office, dubbed "the Oubliette." It was a place where suspected high-level criminals were detained and interrogated. The detention room was comparable in size and amenities to a high-ranking officer's private suite on a spaceship. It was, he thought, far preferable to the room he had been thrown into at the time of his hearing two years before, although the comparison did little to console him.

The public prosecutor was a dignified man past middle age, but the daggers in his eyes cut against the grain of his gentlemanly good looks. To him, there were only two types of people: those who'd committed crimes and those who'd yet to try. After dispensing with a customary greeting, the prosecutor looked at the young black-haired marshal like a chef eyeing his ingredients.

"I'll get straight to the point, Admiral. Recently some odd rumors have come our way."

"Is that so?"

It seemed the prosecutor hadn't been expecting that answer. He'd rather expected Yang to deny it.

"Do you even want to know the nature of the rumor?"

"Not really."

The prosecutor flung needles of hatred from his squinted eyes, but Yang ignored them with characteristic nonchalance. Even under the unilateral prosecution of his trial, he'd never deferred to intimidation. The prosecutor, for his part, stumbled over Yang's renown and status, and decided it was better to dial down on the bad-cop routine.

"People are saying that Admiral Merkatz, supposedly killed in action during the Vermillion War, is, in fact, still alive."

"First I've heard of it."

"Oh, is it now? The world must always be so full of surprises for you, eh?"

"Indeed. I live every day as if it were the first."

The prosecutor's cheek muscles twitched. He wasn't used to being mocked. Usually the ones who came before him were in a much weaker position.

"Then it should be the first time you're hearing of this as well. There's a rumor going around that the one who faked Admiral Merkatz's death and aided in his escape is none other than you, Admiral Yang."

"Oh, so I've been arrested on nothing more than a passing rumor without a shred of evidence to support it?"

Yang was raising his voice, half-earnest in his anger. He'd relented when presented with an arrest warrant and had succumbed to being questioned, but if the warrant was founded on nothing, then who in the government had sanctioned it? As if to underscore Yang's uneasiness, the prosecutor went silent.

Around the time of Yang's arrest, an official notice was sent out to the following effect:

"Regarding the arrest of retired marshal Yang, there is a possibility that his old subordinates will transgress our lawful order and resort to taking matters into their own hands. Regardless of whether they are active or retired, you are to keep a close eye on the Yang fleet's old leaders and put a stop to any potential danger before it develops."

This notice was a double-edged sword. Vice Admirals Walter von Schönkopf and Dusty Attenborough, who'd retired from service to become ordinary civilians, had already guessed as much by the sudden appearance of surveillance guards. But von Schönkopf's feelers were much longer and more sensitive than the government could imagine. He had, more boldly and more meticulously than Yang, been carrying out underground activities of his own as a conspirator.

On that day, at eight o'clock in the evening, Attenborough was called by von Schönkopf, whereupon he headed for the restaurant known as March Hare. On the way, he turned to look behind him several times, bothered as he was by the guards tailing him. Upon entering the restaurant, a gentlemanly mustached waiter led him to a corner seat. Wine and meals were waiting for him at the table, as was von Schönkopf.

"Vice Admiral Attenborough," he said, smiling. "I see you brought an entourage with you."

"Retirement does have its perks."

They noticed that both surveillance teams had come together along a wall not ten meters from their table.

It wasn't as if the alliance government had the wherewithal to surveil every retired military leader, and neither did the Imperial Navy. The lenses of prejudice and caution, mused Attenborough, were focused solely on the Yang fleet's staff officers.

"Is it true that Admiral Yang has been arrested, Vice Admiral von Schönkopf?"

"I heard it directly from Lieutenant Commander Greenhill—Mrs. Yang, that is. It has to be true."

"But they have no right. What excuse could they possibly have to…"

Attenborough broke off there. He couldn't stop the powerful from doing whatever they wanted when they believed in their right to monopolize interpretations of "justice" and to alter the dictionary as it suited their needs.

"Even so, to execute Admiral Yang at this point would give those aimless, smoldering anti-imperial tendencies a symbol around which to rally, then erupt. Then again, knowing them, I'm sure they're aware of that already."

"If you ask me, that's exactly what the Imperial Navy is hoping for."

Attenborough caught his breath at von Schönkopf's answer, letting out a sound like a whistle that ended before it began.

"You mean they'll use this as a reason to round up the entire anti-imperial faction?"

"And Admiral Yang will be their bait."

"How very cunning."

Attenborough clicked his tongue loudly. The empire, he thought, wouldn't be satisfied until it had gained total domination over the alliance, and the very thought of the underhanded methods they'd used to deceive their commanders made his skin crawl.

"Will the alliance government allow itself to be taken for that ride?"

"About that…Cunning as the trap may be, I can't believe anyone in the alliance government won't see right through it. The kicker is that everyone will have to go along with it, knowing it's a trap all the while."

Attenborough agreed with what von Schönkopf left unsaid.

"I see. So, if the alliance government refuses to execute Admiral Yang, that's an automatic violation of the Bharat Treaty?"

And an ideal excuse for the empire to conquer the alliance once and for all. The alliance government couldn't afford another war. According to their logic, the unfair death of a hundred people was preferable to the unfair death of a hundred million. Attenborough frowned.

"Of course, now I get it! The alliance government has only one choice, and that is to prevent the Imperial Navy from sticking its nose into this and to dispose of Admiral Yang by their own hands."

Von Schönkopf praised this colleague five years his junior for his acumen. Since receiving Frederica G. Yang's transmission, which had likely been tapped, the alliance government had been trying to read through a hastily cobbled script to deal with the situation. In his head, a completed crossword would look something like this:

"Here we have a group called the anti-imperial extremists," explained von Schönkopf, lowering his voice. "Without knowing what the alliance government has done to stave off total subjugation on the part of the empire, all they can do is shout their democratic principles from the rooftops. They put Admiral Yang on a pedestal as national hero and try to bring down the current alliance government as a challenge to the empire, regardless of the consequences."

Von Schönkopf went on:

"And yet, as an apostle of democracy, Admiral Yang refuses to bring down the government through violent means. Enraged, the extremists denounce Admiral Yang as a traitor and ultimately kill him. The Alliance Armed Forces rush in but are too late to rescue Admiral Yang, even if they are successful in annihilating the extremists. Admiral Yang becomes an invaluable human sacrifice toward protecting the democratic principles of his motherland. It's pretty seamless, don't you think?"

Von Schönkopf smiled bitterly. Attenborough lightly brushed his brow, transferring cold beads of sweat to his fingertips.

"But does the alliance government have the guts to pull it off?"

Von Schönkopf turned to someone who wasn't there with a look of contempt.

"A despotic government and a democratic government may wear different clothes, but people in power never change. They feign innocence for the wars they started, claiming only the achievements of bringing those wars to an end. They sacrifice anyone outside their circle, shedding their crocodile tears. Such performances are their forte."

Attenborough nodded and brought the whisky glass to his lips, but his hand stopped in midair and he lowered his voice further.

"Then whatever are those of us shouldering the honor of being extremist military leaders supposed to do?"

Von Schönkopf seemed pleased with his young colleague's discernment.

"Then you also think we have a part to play in their little scenario?"

"It's pretty obvious. They'd even use Admiral Yang and throw him away like unwanted trash, so you can be sure they'll use us as well to the best of their advantage."

Von Schönkopf nodded and smiled, throwing a cold stare at the plain-clothes guards still eyeing them from across the room.

"I wouldn't be surprised if those bastards thought we were discussing a rebellion against the government at this very moment. In fact, they're *hoping* for it. In which case, it's our duty as actors to play our parts to the fullest."

Attenborough was riding in von Schönkopf's landcar, heading down the highway at night toward his house in the suburbs. Because both were full of alcohol, naturally they'd engaged the automatic driver. Von Schönkopf asked Attenborough what was weighing on his mind.

"I'm a man without attachments. I've got nothing to live for, nothing to hold me back. Is that true in your case, too?"

"I have a daughter."

The shock Attenborough felt from this casually delivered remark was probably the biggest of the night.

"You have a daughter?!"

"Going on fifteen…ish."

Attenborough was about to stress the fact that he wasn't married but quickly realized how impolite that would be and chided himself for getting so riled up. For while von Schönkopf may not have boasted of having "a lover on every planet" like Olivier Poplin, it would empty an artist's paint box to depict his varicolored history with women.

"Do you know her name?"

"She has her mother's maiden name: Katerose von Kreutzer. I hear she goes by Karin."

"Judging by that name, I gather her mother must've been a refugee from the empire, like you."

"Could be."

When Attenborough asked, in a somewhat suspicious tone, whether he didn't remember, von Schönkopf heartlessly told him that he couldn't very well bring to mind every woman he'd slept with.

"Just thinking of the stupid things I did, back when I was nineteen or twenty…"

"Makes you break out in a cold sweat?"

"No, I just never want to go back to that time. The very existence of women seemed so fresh to me back then."

"And how is it that you know you have a daughter?"

Attenborough couldn't resist bringing the conversation back around to that topic.

"Right before the Vermillion War, she told me in a letter that her mother had died. There was no return address. Although I'd been an irresponsible father, at least she'd taken the initiative to let me know *that* much."

"You never met her?"

"And if I did, what would I do then? Tell her how beautiful her mother was?"

Von Schönkopf's bitter smile was lit by flashes of light through the window.

"This is the police. Pull over your landcar immediately."

The two of them checked the gauge to see if they were speeding and noticed several lights in the dark screen of the rear monitor. Attenborough let out a nervous whistle.

"They're demanding we pull over. What should we do?"

"I like giving orders, but I hate taking them."

"That's a good philosophy."

The police car, having been duly ignored, raised the shriek of its overbearing siren and closed in on them. From behind, several backup vehicles joined in the pursuit, and armed soldiers emerged from their reinforced glass windows.

V

Immediately after his tasteless, largely untouched meal was cleared away, Yang was told he had a visitor. For a moment, he thought it might be Frederica, but just as quickly, he abandoned that hope. The authorities would obviously have rejected Frederica's request for a meeting. *Maybe it's him*, Yang thought, none too happy about the prospect.

Chairman of the alliance council João Lebello appeared before the young imprisoned marshal. When the door opened, a dozen or so military police officers were right behind him.

"It's truly a shame that we should be meeting in a place like this, Marshal Yang."

His voice was well suited to the pensive mask he wore, but it made no impression on Yang either way.

"I'm sorry you feel that way, but I didn't exactly ask to be here, either."

"Of course you didn't. Mind if I sit down?"

"Go right ahead."

As he took a seat on the sofa opposite, much more uprightly than Yang, Lebello answered the unspoken question.

"You have violated the Insurrection Act and become a danger to the survival of our nation. These are the charges brought against you by the imperial high commissioner's office."

"And does the chairman agree with the charges?"

"I'm not sure yet. I was hoping you'd do me the favor of denying these allegations outright."

"And if I did, would you believe me?"

Yang could tell this conversation was going nowhere. Lebello's face went dark.

"Personally, I've always believed in you, but I can't very well deal with this situation on a purely emotional or moral level. The survival and safety of our nation has nothing to do with our one-on-one relationship."

Yang vented a sigh.

"You can stop right there, Chairman. You've always been known as a fair-minded politician, as your many actions attest. So how can you think it's at all natural to sacrifice individual rights of citizens for the sake of the nation?"

Lebello's expression was like that of someone with a respiratory disorder.

"You know I don't think that. But isn't that how it goes? Self-sacrifice is the most noble of human deeds. You've truly devoted yourself to the nation. If you realize that way of life to the very end, then posterity will value you even more."

Yang was ready to object. Lebello was in a tough position, to be sure, but even Yang had a right to assert himself. The way he saw it, reality wasn't reflected in the civil servant's mirror, and yet he'd always gone above and beyond what his salary required. What's more, he'd always paid his taxes. After already being cursed as a "murderer" by bereaved families of subordinates who'd been killed in action under his command, why did he have to sit there and be lectured by a representative of the very government for whom he'd made all those sacrifices?

Yang chose not to speak what was on his mind. He gave a small sigh and sat back into the sofa.

"What would you have me do?"

There was nothing admirable in asking for such instruction. Yang wanted to know what Lebello really thought. Lebello's response was more abstract than it needed to be and set off loud warning bells in Yang's head.

"You're so young to have gotten so far. You've never once met defeat at the hands of even the most formidable opponents. Time and again, you've saved us from certain danger and kept our democracy from crumbling. Present and future generations will intone your name with pride."

Yang stared at Lebello. There was something almost palpable that Yang couldn't ignore in his far-too-formal way of speaking. Was Lebello reading off Yang's epitaph? Lebello wasn't speaking to the Yang of the present, but justifying his use of the term "present and future generations."

Yang's mental roads were suddenly jammed with traffic. In fact, many fruits in the orchard of his intellectual activity had ripened, and among them hung the very conclusion that von Schönkopf had also reached. He didn't want to believe it, but the situation was beyond his control. Yang reprimanded himself for being so naive. He'd had an inkling for the past five or six years that something bad was going to happen, but the situation had now thrown on a pair of roller skates and amped up to full speed, and it was as if the brakes of his shame were no longer operational.

"Naturally, good citizens should obey the law. But when their nation seeks to violate individual rights by laws they've set up only for themselves, it would be an outright sin for those same citizens to go along with them. The people of a democratic nation have the right and responsibility to protest, criticize, and oppose the crimes and errors committed by the nation."

Yang had once said as much to Julian. Those who opposed neither unfair treatment nor the injustice of the powerful were no more citizens than they were slaves. And those who didn't fight back even when their own equitable rights were violated were certainly never going to fight for the rights of others.

If the alliance government was going to try Yang for "commandeering military vessels and ordinances belonging to the Alliance Armed Forces," he could only be resigned to his fate. But what of his opinion? The law was the law, and if he'd broken it in any way, he had a right to stand before a jury. But Yang wasn't ready to give in just yet.

They wanted him dead, and this was the only way they could get away with it. The government's power structure enabled laws through due process and punished criminals in accordance with those laws. Premeditated murder was an unjust use of their authority, and the act itself was proof of the ugliness of their motive.

Even more deplorable was that his accuser was the very government for which he'd performed his many duties. Even knowing that Lebello's hand had been forced, Yang found it hard to sympathize. It was an unthinkable story, but it stood to reason that the one being killed should be worthier of sympathy than the one doing the killing.

Even if the government did have the right to kill him, he wasn't obligated to go down without a fight. Because Yang was weak on narcissism, he agreed with the sentiment of Lebello's "epitaph," but not out of some masochistic allegiance to the idea that death by self-sacrifice was more meaningful than death by resistance. He looked through the figure of this unwilling actor to Frederica's hazel eyes in the background. She wasn't going to just stand and watch as Yang died a useless death or was unjustly abducted. Rescuing her good-for-nothing husband would take every ounce of courage and scheming she had. Until then, Yang would need to buy some time. Yang turned these thoughts over in his mind, barely noticing that Lebello had already stood up and bid his farewell.

⁂

Admiral Rockwell, seated as director of Joint Operational Headquarters after the establishment of the Lebello administration, had yet to return home, waiting as he was for a certain report in his office. The Joint

Operational Headquarters building had just the other day been decimated from the ground up by a missile attack from the imperial Mittermeier fleet, and minimal operations were still being conducted in several of the underground rooms.

At 11:40 p.m., a transmission came via Captain Jawf, commander of special forces. Jawf had failed to bring vice admirals von Schönkopf and Attenborough into custody. The admiral chewed out Captain Jawf, making no efforts to hide his disappointment.

"Vice Admiral von Schönkopf is an expert in hand-to-hand combat. I'm sure Vice Admiral Attenborough can hold his own as well. But aren't there only two of them? I guess I should've lent you two squads."

"But it wasn't just the two of them," Captain Jawf corrected in a gruff yet dejected tone. "Rosen Ritter soldiers came out of nowhere and attacked us, and so they escaped. Highway 8 is covered in flaming cars and dead bodies. See for yourself…"

The captain leaned out of frame to reveal a flurry of silhouettes moving about orange flames painted on indigo canvas. Rockwell's heart did a triple axel in his chest.

"The entire Rosen Ritter regiment was in on it?!"

Captain Jawf rubbed the light-purple bruises on his cheekbones. *As you can see*, he wanted to say, *it took a lot out of us*.

"Their membership hasn't been replenished since after the Vermillion War, and yet there are still more than a thousand soldiers attached to that same regiment. And not the usual thousand, either."

Admiral Rockwell shivered. No exposition was needed. The Rosen Ritter regiment may have been exaggerating when they said their combat abilities were comparable to those of an entire division, but they clearly had enough resources to substantiate that claim.

"Your Excellency, I'm fine with starting the fire, but I wonder if we have everything we need to extinguish it."

After voicing this half-sarcastic musing, Captain Jawf waited for his superior's answer, knowing beyond the shadow of a doubt that the spread of fire was inevitable in this case. Admiral Rockwell's face was like a dozen sour expressions in one.

"Beats me. Go ask the government."

CHAPTER 6:

I

THE PLATEAU WAS FOUR THOUSAND METERS above sea level and had been scorched bare by excessive sunlight through a thin atmosphere. Julian Mintz sat on solid earth that had been eroded more by time than by wind or water, watching the rhythm of the waves gently breaking and receding along the shore. The opposite shore was well beyond the horizon, imperceptible to Julian's naked eye. The strong wind blew his flaxen hair into disarray.

This lake was called Namtso, located one thousand kilometers inland from the southernmost coast of this continent. It had an area of nearly two thousand square kilometers and served as a landing spot for merchants and pilgrims alike. After acclimating themselves to the altitude, new arrivals would head out in landcars or on foot to the holy land, where an eight thousand–meter mountain called Kangchenjunga served as the Church of Terra's stronghold. People in black clothes dotted the landscape, barely moving in the distance. Julian had been watching them for the past three days.

The bluish-purple sky drew his gaze upward as if by magnetic attraction. As he gazed upon that sky, Julian recalled the eyes of the girl Poplin had introduced him to on Dayan Khan supply base in the Porisoun star zone. Her eyes had glistened as if under immense pressure and had convinced Julian there was no room in them for himself. Her name, if he remembered correctly, was Katerose, nicknamed Karin. Her surname escaped him, but he was sure he'd seen her before. She was a beautiful girl, impressive in every way and impossible to forget.

Someone sat down next to him. Out of the corner of his eye, he caught a glimpse of Olivier Poplin's grin.

"You don't have a headache?"

"I'm fine. I'm younger than you, Commander. I adapt better."

"I guess you are fine if you can talk back like that," Poplin snorted.

As Poplin stretched out his long legs in front of him, he squinted and looked at the vast bluish-purple dome above them. He'd only ever had an interest in everything beyond this so-called sky, and since landing on the surface of this "worthless planet," three days had been enough to make him homesick for what lay on the other side of the atmosphere. The ace pilot said he was never meant to live on land, but that was just his ego talking. Julian felt no homesickness for the time being. But sooner or later, thought the boy, he would come to agree with Poplin.

On July 13, Julian, along with four fellow travelers, hopped in a reserved landcar and set out for Mount Kangchenjunga, 350 kilometers to the south. Accompanying him were Commander Olivier Poplin, Captain Boris Konev, Ensign Louis Machungo, and a crewman with the overly decorous name of Napoleon Antoine de Hotteterre. *Unfaithful* was left in the capable hands of its administrative officer, Marinesk, and its astrogator, Wilock. Such precautions allowed them to leave the planet at a moment's notice should something come up.

Marinesk and Wilock bade farewell, left the others on the shore of the lake, and crossed over a massive landform protruding in the distance.

The ground was like something out of a black-and-white movie, interrupted only by the Technicolor brown of high mountains. By the time the Creator had gotten to this desolate land, his supply box had surely been almost empty. The atmosphere and sunlight played harshly on the skin. The panoramic ridgeline of the mountains was precise enough to have been rendered by hand.

Realistically, it would take them twelve hours to reach Mount Kangchenjunga. Along the way, they would pitch tents and camp for a night. In such high altitude, it was impossible to overestimate one's own stamina. Making a journey of ten thousand light-years to Earth only to collapse from altitude sickness had all the makings of a morbid joke.

They'd packed the back of the landcar with space food, medicine, and a modest selection of silver ingots for "alms." Boris Konev, who'd brought several groups of pilgrims, knew from experience that such alms held currency value as commodities and would only work in their favor. According to him, everyone here was happy to receive even a simple gift.

Along the way, they occasionally came across returning pilgrims and exchanged casual greetings with them. Meanwhile, Konev shared the various bits of knowledge he knew about Earth.

"The United Anti-Earth Front was nicknamed the Black Flag Force, but even after their indiscriminate attack, there were about a billion people left alive. But even that number dropped in the blink of an eye."

Nearly all of them had abandoned their barren homeworld for other planets, but bloodshed was rampant among those who remained on the surface, first out of a need for survival and subsequently for their beliefs. Boris Konev didn't know the specifics. What he did know for sure was that those Earthers who fell from high positions of authority only fought among themselves to satisfy their belligerence and lust for power.

"So, Earth's present degeneration can be traced back to that meaningless conflict?" asked Julian.

"Who knows? It's been eight hundred years since the Western calendar ended. And this is an isolated and introverted society. I'd be surprised if it *hadn't* degenerated."

More surprising was that this incessantly degenerate Earth had reverted to the same methods of influence that had brought about its downfall in the first place.

"I'm hoping there's some sort of reference room at the church's headquarters," mused Julian.

"Even if there is, we may not be allowed inside."

"If security is too tight and we try to break in, we'll get what's coming. That might just be our chance."

Either way, Julian knew they couldn't do much of anything until they'd gathered more information and acted efficiently, and with better judgment. But Admiral Yang, who was surely aware of these developments, had only allowed this reckless plan because he thought there was something useful to be found within the scope of Julian's capability.

The following afternoon, Julian and the others reached the Church of Terra's base of operations. More than a thousand meters of Mount Kangchenjunga's summit, which at one time had pierced the azure sky, had been blown off by missiles, giving it the appearance of an abandoned, half-built pyramid. A deep ravine cut its way between the plateau and the mountain peak. Julian's group would need to leave the landcar behind and scale the cliffs until nightfall.

Inside the enormous door, sixty centimeters thick and made of multiple layers of steel and lead, they found themselves in a spacious room of bare concrete. A throng of believers, each cloaked in black, sat waiting to be led in. Julian guesstimated about five hundred of them. As he sat down to join them, an elderly man with white hair who'd clearly been sitting on his blanket for a while held out his basket with a kindhearted smile. Once he caught the meaning of this gesture, Julian thanked him and accepted a piece of rye wheat bread, then asked where he was from.

The elderly man gave the name of a planet Julian had never heard of.

"And where are you from, young man?"

"Phezzan."

"That's much farther. I'm impressed, especially for someone as young as yourself. Your parents must have taught you well."

"Thank you…"

Julian looked even less favorably on the Church of Terra's cultish ways now that he'd seen the simpleminded people whose piety they were taking advantage of just to restore their selfish power.

While Julian took stock of his surroundings again, a low inner door opened to reveal a small congregation of what appeared to be lower-level acolytes or clergymen in the middle of their ascetic practices. They began mingling with the believers, whose plain black clothing matched their own. In exchange for waterproof sacks filled with alms, which they received with chants of blessing, they handed out guidebooks to the compound. Julian did as the other pilgrims did, trying to hide his face as much as possible.

"This is an underground shelter," said Boris Konev with blunt scorn when they'd first entered the room. "At one time, the Global Government's top army brass secluded themselves in this fortress while directing the war with the colonies. You may have heard good things about this place, but…"

Secure in their fortress of thick bedrock, massive firearms, and air purifiers, these military leaders had watched as tragedy unfolded on the surface. They had plenty of wine and women, to say nothing of food, and expected to enjoy the tranquility of their underground paradise for years to come. This enraged the Black Flag Force's commander, who, realizing that a full-on attack would be futile, instead blew up one of the giant irrigation channels running beneath the Himalayas, sending millions of tons of water into their underground den of sin. Of the twenty-four thousand people trapped inside, only a hundred had escaped a death by drowning.

Julian examined the guidebook handed to them, thinking it might have the whole incident recorded inside. Then again, no religious organization, past or present, had ever thrown open its infrastructure, financial affairs, and full backstory to believers. Whatever was written there was probably a lie.

The grand chapel, crypt, bishops' assembly hall, archbishops' assembly hall, Grand Bishop's audience room, confessionary, meditation room, interrogation room, and several larger and smaller rooms besides were included in the guidebook. There were, of course, also the pilgrims' quarters and mess hall, but no reference room was mentioned.

"Hey, find any nuns' quarters in there?"

"Afraid not, Commander."

"Does that mean men and women bunk together?"

"I'm amazed, perhaps even a little jealous, that you can still go there, given the circumstances," said Julian half-jokingly, standing up with his rucksack in one hand.

At the clergymen's signal, the pilgrims obediently formed a line and made their way slowly through the doorway. As they followed suit, Julian and the others were handed small tags, each printed with a room number.

Julian, Poplin, Konev, Machungo, and de Hotteterre quickly confirmed each other's lodgings. Machungo and de Hotteterre were in the same room, while the rest were in separate ones. *Was this by chance or design?* Julian wondered. Before he could trace the implications of that thought further, whispers of elation and excitement swept through the fluorescently lit hallway as believers fell to their knees along the wall. The reason for their obeisance became clear when Julian noticed the solemn approach of a black-clad procession.

"It's His Grace the Grand Bishop," came waves of whispers.

Julian followed their example and knelt in kind, warily observing the figure at the center of the procession.

He did more than wear black. It was the black clothing that gave him any sense of form at all. That was how little presence this old man had. So little, in fact, that Julian found himself wondering if he was looking at a hologram. His feet made almost no sound. His skin color was almost indistinguishable from the fluorescent lighting. His eyes seemed to be fixed on something way beyond this transient world. Julian wanted to know if there was anything inside his body. He *had* to know.

"To witness the countenance of His Grace the Grand Bishop," whispered an old believer standing next to Poplin, tears of gratitude streaming down her face, "is a chance one might not get in a lifetime. What a fortuitous blessing."

"If I could," muttered a dejected Poplin to himself, "I'd rather go through life not having seen him at all."

Poplin saw no evidence of wrinkles or even muscles in the Grand Bishop. He was a dry shell of a man who looked like he'd burn that much more quickly if one cremated him, mused the ace pilot.

The archbishop was around thirty years of age. His exceptional promotion was a result neither of his command of doctrine nor depth of faith, but rather his abilities as a natural-born man of the world. Had there been a bureaucratic society on Earth, he might have ruled from its summit. But because no such structure existed anymore, he'd entered the Church of Terra and secured his position as archbishop in the space of one or two years. He knew better than to tell anyone that the only thing he worshipped was his own resourcefulness.

"I understand our branch on the planet Odin has been annihilated?"

"Regrettably, it would seem so, Archbishop de Villiers."

His superior lowered his head solemnly.

"Baron von Kümmel is dead, and it seems everyone in the sect martyred themselves."

"Baron von Kümmel, you say? What a worthless man. What did he live for, and what did he die for?"

A gloomy cloud of disappointment crossed the archbishop's face. His office was a low-ceilinged yet spacious room, filled nine centuries ago with the souls of those who had drowned—the very thought of which, if you asked him now (not that he'd tell you), was laughably absurd.

"Even if Baron von Kümmel is to blame for our failure, aren't we taking things a little too fast?"

The old bishop's voice was like that of an emperor criticizing his highest general's tactical error. At least that was how the archbishop chose to interpret it as he glared at his much older subordinate with venom in his eyes.

"The Imperial Navy's invasion is imminent. Such failures are therefore nothing to worry ourselves about. We can revisit the emperor's assassination once we're out of harm's way."

"Indeed. We cannot allow our holy land to fall into the evil hands of those heretics."

"Don't worry. His Grace the Grand Bishop already has taken measures."

The archbishop's lips made a half-moon smile. "Knowing we were able to get that close to an emperor, there's no reason to think we can't get close to an admiral."

II

On July 24, the 5,440 vessels of Senior Admiral August Samuel Wahlen's punitive expedition to Earth entered orbit on the outer edge of the solar system. After receiving his orders, Wahlen had quickly assembled a regiment of cruisers, managing the difficult task of putting them into formation along the way.

August Samuel Wahlen had been instrumental in helping to establish the Lohengramm Dynasty. And while he had a few defeats on his military record, his victories were overwhelmingly many. His ingenious determination as a tactician and his manly fortitude instilled confidence in his soldiers.

If one defeat brought him shame, it was his loss in March of that year, when, near the Free Planets Alliance's Tasili star zone, he had fallen prey to Yang Wen-li's tricks and had been unilaterally crushed. One would think his every vein would have burned with regret at the time, but in terms of recognizing his opponent's worth, Wahlen was even more flexible than his comrade Lennenkamp. And while he admired Yang's ingenuity with a bitter smile, he bore no grudge against him. He was simply determined to never let it happen again.

He was greatly pleased by Reinhard's order to capture the Church of Terra's stronghold. He'd never expected to have the chance to redeem himself so soon. He had to satisfy Reinhard's favor at all costs, especially since the emperor had chosen him over Wittenfeld to do it.

If the Church of Terra was indeed nothing but a cult, he would have no trouble banishing them to some frontier planet like the Galactic Federation of States had done eight centuries ago. But there was no way he was going to take their political influence, organizational abilities, and assets for granted, especially considering they'd almost gotten away with regicide. There was no sound reason to pardon any terrorist group just because they acted in the name of religion.

Wahlen was thirty-two years of age, the same as Yang Wen-li and Oskar von Reuentahl. He was a tall and burly man with hair of bleached copper wire. Five years ago, he'd gotten married. A year later, their son had been born, but his wife had died due to complications in the delivery. Their son was being brought up by Wahlen's parents. They'd spoken to him of remarrying as many times as he had fingers and toes, but he had no interest.

The frontier planet which humanity had abandoned nine hundred years ago was reflected on the flagship's main screen. His chief of staff Vice Admiral Leibl, chief intelligence staff officer Commodore Kleiber, and others had assembled around their commander to plan their method of attack in front of the 3-D display.

"I see. Under the Himalayas, is it?"

"Their underground headquarters is protected by a hundred trillion tons of dirt and bedrock. We could attack it with ELF missiles and be done with it in one or two sweeps."

"You mean blow up the whole mountain? Where's the art in that? Besides, the emperor was explicit about not sacrificing any innocent civilians."

"All right, then. Shall we send in our armed grenadiers? It wouldn't take very long."

Wahlen looked to his chief of staff.

"How many exits and entrances does their underground base have? Unless we determine that, they'll just escape the moment we come barging in. Destroying their base and killing any fanatics we can find, only to let their ringleaders get away, would undermine the emperor's good graces."

"Then what do you—"

"Relax," said Wahlen, reining in his chief of staff's impatience. "The Earth isn't going anywhere, and neither are they. We have until we reach Earth's orbit to come up with a solid plan. I've got a prized 410-year-old white wine to present as a trophy."

After releasing his staff officers, Wahlen leaned against a wall and folded his arms, savoring the opportunity to see the screen from anywhere but his commander's seat. It was a habit he'd kept since his days as a recruit. He was too absorbed to notice that one of his noncommissioned officers was cautiously approaching him.

"Admiral!" cried out one of his staff officers.

Wahlen wrenched his tall body just in time to dodge a glint of light drawing a diagonal across his field of vision. He recognized it as a battle knife as he rammed against the wall behind him.

At once, Wahlen lifted his left arm to protect his throat. The fabric of his military uniform ripped audibly, the blade sending a searing pain through his muscle tissue. He waited a moment for it to cool into a throbbing pain.

As splattered blood from his wound temporarily blinded the raging eyes of his would-be assassin, Wahlen pulled the trigger of the blaster in his right hand, sending rays of light into the man's right shoulder where it met his arm.

The assassin threw his head back, his hand still holding the knife high, and let out a shriek of agony.

The staff officers, who until then had held fire for fear of hitting their commander, wasted no time in leaping upon the assassin, forcing him to the floor.

Wahlen's face was pale from blood loss and pain, but he managed to get to his feet and bark his orders.

"Don't kill him! Keep him alive. I want to know who he's working for."

But then a white light burst in a corner of his consciousness, and the expeditionary commander fell against the wall and slid to the floor.

The medic who rushed to his aid determined that the knife had been coated with an alkaloidal poison and that if they didn't amputate Wahlen's left arm, his life would be in danger.

The surgery left Wahlen minus one arm in exchange for his life. A lingering trace of the toxin left him feeling feverish, conversely making the hearts of his staff officers run cold.

Wahlen pulled through a serious injury and fever that might've brought anyone to death's door, regaining total consciousness sixty hours later.

After drinking the nutrients given to him by the medic, Wahlen said not a single word about the left arm he'd lost but instead had the non-commissioned officer who'd attacked him brought into the sick bay. The assailant, propped up between two soldiers, had a bandage around his shoulder and appeared to be in worse shape than he was.

"We didn't torture him. He just won't eat anything."

Wahlen nodded at his subordinate's explanation and looked straight into the man's eyes.

"Now then, you feel like telling me who sent you to kill me?"

In the eyes of the assassin, clouded by ashen fog, the crimson flames of bloodlust rose again.

"No one ordered me. Those who refuse to let the sanctity of Mother Earth alone must suffer by the transcendental will that governs the entire universe."

Wahlen gave a fatigued smile.

"Spare me your theology. I just want to know the name of the one who ordered you to assassinate me. I'm guessing it's someone affiliated with the Church of Terra. Is he aboard this ship?"

Tension had an eagle grip on everyone in the sick bay. The assassin let out a maddening scream and began to struggle. Wahlen shook his head once, raising his remaining hand and ordering the man back to his isolation cell. His chief of staff looked anxiously at his commander.

"Shall we interrogate him again, Your Excellency?"

"I doubt he'll talk. That's the way religious fanatics are. By the way, when can you get me a prosthetic arm?"

"In a day or two," the medic said.

Wahlen nodded, looking down at where his left arm used to be, but soon turned away his emotionless gaze.

"Speaking of which," he said abruptly, "isn't there another officer with a prosthetic arm on this ship?"

To which his staff officers exchanged bewildered glances, but Commodore Kleiber's superlative memory was triggered.

"That would be Commander Konrad Rinser, one of the staff officers aboard the flagship."

"Yes, Konrad Rinser. I was introduced to him by Siegfried Kircheis during the Battle of Kifeuser. Right, call him in."

Thus, Konrad Rinser, imperial commander, came to be under Senior Admiral Wahlen's command, landing on Earth before the main force to scout out the Church of Terra's headquarters and clear the way for companion forces to invade.

III

On Earth—or rather, under it—time passed idly for a spell. The date was July 14, ten days after infiltrating the Church of Terra's underground base, and Julian found nothing of worth during his stint as a faux believer.

Surveillance cameras were installed everywhere, rendering meaningful exploration of the compound impossible, and any stairways or elevators leading to the lower levels were invariably guarded. Being separated from his fellow travelers meant Julian couldn't freely associate with them. Thinking he had no choice but to gain the trust of his hosts, he'd engaged in a sort of involuntary servitude. In between worship, prayer, and sermons, together with other believers he cleaned the hall and sorted the provisions storehouse, all the while committing the layout of the underground base to memory. But even Julian couldn't help but feel like a fool and could only imagine that Poplin and Boris Konev were in especial agony without a defined sense of purpose.

On the night of the twenty-sixth (not that either noon or night meant anything underground), Julian was finally able to sit across from Poplin in the buffet-style mess hall and speak to him quietly.

"So, any young beauties caught your eye yet?"

"No way. Just some antiques that might've been women half a century ago."

Poplin sipped his lentil soup with a sour face. The mess hall had passed its peak time slot, so there weren't many other people around. The two of them were afraid of what others might think if they talked for too long, but at least they *could* talk.

"More importantly, did you find any sort of reference room or database?"

"Nothing. Anything like that is more likely to be another level down. I'm sure I'll find it soon."

"Don't get your hopes up."

"I won't."

"I haven't said anything about it until now, but even if you *do* find a reference room, there's no guarantee it'll have what you need. These guys might be nothing but a cult of megalomaniacal crazies."

Poplin closed his mouth, looking past Julian's shoulder in that way he did when talking about women. Julian turned around. The moment he did so, a piercing racket assailed his eardrums. A male believer stood with his arms overhead, while another was writhing under an upturned table. Elderly and female believers screamed and dispersed. The man's eyes, which betrayed a long-lost mind, glimmered from underneath his black hood. He lifted the table with surprising strength, throwing it into the crowd of believers. Another crash, and more screams.

Someone must have notified the authorities, because five or six clergymen armed with stun guns jumped in through the door and surrounded him. Thin cords shot out from their guns and pierced the man's body. A low-output, high-voltage current sent him flying into the air before he hit the floor with a short scream.

Poplin's face, half-concealed by his hood, went completely pale, as if some ominous suspicion had been realized.

"Dammit," groaned Poplin. "So *that's* it. How did I not see it before?"

Poplin grabbed Julian by the wrist and led him out of the mess hall, hurrying his pace against the crowd running over to see what the commotion was all about. When Julian finally asked what was going on, Poplin shot him a serious look.

"We need to find a bathroom fast and throw up everything we just ate."

"Are you saying we've been poisoned?"

The ace pilot took a moment to answer.

"Something like that. That man who went berserk in the mess hall just now? That was a classic reaction to a psychotropic drug called thyoxin."

Julian's voice caught in his throat. Amid the cymbals of shock crashing in his head, fine singing voices of reason told him the truth. The food they'd been eating for the past twelve days in the cult's headquarters had been laced with narcotics, the same addictive synthetic drug that both the empire and the alliance had secretly collaborated on.

"It's the reason why the Church of Terra's followers are so damned docile, like slaves," said Poplin, shifting the focus to the other believers, if only to ignore his growing uneasiness. "A long time ago, revolutionaries used to call religion the opiate of the masses, but this is a whole other level."

When they entered the bathroom, they jammed their fingers down their throats and vomited up their meals. While rinsing out their mouths, Julian was warned not to drink the water, as there was a possibility that the entire water supply was laced with the drug.

"Don't eat anything else today or tomorrow, although if we happen to go into withdrawal, we might not have much of an appetite anyway."

"But the others…"

"I know. We need to let them know as soon as possible."

The two of them were on the same page. They could only hope they weren't being monitored right now. They had to find a way, however risky, to avoid suspicion. But if they continued eating the food and became addicted to the drug, they would become nothing more than livestock for the Church of Terra. They were hung on the horns of a dilemma.

"At any rate, Commander, you sure do know a lot."

Poplin cocked a half smile in response to Julian's praise.

"Women aren't the only thing I pursue. I'm a regular walking museum."

That night somehow passed without incident. Perhaps it was because these lodgings were intended for soldiers that this room of exposed bedrock was large enough to fit fifty three-tiered beds. Curtains of tattered cloth were their only barriers for privacy. At some point, Julian managed to fall asleep, caught between real hunger and imagined withdrawal.

From noon onward the next day, Julian sensed that his physical condition and mood were beginning to deteriorate. He was racked with chills, broke out in hot flashes, and was becoming generally uncomfortable. He was lax in his chores as well, made even more challenging for the lack of nourishment.

Full-on withdrawal set in that same night.

He knew it was coming when something snapped inside him, and his body began to tremble violently. Chills ran up his spine, his heartbeat spiked, and he began coughing violently in a way he hadn't since he was a baby.

Someone grumbled from another bed, but he couldn't stop the cough no matter how much he tried. Wrapping his head in a blanket was all he could do to muffle it. During one of the brief interims that it abated, as he was fervently steadying his breathing, the kindly voice of an old believer came from the bunk above him.

"Young man, are you okay? Should I take you to the infirmary?"

"No, I'm fine. Thank you."

His voice was barely audible. His neck and chest were soaked in cold sweat, and his shirt was stuck to his skin.

"Don't push yourself too hard."

"I'm fine. Really, I'm okay."

Julian wasn't just being modest. If the doctors examined him and saw that he was experiencing withdrawal symptoms, they were sure to pump him full of something stronger and turn him into a total junkie. The cult was in on it.

The urge to vomit jumped up from his stomach to his throat. Anything that came up was pure digestive acid. He pressed the sheets to his mouth and finally forced the bitter liquid back down. After that first wave, he was again wracked by violent coughing, now to the accompaniment of stomach pains.

The other four—Poplin, Konev, Machungo, and de Hotteterre—were surely braving the same storm, and Julian knew he wasn't alone. Even so, he couldn't bear the eagle's grip of pain and unpleasantness wrapped around his body. In the middle of a nasty coughing fit, he felt like he was in the harshest G-force training. Beneath his damp skin, the cells of his muscles began running wildly in all directions. His internal organs and nervous system shouted a hysterical resistance song as Julian's sense of self was thrashed about by strong winds and thunder. The pain and unpleasantness of it all radiated from his core, bouncing off the underside of his skin and back to his core. Shooting stars streaked across the black canvas of his inner eyelids, bursting into supernovas and battering Julian's consciousness.

A voice feigning kindness flowed into his ear canal:

"Whatever is the matter with you?"

Julian stuck his pale face out from under the blanket. After who knows how long, the storm inside him was slowly but surely giving up its seat to calm. Two men were looking at Julian with courteous sympathy.

"I heard from other believers that you're really suffering. We share the same faith. Our hearts go out to you. There's no need to hold back. Come with us to the infirmary."

The men had white square patches sewn onto their black robes, designating them as the church's medic unit. Try as he might to deny it, Julian felt a divine presence. Was this how he was supposed to react? He nodded obediently and got to his feet. Taking that as a signal, his pain and discomfort retreated into the domain of the past. Now more than ever, his act would need to be convincing.

IV

Upon entering the infirmary, Julian knew that the door to Ali Baba's cave had at last opened before him. Two preceding visitors were in the examination room—a refined young man with green eyes and a hulking giant who appeared more bovine than human. Although they were both emaciated, their eyes flickered with hope when they locked on Julian, who found that he was recovering confidence and energy with every passing second. In his mind, fate was still showing her gentle old woman's profile.

"What's with all the sick believers today?" grumbled a middle-aged doctor whose white clothing stood out in a sea of black.

Perhaps it was Julian's own preconception getting in the way of his thinking, but he didn't look much like a man who'd devoted his life to medicine.

"I wonder if something is making you all sick."

One by one, the doctor placed a dozen syringes on a silver tray. Poplin kicked one to the floor.

"There is," he said calmly.

"Oh? What could that be?"

"Because you made us eat ketchup laced with thyoxin, you damned charlatan!"

The doctor tore off his mask and sprang at him with a laser scalpel in his hand. But Poplin's agility wasn't up to snuff. The young ace flicked his wrist instead, sending a hypodermic needle straight into the doctor's right eye. The doctor let out a bloodcurdling scream. The door opened and two men from the medic unit came bursting in.

Before one of them could reach for his stun gun, Julian's right foot sank into the abdomen of his black robe and sent the man flying without a sound. The other was restrained in Machungo's iron grip, only to kiss the wall at ten meters a second.

Poplin dissolved the white powder he had taken from a desk drawer in a cup of water, then filled the biggest syringe he could find. He knelt in front of the doctor, who was sprawled on the floor, clutching his right eye and struggling in pain and anger. Machungo pinned down one of the doctor's arms and wrapped a rubber tube around it. Poplin spoke softly.

"I'm sure I don't need to tell you that once I inject this much thyoxin into your bloodstream, you'll die from shock in under a minute."

"Please, stop."

"I'd like to, but life doesn't always go the way you want it. Sometimes, growing up means separating what you want to do from what you've got to do. Well then, bon voyage."

"Stop!" the doctor cried. "Spare me, and I'll tell you anything you want to know. Just stop."

Poplin and Julian exchanged sinister smiles. Julian knelt beside the ace.

"I want to know what the Church of Terra is hiding. First, tell me, in no uncertain terms, where I may find the church's financial base of operations."

The doctor's left eye moved in Julian's direction, exuding fear and panic. The nonchalance with which Julian had made his demand only made the doctor tremble more.

"I have no idea about such things. They don't give me access to that information."

"If you don't know, then I want you to tell me, if you can, about those who do."

"I'm just the doctor."

Poplin laughed through his nose.

"Are you now? Then you serve no purpose here. In which case, I'll make a corpse out of you."

The doctor's final scream was drowned out by an alarm. An electric current of tension ran through the three of them as gunshots and explosions filled the air.

The door opened again. This time, the bishop-level clergymen who came tumbling in took one look at what was happening in the room and yelled as loud as they could.

"We've been invaded by heretics! I found some here, too. Kill anyone who violates the sanctity of—"

Before he could finish his sentence, he was thrown against the wall and slid to the floor as if refusing the wall's embrace.

"You call yourselves clergymen, yet you traffic innocent people and who knows what else. Repent before God of your impoverished hearts," sputtered Poplin as he began tearing off the bishop's robe for a disguise. "It's not so easy taking off a man's clothes. There's no payoff for doing it. Was this the reason I came all the way to Earth? Meanwhile, Marshal Yang is living it up with his beautiful new wife. Totally unfair."

Poplin continued to deride the situation, but when he peeked out of the half-opened door, he let out a soundless whistle and stepped back a few paces, clutching his black robe. He shook his head in exasperation.

"You know, Julian, things don't always go the way you'd like them to at first."

"But over time…?"

"They usually get worse."

Poplin pointed to a group of imperial soldiers taking full advantage of their heavy artillery to barrel their way through the cross fire.

CHAPTER 7:

I

WALLS OF ORANGE FLAME had turned one section of the highway into a living oil painting. Fire brigadiers and rescue workers were moving about between the corpses and car fragments, sirens heightening people's uneasiness all the while. The night was filled with tension, spreading out over the alliance capital of Heinessen.

On a hill one block away, a group of armed soldiers was gazing at the carnage with both the naked eye and night vision binoculars.

Three former Alliance Armed Forces soldiers in military garb stood in the center of the group: retired vice admiral Walter von Schönkopf, retired vice admiral Dusty Attenborough, and retired lieutenant commander Frederica G. Yang, now commanders of a "rebel force" against the alliance government. When Frederica had married Yang and the other two had handed in their letters of resignation, they'd already made their choice between Yang Wen-li and the alliance government.

Going by the definition that "strategy is the art of creating a situation, and tactics the art of taking advantage of a situation," it was safe to say von Schönkopf and Attenborough had acted as top-notch strategists tonight.

"First, we incite a big uproar."

The alliance government was secretly planning to kill Admiral Yang, whom it had wrongfully arrested with no evidence. Fear of an Imperial Navy invasion was mounting into panic, and even without Admiral Yang's involvement, they were deluded in thinking they could keep the nation from harm. At this point, the rebel force's objective was to bring about an imperial invasion, thereby allowing them to rescue Yang.

"Second, we control that uproar."

If the ensuing chaos went unchecked, then their dealings with the Imperial Navy would also become too large to handle, and they might end up summoning not Commissioner Lennenkamp the fox, but Emperor Reinhard the tiger. By streamlining the chaos, as it were, Lennenkamp would feel confident enough to take them on himself. In any event, they would need to buy some time.

Once they had Yang in their possession, they would flee Heinessen and link up with Merkatz and the rest.

What came next was Yang Wen-li's idea. Which was why they were rescuing him in the first place—to make that idea a reality.

"The problem is whether Admiral Yang will say yes."

"He probably won't say yes, even if we press him. Naturally, it'll be different if his wife is the one who proposes it. Otherwise, he can rot in prison, and then no one will be able to save him."

As von Schönkopf said this, Attenborough shrugged his shoulders.

"I feel sorry for Admiral Yang. He'd finally gotten out of that uniform and was duly blessed with a wife and a pension."

Von Schönkopf winked at Frederica.

"Gardens exist only to be devastated by scavengers. No one should keep a beautiful flower all to themselves."

"Oh, why thank you very much. But maybe I *want* to be kept all to someone's self."

Both retired vice admirals then noticed the suitcase at her feet.

"What's with the suitcase, Lieutenant Commander?" Attenborough asked.

"It's his military uniform," responded Frederica with a forthcoming smile. "I think it suits him better than any formal clothing."

Then no other clothes suit him, no matter what he wears, von Schönkopf mused to himself.

"Maybe I should renounce my bachelorhood as well," whispered Attenborough to the night sky.

"Sounds good to me. But before you do, let's get this one job over with, and fast."

Von Schönkopf let out a shrill whistle, spurring his armed soldiers into action. Fearing the alliance government would be notified of the situation by the Imperial Navy, they doubted if there was anything they could do to cover it up, and so they decided to march headlong into the storm. Perhaps this rebel force would be successful after all.

Free Planets Alliance council chairman João Lebello first got word of the incident just as he was about to leave his office for the day. The stiff face of Admiral Rockwell on his comm screen glared at the chairman, who was amazed to learn of the Rosen Ritter regiment's mutiny, and concluded his report.

"I humbly take full blame for this failure, although for the record I've always been against these kinds of sly tactics."

"It's a little late to be saying that now."

Lebello barely managed to keep himself from yelling with rage. He'd been assured there'd be no technical problems in the execution stage. And before he shirked any responsibility, he had to take down this rebel force.

"Of course, I *will* take them down. But if the situation gets out of hand and the Imperial Navy gets wind of it, they'll intervene for sure. It would behoove you to keep that in mind."

Rockwell already saw little need in trying to earn the chairman's respect. His shameless expression disappeared from the screen.

After a few seconds of deliberation, Lebello called the man who'd instructed him on this "sly tactic," Central Autonomous Governance University president Oliveira. He'd already returned home, but when he'd learned that von Schönkopf and the others had gotten away and launched a full-on counterattack, and after being scolded for his failed plan, he'd sobered up from the fine brandy he'd been nursing.

"How can you say such a thing?"

Now it was the brains behind the operation calling him out for unfairness. He'd always interpreted the law as it was written, and in the best interests of those enforcing it. For legalizing certain privileges, he'd reaped small rewards, and he had never taken responsibility for any trickle-down effect of his decisions. He simply proposed plans and left the implementation to others. He praised his own planning skills even as he disparaged others' abilities to get things done.

"Chairman, I don't recall twisting your arm when I gave you my proposal. Anything that's happened since then is the result of your own judgment. In addition, I demand some armed protection so that no harm comes to me."

Realizing he could count on neither the brawn nor the brains, Lebello left the council building and got into his landcar. He was a sinking ship. No, he told himself, the alliance government was the ship, and he was its incompetent captain.

For Lebello, it was nothing more than karmic retribution that he was scheduled to see an opera that night with the imperial high commissioner. If he didn't show up, the commissioner might suspect foul play. And so, he made his way to the National Opera House to waste the next two hours of his life.

Lebello's landcar was sandwiched by escort vehicles on either side. Where normally one car was standard, such protection increased in proportion to a decline in governability. By year's end, four cars would probably turn into eight. His regret grew with each passing second. Lebello folded his arms and scowled at the back of the driver's head. The secretary riding with him was trying his best to avoid looking at his boss, directing his attention instead to the nightscape outside, when he suddenly raised his voice. Lebello turned his gaze to the window and froze. Several landcars had made sudden illegal U-turns and were rushing toward them against traffic. They'd apparently disengaged their automatic controls and were driving completely manually.

The drivers shouted insults at the secretary. From the sunroof of a car closing in on them, they saw a soldier emerge with a hand cannon.

The man shouldered the cannon, met Lebello's eyes with his own, and laughed without a sound. Lebello felt a lump of ice slide down his back. As someone in a high position of power, he'd been resigned to being a terrorist target, but having the muzzle of such a large weapon aimed at him crushed his theoretical determination and summoned a deep-seated fear in its place.

Fire arrows were unleashed, and a thunderous roar tore through the night. The escort landcars went up in balls of yellow flame, rolling across the road. At almost the same moment, those two balls of flame split into four, encircling Lebello's landcar in a dazzling ring.

"Don't stop. Just keep going," Lebello shouted, his voice scaling upward.

But the driver chose to surrender. Lebello's command was ignored, and the quickly changing scenery outside his window came to a halt. Surrounded by unfamiliar vehicles, Lebello stepped out of his landcar at their center, feeling little dignity in doing so. The council chairman, on whose shoulders now weighed a sense of defeat, was approached by the same man who'd just blasted away the escort cars with a hand cannon. His shoulders were now free of their burden.

"High Council Chairman, His Excellency Lebello, I presume?"

"And who are you?! What's the meaning of all this?"

"The name's Walter von Schönkopf, and as of this moment, you've just become our hostage."

Lebello tried frantically to calm his heart and lungs.

"I've heard a lot about you."

"The pleasure's all mine," responded von Schönkopf without an ounce of zeal.

"Why all the theatrics?"

"I should ask the same of you. Between you and me, can you really say with any pride that you've treated Yang Wen-li fairly?"

"As much as it pains me to say this, the destiny of a nation isn't something to be examined through the prism of a single individual's rights."

"A nation that does everything it can to safeguard individual human rights would be a democratic nation, would it not? To say nothing of the fact that Yang Wen-li has done more for this nation than all of us put together."

"Do you think my heart is not aggrieved? I know it's unfair. But ensuring the survival of our nation supersedes all."

"I see. So, you're an upright politician when it comes to the greater good?" A bitter smile ran obliquely across von Schönkopf's graceful face. "And yet, in the end, you bigwigs always end up standing on the side of collateral damage. Cutting off your hands and feet is painful, to be sure. But from the perspective of those same appendages, any tears you shed just come across as hypocritical. What a pitiable man—no, a great man—you are for having killed your own self-interest in sacrifice to your nation. How does that saying go? 'Shedding tears as you put down your horse'? Hmph. So long as you can get by without sacrificing yourself, you can shed as many tears of joy as you like."

Lebello was done trying to justify himself. Clearly, submitting to dishonor was nothing more than the hubris of a man in power.

"And what do you intend to do now, Vice Admiral von Schönkopf?"

"Only what's most sensible in this situation," said the retired vice admiral calmly. "Yang Wen-li was never suited to play the part of the tragic hero. As an audience member, I have a mind to finagle the script. I'm not averse to using violence, as the situation demands. And the situation," von Schönkopf added with another smile, "indeed demands it."

Lebello sensed no compromise or conciliation in that smile. He had never signed up to be a tool for others.

II

Until he had been seated as the Free Planets Alliance High Council chairman following Job Trünicht's resignation, the value of João Lebello's ability and character had been far from low. By SE 799, at the exact age of fifty, he'd already served under two cabinet ministers, showing a rare talent for administration and policy making in the fields of finance and economy. He'd always been opposed to reckless foreign campaigns, had kept the military from overgrowing, and had striven to improve diplomatic relations with the empire. His political opponent Job Trünicht often cursed Lebello's "honeyed words," but never his character.

On this night, he'd become a target of intense criticism for buckling under the pressure of imperial high commissioner Lennenkamp and attempting to take out Yang Wen-li. Now he saw truth in the saying, "A capable man in times of peace reveals his true colors in times of crisis."

But this kind of worldview was more apt to consider a "profitable man in times of crisis" versus a "capable man in times of peace." Had Yang and Lebello been born half a century earlier, the latter would have served the Free Planets Alliance as a capable and noble statesman, while Yang would have been a second-rate historian scolded by the PTA for not taking teaching seriously enough and making students learn everything on their own. And that's probably just what Yang would have preferred.

In any event, there was no doubt that Lebello was a most capable hostage. For now, nothing else mattered to von Schönkopf and Attenborough.

From his landcar, von Schönkopf cut in on a channel reserved exclusively for military use. On the cloudy portable visiphone screen, chromatic and neutral colors resolved themselves into the shocked expression of a middle-aged man with thick eyebrows and an angular jaw. Incredibly, they'd managed to connect to Admiral Rockwell's office at Joint Operational Headquarters.

"This is the lawless, villainous rebel force. It is with the utmost sincerity and courtesy that we present you with our demands, Your Excellency. Listen carefully."

One of von Schönkopf's special skills was adopting an attitude and tone of voice that sent his opponents flying into a genuine rage. This time, too, Rockwell felt every fiber of his being creaking with anger at the arrogance of this unexpected talking head. Rockwell was in his midfifties and in perfect health, a slightly elevated blood pressure his sole cause for concern.

"I take it that you're von Schönkopf, head of the Rosen Ritter regiment. Don't go recklessly wagging your tongue, you damned rebel."

"I don't know much about ventriloquism, so I'll wag it as I please. May I proceed with the particulars of our demands?"

Having uttered this affected request for approval, von Schönkopf waited for no answer before going on.

"The honorable alliance prime minister, His Excellency João Lebello, is currently being put up in our luxury prison. In the event that our demands aren't met, we'll be forced to banish His Excellency Lebello to heaven and put an end to this despair by attacking the Imperial Navy in the name of the alliance, starting a magnificent war in the streets, civilians and all."

A war in the streets between the Imperial Navy's armed grenadiers and the Rosen Ritter regiment! Just the thought of it made Admiral Rockwell shudder. Part of him relished the prospect of engaging his romantic bloodlust, a fault common to all military men, while most of him fell under the influence of fear and uneasiness.

"You'd involve innocent civilians in your pointless showdown just to save yourselves?"

"And what about you? You'd kill an innocent man just to save *yourselves*?"

"I have no idea what you mean. Don't slander us without anything to go on."

"Then let's get back to our demands. Assuming you don't feel like attending Chairman Lebello's state funeral, you are to release Admiral Yang, unharmed. Oh, and a hundred cases of the finest wine you can get your hands on."

"It's beyond my station to make that call."

"Hurry up, then. If no one in the alliance government has the proper qualifications, then we might as well negotiate directly with the imperial high commissioner."

"Don't be rash. I'll get back to you ASAP. You are to negotiate only with the alliance government and the military. At least that's what I hope you'll do."

Von Schönkopf threw a vicious smile at the HQ director and cut the call. Rockwell turned his fuming gaze from the screen to his aide, who threw up his hands in exasperation. He'd been unable to trace the source of the call. Rockwell clicked his tongue loudly, throwing his voice at the screen like a stone.

"Traitors! Unpatriotic bastards! That's why we can never trust anyone who defects from the empire. Merkatz, von Schönkopf, the whole lot of them."

And now Yang Wen-li, the very man who'd appointed them to their posts. He should never have counted on that disloyal, unpatriotic bunch for their talents alone. Those who fought to live were useless, nothing more than brainwashed livestock who spent their days happily, embracing neither doubt nor rebellion as capable men for the nation and the military. This wasn't about safeguarding democracy. It was, however, about safeguarding a democratic nation.

Rockwell's eyes flashed. An unfair yet proper solution to the situation tempted him with irresistible sweetness. It would be difficult to extricate Chairman Lebello from imprisonment. But if they ignored his capture, couldn't they just leave it up to the alliance government to deal with the rebel force? Yes, protecting the nation was paramount. And no sacrifice, no matter what kind or how large, would be spared to achieve it.

⋰ ⋅ ⋅

While Rockwell's mental temperature was busy rising and falling, the empire's high commissioner Lennenkamp, clad in his formal military uniform, was just settling into his luxurious box seat at the National Opera House.

Although he hadn't even an ounce of his colleague Mecklinger's affection for the arts, he knew when to be polite and had therefore arrived at the Opera House just five seconds before the appointed time. Nevertheless, Mecklinger's natural anger was aroused when their host appeared to be late.

"Why has the chairman not shown up yet? Is he too proud to sit with us uniformed barbarians?"

"No, I'm sure he has already left the council building and is on his way as we speak."

Lebello's chief secretary servilely rubbed his hands. If there was one bad attribute of bureaucrats, it was that they could only grab on to human relationships as rungs for going up or down. Lebello stood on Lennenkamp, and Lennenkamp on Lebello. To whoever was in the higher position at any given time, the other could bow and scrape without even the slightest injury to his pride.

Just as Lennenkamp's displeasure was reaching a breaking point, he received a visiphone call. Everyone looking after the high commissioner went out into the hallway reverently like manservants as Lennenkamp heard out a report from Vice Admiral Zahm, a chief officer in the commissioner's office. Chairman Lebello, he now learned, had been taken captive by Yang's subordinates.

The lips half-hidden by Lennenkamp's mustache curved upward. It was a better excuse than he ever could have hoped for. The chance to openly blame the alliance government for its lack of ability to handle things, get rid of Yang, and compromise the alliance's autonomy on the home front had jumped right into his pocket.

Lennenkamp shot up from his overly soft chair, having no need to cover up his disinterest in the performance. Arrogantly ignoring anyone connected with the flustered alliance government and the theater, Lennenkamp took his leave. He was about to star in an even more magnificent opera of bloodshed.

III

At some point in the future, Dusty Attenborough would wax poetically about what happened thereafter, as if he'd been a witness to history:

"At the time, I didn't know which side had the upper hand. The people of Heinessen were blind for all the smoke, running around in a panic and crashing into each other at every turn."

Then again, it was Attenborough and his comrade von Schönkopf who'd been throwing oil into the flames of that confusion from the start. The side on which said oil was being poured was in a total frenzy. And while both the galactic imperial high commissioner's office and alliance government were spinning their own webs of conspiracy, they were unable to grasp the full picture of the chaos, trying as they were to find and exploit a weak point in their opponents. Above all, the alliance government objected to any obvious movements on the part of the Imperial Navy. In the chairman's absence, Secretary of State Shannon became his representative.

"This is a problem that should be resolved within the alliance. The Imperial Navy had better not stick its nose into this one."

The Imperial Navy's response was high-handed.

"But the alliance government can't seem to maintain its own public order. It's therefore in the empire's interest to defend the council's well-being by mobilizing our own forces. I can assure you that anyone who interferes will be treated as an enemy of the empire, no questions asked."

"If the situation does get out of hand, we'll ask for your assistance. I hope you'll wait until then."

"Then I'd like to negotiate directly with the highest person in charge of the alliance government: His Excellency the council chairman. And just where *is* the chairman?"

There was no point in dignifying such mockery with an answer.

Under provision of the Bharat Treaty, viz the "Insurrection Law," government surveillance had kept Yang in check for allegedly disturbing the amity between the alliance and the empire. But no provision in the treaty stated that any criminals who violated the Insurrection Law had to be handed over to the empire. So long as no harm came to the empire and those affiliated with the high commissioner's office, there was no reason for them to interfere. The defeated alliance government had never abused this treaty, which had been forced upon them, and had necessarily, yet with utmost courtesy, rejected the Imperial Navy's offer to help. Lennenkamp, too, had forcibly ignored the treaty to the point where his hands were tied.

In any event, the view on both sides was extremely narrow, and their myopia was only worsening. From where Yang sat, he'd all but succeeded. If the chaos and confusion escalated any further, both the alliance government's ability to maintain public order and the imperial high commissioner's office's ability to cope with crisis would be called into question. Another solution was to call a draw before the situation escalated beyond Heinessen, clap their hands, and be done with it. But both Lebello and Lennenkamp had no such audacity, and so they swam desperately on, tumbling down a waterfall into catastrophe.

Yang couldn't help but sympathize, at the same time discerning one contributing factor in all of this: namely, that von Schönkopf was fanning the flames.

"Some people just can't leave well enough alone," Yang said to himself, ruffling his dark hair in his holding cell at the Public Prosecutor's Office.

The steel door opened, and in walked a man that had "military poster child" written all over him. Crew cut, sharp gaze, stubborn mouth. The lieutenant was slightly younger than Yang.

"It's time, Admiral Yang."

The officer's voice and expression were more gloomy than pensive. Yang felt his heart do an unskilled dance. His worst fear had dressed itself up and manifested, ready to lead Yang to the coldest place imaginable.

"I'm still not hungry."

"It's not time to eat. From this point, you'll never have to worry about food or nourishment ever again."

Seeing that the officer had pulled out a blaster, Yang took a breath. This was one prediction he was most unhappy to see come true.

"Do you have any last requests, Your Excellency?"

"I do, actually. I've always wanted to try a vintage white wine from SE 870 before I die."

The lieutenant took a full five seconds trying to process the meaning of Yang's words. When at last he understood, his expression grew angry. It was only the year 799.

"I cannot grant any impossible requests."

Yang changed tactics by voicing a fundamental doubt.

"Why do I have to die in the first place?"

The lieutenant straightened his posture.

"So long as you're still alive, you'll always be the alliance's Achilles' heel. Please, give up your life for your country. It's a death worthy of the hero that you are."

"But the Achilles' heel is an indispensable part of the human body. There's no point in singling it out."

"Save it for the afterlife, Admiral Yang. Just take it like a man. I can assure you that dying like this will not bring shame to your renown. I know I'm unworthy, but I'm here to help you."

The one saying those words trembled with extreme narcissism, while the one being forced into an undesirable death felt neither joy nor deep emotion. As he looked at the muzzle with a feeling more transparent than fear, he told himself he was ready. The lieutenant posed for effect, took a deep breath, and stretched out his right arm. He aimed at the center of Yang's forehead and pulled the trigger.

But the beam of light shot through empty space, exploding off the opposite wall and scattering in particles of light. Shocked at his failure, the lieutenant's gaze tore up the room in search of a prey that should've been cornered. Yang had, one fraction of a second before being killed, fallen to the floor, chair and all, as he evaded the blaster ray.

As those in the know would later say, even Yang was impressed with his own performance. But he'd only run into a blind alley. Once he fell to the floor, he made no attempt to move. Seeing the cruelty flickering across his executioner's face, it seemed he'd only succeeded in moving the spot where he was going to die a meter downward.

"You're pathetic, Your Excellency. And they have the nerve to call you 'Miracle Yang'?"

Looking down into the abyss of death, Yang was furious. And just when he was about to say something back to his assassin, the glint of the steel door as it opened behind the lieutenant caught his eye. A moment later, a ray of light sprouted from the man's thick chest. The lieutenant's scream hit the ceiling as he threw his head back, his hefty body doing a half turn and falling headfirst onto the floor. Yang pulled himself onto the shore of life to see golden-brown hair, hazel eyes brimming with tears, and lips repeatedly calling out his name. Yang stretched out his arms and embraced the slender body of the one who saved him.

"I owe you my life. Thank you," he said at last.

Frederica just nodded, barely able to comprehend her husband's words. A veritable explosion of emotions had liquefied into tears. He wiped away her tears, but she went on crying like that child he had briefly met eleven years ago.

"Wait, you'll spoil that beautiful face of yours. Hey, don't cry…"

Yang stroked his wife's face, feeling even more bewildered than when he was being attacked by a fleet of ten thousand ships from the rear, when a boorish intruder appeared to take control of the situation.

"Our dearest marshal, we have come for you."

With refined boldness, the former Rosen Ritter regimental commander saluted. Yang held Frederica with his right arm, only now saluting back unabashedly.

"My apologies for all the overtime I've put you through."

"It was my pleasure. Even a long life has little meaning if one doesn't live it fully. That's why I'm here to save you."

Von Schönkopf had taken his tactical actions to the extreme. He'd informed the military he'd taken the chairman hostage and given them some time to answer, all the while rescuing Yang by force. Rockwell had been duped. By stalling, he'd accommodated von Schönkopf's actions to fruition. But not even von Schönkopf could have predicted that Rockwell would go so far as he did to seize this rare opportunity to "deal with" Yang. In theory, he'd had more than enough time to quietly rescue Yang, when in reality he'd gotten there in the nick of time.

"Well, maybe it won't be of much use to you, but please, take this blaster just in case," said Commander Reiner Blumhardt, handing over his weapon.

Technically speaking, Commander Blumhardt was now official commander of the Rosen Ritter. While it was only natural that a thirteenth-generation regimental commander like von Schönkopf should ascend to admiral, he was unable to become a commander of one regiment. Fourteenth-generation regimental commander Kasper Rinz had led half of his troops and thrown himself into Merkatz's fleet, officially MIA during the war. Upon returning to the capital, Blumhardt had received notice that he was to be acting regimental commander, but since the alliance had surrendered to the empire, the chances of keeping an organization composed of young refugees going were slim. It was probably better to just dissolve the regiment altogether than to be targets of vengeful punishment. In the same way that Yang was liable for Merkatz and the others, von Schönkopf was responsible for his men, and on this day he'd bound his future to theirs. There was no turning back now.

Outside the door, there were signs of guards on the move.

"We are the Rosen Ritter regiment," said Blumhardt proudly through a megaphone. "If you *still* wish to fight us, then write your wills and come at us. Or we can write your wills for you, in your own blood."

It was a bluff, but the formidable track record of von Schönkopf and the Rosen Ritter was enough to strike fear in the Central Public Prosecutor Office's guards. Their belligerence quickly went extinct, as short-lived as their bravery and audacity. Although the alliance government used to exaggerate the ferocity of von Schönkopf and his gang to strike fear into enemy nations, now it was their former allies who'd grown afraid of the thorns.

The moment Yang changed into his military uniform in the back seat of a landcar rushing through the night, his short stint as a pensioner ended. He reverted to the man he once had been on Iserlohn Fortress. Frederica looked happily upon the gallant figure of her husband.

"Mind telling me what tonight's 'volunteer work' was all about, Vice Admiral von Schönkpopf?" asked Yang of the principal offender as his wife adjusted his black beret.

"I've always had a great interest in how order-following, law-abiding men such as yourself think and act when they escape the kind of bondage you were under. Isn't that reason enough?"

Without answering, Yang fiddled with the shortwave emission device that was disguised as a cufflink, a little something Frederica had attached to the safari jacket she'd given him when he was arrested. It had alerted his wife to his location and saved his life. As he put this accessory to which he was so indebted into his pocket, Yang's mind was elsewhere. He asked an unrelated question instead.

"You've always supported me, telling me I should grab power by the reins. But what happens when I take power into my own hands and my character changes?"

"If you *do* change, you'll be no different than anyone who came before you. History would repeat itself, and you'd be just another character in textbooks who will trouble future middle schoolers for centuries to come. Anyway, why not try a bite before you go criticizing the flavor?"

Yang folded his arms and groaned quietly.

Even his Officers' Academy junior Dusty Attenborough nodded with a grimace.

"Vice Admiral von Schönkopf is right. Admiral Yang, at the very least you have a responsibility to fight for those who fought for you. You don't owe the alliance government anything anymore. It's time you went all-in."

"Sounds like a threat to me," grumbled Yang, only half-serious.

From the moment his life was saved, Yang had ceased to be his own property.

"You're being too optimistic," Yang continued. "Anyone who thinks he can survive with both the empire and the alliance as his enemies is beyond mad. Tomorrow, I might very well be part of a funeral procession."

"Well, I suppose that could happen. You're not immortal. If I had to die, I wouldn't mind going out that way myself. I'd rather die as a staff officer for Admiral Yang the famous rebel than as the slave of a slave of the empire. At least my descendants will remember me fondly."

At this point, it was Yang's stomach, not his mouth, that protested. He hadn't eaten in more than half a day. With a knowing look, Frederica took out a basket.

"I brought some sandwiches. Here you go, dear."

"Wow, thanks."

"Of course. I've got black tea, too."

"With brandy?"

"Of course."

"Are we having a picnic now?" muttered Attenborough, stroking his chin.

Von Schönkopf responded with a bitter smile.

"Not even. A picnic would be a lot more involved."

When Yang Wen-li's figure seized the center of his vision, João Lebello reflexively did a double take. It was because of him that the alliance's prime minister had necessarily upheld dignity and advocated for justice. Seeing Lebello's elated figure puffed up with pride, it was Yang who couldn't suppress a sigh. While he respected Lebello as a public figure, he just couldn't abide by him as a man.

Their secure hideout was a room in a building the Rosen Ritter had boldly set up not one kilometer away from the Hotel Shangri-La, which housed the imperial high commissioner's office. Its owner had gone bankrupt before it had even been finished, and the building had been abandoned ever since. Its bare inner concrete walls were soundproofed. As a welcome space for a prime minister, it left much to be desired.

The prisoner in question was the first to speak.

"Admiral Yang, you do have some sense of the crimes you've committed, right? Breaking the law with force, wounding our national sanctity, showing contempt for public order. Need I go on?"

"And just how have I broken the law?"

"Are you really going to cajole me into pardoning you after you've unlawfully imprisoned me like this?"

"Ah, I see."

A bitter smile crossed Yang's face, like that of an assistant professor who'd just pointed out a grammatical error in a student's essay. Attenborough laughed at Lebello. That's when Lebello understood. He went pale with humiliation.

"If you don't want to add to your crimes, I suggest you release me at once!"

Yang took off his black beret and ruffled his hair, taking on the expression of a drama teacher scrutinizing his protégé's performance. Daunted, Lebello relaxed his shoulders.

"Do you have any demands? If so, then just tell me."

"The truth."

Lebello said nothing.

"Just kidding. I would never ask for something so pointless. I only ask that you guarantee our safety. Not indefinitely, but within a given period of time."

"You are public enemies of the state. I cannot make any deals that would defy justice."

"Are you saying that so long as the Free Planets Alliance government exists, my friends and I will never know peace?"

Lebello gave no immediate reply, having sensed something akin to danger in Yang's tone.

"If that's the case, I must also become a disciple of egoism. If necessary, I might even sell my own nation to the empire for next to nothing."

"Do you think I'd allow you to do something like that?! As an admiral, you also held an important position in the state. Does your conscience harbor no shame?"

"Now there's a fine piece of logic," von Schönkopf interjected, fixing his gaze on Lebello. "It's okay for a nation to sell individuals, but not vice versa?"

Yang cleared his throat slightly.

"So, will you at least consider my proposal?"

"Proposal?"

"We take Commissioner Lennenkamp hostage, then leave planet Heinessen. The alliance government will go through the motions of pursuing us without actually doing so. I will take full responsibility for any conflict with the empire. Should the alliance bow to the empire and ask them to rat out and arrest Yang Wen-li, you'll end up saving face."

Lebello mulled over Yang's proposal in silence. His self-interest was running around a maze in his heart, looking for a safe exit.

"I have one more condition. I should hope you won't punish anyone who has remained in the alliance government. Those who served under me—Caselnes, Fischer, Murai, Patrichev, and many others besides—had absolutely nothing to do with this whole ordeal. If you can swear to me, by all the dignity invested in you by the alliance government and democracy, that no harm will come to them, then I will leave Heinessen. Of course, we will release you, Chairman, and bother the people no longer. Does that sound reasonable?"

It wasn't the government but the part about "the people" that spoke for Yang's sentiments. Lebello heaved a sigh. It seemed he'd found an exit after all.

"Admiral Yang, I have no intention of apologizing to you. I've been entrusted with the heaviest of responsibilities in the most difficult of times. For the sake of ensuring the survival of the Free Planets Alliance and the generations to come, I will resort to any method, no matter how underhanded. I am, of course, resigned to any censure that arises from my actions."

"In other words, you agree to my proposal to take Lennenkamp hostage," was the ever-prosaic Yang's response. "Then that's that. Vice Admiral von Schönkopf, I leave you in command."

"You can count on me."

Von Schönkopf nodded happily. Lebello wanted nothing more than to call them warmongers, but instead asked when he could expect to regain his freedom.

"When His Most Unfortunate Excellency Lennenkamp loses his."

A member of the group, Captain Bagdash, who'd been observing from the sidelines, walked up to von Schönkopf and whispered in his ear.

"It's not my place to say so, but I don't think you should trust them. Not only Chairman Lebello, but all those powerful men he surrounds himself with. They bow only to the highest bidder."

"Does that mean they'll deny Admiral Yang's proposal?"

"They'll say 'yes,' if only because they failed to conceal the incident itself and they want to strong-arm Admiral Yang and everyone responsible. But who knows how the situation might change? If it's to their advantage, I wouldn't put it past them to erase Lennenkamp and all of us with him."

Bagdash was an expert in intel and subversive activities, and had once belonged to the camp that antagonized Yang, so even after having his name entered as Yang's staff officer, he was constantly being frowned upon. In this instance, however, he'd been instrumental in the gathering and analysis of information, and in planning the attack on Lebello, and by those services rendered had established a foothold and trust within the group. Maybe they'd missed their chance after all.

"What worries me is Admiral Yang's lingering affection for the alliance's democratic government. I'd be concerned if he thought his punishment would have any positive effect on the alliance."

"I think everything will work out. Even if he regrets it now and goes back, he can kiss his pension goodbye. He'll have to give it up and become self-reliant."

"And you? Have you given it up?"

"Giving up is one of my redeeming qualities. It was the same when Your Excellency von Schönkopf saw through my plans two years ago."

"The sun will be out any second now."

From the thick summer clouds, Bharat's sun cast its first beams. The night was quickly retreating, but left behind chaos in its wake, making no attempt to dispel the deep black shadows. Traffic was intercepted throughout the city as alliance troops and police ran wild under a broken chain of command.

"All right, then, shall we begin our assault at dawn?"

Von Schönkopf picked up his helmet.

"The Hotel Shangri-La it is."

Commander Blumhardt tore up the pavement of his memory, on the underside of which was recorded some beneficial information. He smiled knowingly, confident of their success, gathering his company commanders and doling out his tactical commands.

The Hotel Shangri-La had become a bastion of sorts, surrounded as it now was by a sea of fully armed imperial soldiers. At Lennenkamp's instructions, they'd gained control of key locations in the city streets of the alliance capital of Heinessen and assumed battle formation, easily declaring martial law. Since the alliance capital had become prisoner of war to a supposed group of rebel soldiers, any nonsense such as esteem for sovereignty had been thrown down the garbage chute.

The alliance, naturally unaware of the situation brewing in the imperial mainland, had stormed its own capital.

At around midnight, the alliance government had been desperately trying to keep knowledge of these developments from reaching the Imperial Navy. After midnight, the Imperial Navy's occupying forces in Heinessen were anxious about leaking information to their allies.

Lennenkamp, who'd taken up position on the hotel's fifteenth floor, intended to deal with the situation using Heinessen's ground forces—in other words, the sixteen regiments of soldiers under his command. And if that wasn't enough to staunch the flames, then those flames would jump through the abyss of the universe and alight themselves on the torch of Admiral Steinmetz stationed in the Gandharva star system.

In that case, the task of subjugation would revert to Steinmetz, and Lennenkamp's ineffective handling would be denounced. If Lennenkamp, after suppressing Yang's clique and enslaving the alliance government, couldn't gain a new position and power befitting of his achievement, then the mayhem of the previous night would be rendered meaningless.

The group of rebel soldiers, even with the formidable Rosen Ritter regiment at its core, numbered little more than a thousand. Alliance government officials had let rage get the better of them when they tried to rush Yang's execution, only to be beaten at their own game. Even Lennenkamp couldn't fully grasp their movements, unaware that he'd already been sold by Lebello to the Yang camp.

At 5:40 a.m., the thick carpet beneath Lennenkamp's feet undulated for a moment, followed by the sounds of muffled explosions. If not for the early-morning cityscape outside his window, he might've been deluded into thinking he'd sustained a direct hit from an enemy warship cannon. Just as he was considering the possibility of an earthquake, an officer pale with shock burst into his office and announced that the fourteenth floor directly beneath them had been occupied by unidentified soldiers. Lennenkamp jumped to his feet.

Almost like magic, von Schönkopf and his men had gone through the underground communications conduits, then the elevator repair shaft, which ran vertically throughout the entire building, to reach the fourteenth floor. They blew up two elevators and three stairways, but were confronted by imperial forces at the top of the eastern stairway, which they'd barely managed to obstruct. An imperial officer with a captain's insignia shouted at them.

"Stop your useless resistance! If you don't come out, I'll have you swimming in a sea of your own blood."

"Too bad I didn't bring my swimsuit."

The officer's blood pressure shot up at having been ridiculed.

"I'll let that one slide. Now surrender. If you refuse, I can assure you we'll hold nothing back."

"Then show us what you've got."

"Very well. Be prepared to put your scraps where your mouth is, sewer rats."

"Same goes for you. You should've thought twice before blowing things up without listening to everything your opponent has to say."

The captain's open mouth was plugged up by an invisible fist. A subordinate's announcement barely stopped him before he screamed in retaliation.

"Not so fast, we can't use firearms. The concentration of Seffl particles has reached critical mass."

The captain gritted his teeth over the enemy's craftiness, and immediately went to Plan B. Five of his company's armed grenadiers were called into the hotel. They would need to fight their way in using hand-to-hand combat and rescue the high commissioner from his confinement.

⁛   •   •

Von Schönkopf calmly watched through his helmet as a crowd of shining silver-gray battle suits gathered at the foot of the stairs. These figures, who appeared to have left their fear back in the womb, were the living definition of bravery. Even Blumhardt thought as much, and the callousness and pride of the imperial soldiers as they drew near made his entire body grow red hot. When the command to charge was given, the imperial soldiers stampeded up the stairs. The soldier at the front held a carbon-crystal tomahawk which glinted in the light. Von Schönkopf leapt at him, thus setting off what would come to be known by diehard romantics as the "red cascade." The first blood was to be scattered from this unhappy soldier's body. Von Schönkopf ducked under the tomahawk as it cleaved the air. In the following moment, he swung his own tomahawk obliquely, slicing through the helmet and seams of the soldier's uniform to meet the jugular underneath. As blood spewed everywhere, the soldier fell, and a voice filled with anger and hatred spouted from below.

"Vice Admiral," Blumhardt shouted, "it's dangerous for you to be commanding from the front line."

"No need to worry. I plan on living to a hundred and fifty. I still have a hundred and fifteen years to go. I'm not going to die here."

"There aren't any women here, either."

Blumhardt, well aware of the glorious achievements of von Schönkopf off the battlefield, knew his words wouldn't be taken as a joke. There was no time for von Schönkopf to object, anyway. The dreadful sound of many footsteps came rushing up the stairs.

Von Schönkopf and Blumhardt immediately entered a cyclone of bellows and shrieks, metallic impacts, blood and mingling sparks. As carbon-crystal tomahawks drew arcs in the air, fatally wounded imperial soldiers fell down the stairs, covered in blood.

Von Schönkopf wasn't about to make the mistake of taking on several enemies at the same time. His four limbs and five senses were all under the perfect control of his central nervous system, orchestrating short yet severe slashing attacks into every opponent, staving off battle fatigue at every turn.

Dodging one attack with a twist of his tall body, he countered with another to the neck. As each fatally wounded enemy fell to the floor, von Schönkopf was already moving on to the next one.

A tomahawk kicked up wind, while another cleaved that wind. Clashing blades sent sparks and carbon-crystal fragments flying, while spurting blood painted a morbid jigsaw puzzle across the floor and walls. Massive amounts of pain ensued, interrupted only by death. Von Schönkopf at first avoided the spurts of blood from his victims, but eventually could no longer favor aesthetics over perfect defense. His silver-gray battle suit, which reminded one of medieval armor, was covered in several different blood types, fresh from his defeated enemies. Unable to endure their losses, the imperial troops retreated downstairs, even as they ground their teeth with regret. Von Schönkopf clapped Blumhardt on the shoulder.

"Lennenkamp is all yours. Take only ten men with you."

"But, Your Excellency…"

"Do it now! The sand in the hourglass is far more precious than any diamond."

"Understood."

After Blumhardt disappeared with ten soldiers, von Schönkopf led the twenty left behind. Von Schönkopf posed at the top of the stairs, provocatively swinging a tomahawk polished in human blood.

"What's wrong? Is there no one who will stand before Walter von Schönkopf?"

Von Schönkopf was putting on this little performance in the hope it would buy them some time.

A young soldier, full of determination yet obviously lacking in experience, came running up the stairs. Although he brandished his tomahawk with plenty of vigor, von Schönkopf could see how futile the attack was.

Their tomahawks clashed, flashing with sparks. The outcome was decided in a moment as one of the tomahawks clattered across the floor. The soldier with a tomahawk poised at his throat experienced von Schönkopf's laugh as if it were the devil's.

"Do you have a girlfriend, young man?"

The soldier was silent.

"Well, do you?"

"Y-yes."

"I see. Then take my advice: Don't throw away your life so easily."

Von Schönkopf thrust the handle of his tomahawk into the young soldier's chest, sending him tumbling down the stairs, leaving his short scream hanging in the air above the landing. Fresh grunts of anger arose from the bottom of the stairs. As von Schönkopf and his men were delving into that moat, Blumhardt and his were storming into Lennenkamp's room. They surrounded the door and made to pass through a much shallower moat of human blood.

The imperial soldiers' brave yet futile resistance reached its final movement in a matter of seconds. Eight corpses tumbled onto the floor, leaving only the high commissioner.

Light surged out from the blaster in Lennenkamp's right hand. It was not a single flash, but a continuous rapid fire with perfect aim. He had, after all, started out as a soldier.

One of the Rosen Ritter members was hit in the center of his helmet and toppled sideways. He'd been too close to evade the shot. Blumhardt nimbly went around and cut in on Lennenkamp's right flank, sending his blaster to the floor with a single attack, then drove the butt of his blaster into the commissioner's chin.

Lennenkamp stopped himself from falling by putting both hands on his desk, his voice bellowing from a bloody mouth.

"Just kill me already!"

"I'm not going to kill you. You're my prisoner."

"Do you think a low-ranking officer, let alone a senior admiral, would be resigned to becoming a disgraceful prisoner?"

"I'm hoping you will be. I've no interest in your aesthetics or your pride. Your life is all that matters to me. We need you alive."

Blumhardt's words triggered something in Lennenkamp. The commissioner groaned.

"I see. Do you plan on taking me hostage in exchange for Admiral Yang?"

While that wasn't an entirely accurate insight, neither was Blumhardt incorrect.

"I would hope you'd be honored that we recognize you on equal terms with Yang Wen-li."

The one saying those words had no idea how much they'd offended Lennenkamp. It was not because of fear but humiliation that Lennenkamp went pale to the very tips of his splendid mustache.

"Don't go thinking I'd value my life so much as to negotiate with the likes of you."

"That's not what I had in mind, but you aren't the one who'll be doing the negotiating. It will be your subordinates."

"You look like a Rosen Ritter offer, so does that mean you were originally a man of the empire? Aren't you betraying your motherland?"

Blumhardt stared at Lennenkamp, but not because those words made a deep impression on him.

"My grandfather was a republican thinker, and for that was captured by the imperial ministry of the interior, tortured, and finally killed. If my grandfather was a true republican, then I guess he died an honorable death. But my grandfather was just a major complainer."

Blumhardt cocked a half smile.

"The only way I can repay that 'kindness' is with resistance. Anyway, time is more precious than emeralds. Come with me," urged the commander.

The metaphor was accurate. He could already hear the rhapsody of hand-to-hand combat wafting from the floor below. Von Schönkopf and his men had run up from the fourteenth floor, clearing away more enemies.

Three minutes later, the imperial soldiers—soaked in blood, sweat, and vengeance—stormed Lennenkamp's office, only to find it empty. The whole purpose behind their rescue had disappeared along with the one they were trying to kill. Von Schönkopf and his men used the same route by which they'd come and made their successful, if not as quiet, escape. Immediately after, there was an explosion in the elevator repair shaft, and the only route by which the imperial forces might have pursued them was closed off before their very eyes.

IV

Lennenkamp was staring at an empty room. Ceiling above, floor below, walls in front. In that space, despair wore a black robe, gloomily singing a song of ruin. Lennenkamp was still in the rebel force's hideout. The bare concrete walls and floor were all soundproof. Compared to his magnificent office in the Hotel Shangri-La, the differences were staggering.

The imprisoned imperial high commissioner thought this was the end. When he was dragged here, everything made sense. He'd lost not only to Yang's clique, but had also been sold out by Lebello, who supposedly represented the interests of the alliance government.

By what honor could he ever hope to look his emperor in the face again? The emperor had tolerated his failure against Yang Wen-li and given him a high commissioner's post. Lebello strove to meet the expectations of such magnanimity and trust. For the sake of the new dynasty's 1,000-year plan, he'd eliminated obstacles and cleared a path for the empire to subjugate all alliance territory. Until he was taken here, he'd seen a path opening to a superior position. But after being in the same room as both Yang and Lebello, Lennenkamp realized he'd been had. The chairman had been half-averting his eyes behind Yang's back, perhaps out of guilt, but Lennenkamp had lost the will to reprimand him at that moment. It was the only way to avoid the scorn of enemy and ally alike.

His originally narrow view had become even narrower. With eyes devoid of sanity and widened only by a twisted desire for prestige, Lennenkamp looked up at the ceiling.

The soldier who'd brought Lennenkamp lunch found him hanging in the air twenty minutes later. He'd stopped breathing, swaying slowly left and right in his military uniform. Seeing this, the soldier put his ceramic tray warily in a corner of the room and sounded an alarm with his voice. The body, dead by suicide, was taken down by Commander Blumhardt and the men who'd rushed to his aid.

A soldier qualified to be a medic straddled the torso of a man more than ten ranks above him, reaching the limits of what his textbooks and experience told him could be done with an artificial respirator.

"I'm sorry, I can't revive him."

"Out of my way, I'll do it."

Blumhardt did his own inspection of the body, but the result was the same. Against all their efforts, Lennenkamp had shut the door permanently on life. When at last the commander stood up, his complexion as pale as the deceased's, the door opened and spit out von Schönkopf, who'd just returned from releasing Lebello, hands and feet still bound, in a public park. A slight nick appeared in the blade of his usual fearlessness, and his expression became grave. He regretted having to hold off on fulfilling his promise, but at this point it was unnecessary.

"Lennenkamp's death must be kept under wraps. Those alliance government bastards would capitalize on this unique opportunity to mobilize an all-out attack in a heartbeat. Do whatever it takes to make him alive again."

Without a hostage, the Imperial Navy would have no reason *not* to attack the "rebels." But with Lennenkamp dead, the truth would be buried along with him. As for the alliance government, it wanted to set fire to every reality and rumor alike.

When he heard of Lennenkamp's death, Yang thought it over and at last came to a decision with the face of one swallowing a bitter medicine.

"Officially, Admiral Lennenkamp must be kept alive. Profane as it might be, there's no other way."

This one incident guaranteed him, Yang thought, a special seat in hell. Frederica came up with a suggestion. If they applied a little makeup to the deceased's face, it might convince people that he'd only fainted. It didn't seem like a bad idea.

But who was going to do that sickening job?

"I can do the makeup," chimed Frederica. "After all, I was the one who suggested it, and as a woman I'm suited for the task."

The men exchanged glances, but as it was clear they were out of their league when it came to makeup, despite their courage. And so, somewhat inarticulately, they left it to the lone woman of the group to get started.

"This is my first—and last, I hope—experience putting makeup on a corpse. If only he were a little more handsome," Frederica muttered, "then I might not feel so bad wasting it."

It wasn't like Frederica to poke fun at the dead, but it was the only way she could endure the morbidity of this task, despite being the one to propose it herself. As she opened her makeup kit and set to work, the door opened and Yang caught an awkward glimpse of the face.

"Frederica…I, uh…I didn't mean for you to…"

"If that's an apology, I don't want to hear it."

Frederica beat her husband to the punch as her hands worked without rest.

"I don't have any regrets, nor am I angry with you. Not even two months have gone by since we got married, and they've been nothing if not entertaining. So long as I'm with you, I'll never lead a boring life again. Please don't let me down, darling."

"So, married life is entertaining for you?"

Yang had taken off his black beret and ruffled his unruly black hair.

The beautiful young woman who was now his wife never ceased to amaze him. Their life together never seemed all that boring in the first place.

"Be that as it may," Yang muttered indiscreetly, "this doesn't strike me as the right time for such a conversation."

It was the same emotion Frederica had felt before. A third party had been casting a deep, murky shadow across their exchange of courtesies.

Even as Senior Admiral Helmut Lennenkamp, the Galactic Empire's high commissioner, stood on the same planet as Yang Wen-li, his heart was hundreds of thousands of light years away in death. When Yang thought of Lennenkamp's bereaved family, he couldn't suppress a bad aftertaste. The number of people seeking revenge on him had increased yet again.

Yang shook his head and closed the door on his wife's unpleasant responsibility. He thought to himself: *To be forced into an unwilling death or an unwilling life: which is closer to happiness?*

CHAPTER 8:

I

ON JULY 30 OF THIS YEAR—SE 799 and year one of the New
Imperial Calendar—on the imperial capital of Odin, two reports came
in, one bad and one good.

The first was from the punitive Earth force's commanding officer, August
Samuel Wahlen.

"We were imperially commanded to go to Earth, suppress the main
headquarters of the terrorist organization known as the Church of Terra,
and arrest its founders and leaders. But as we breached the Church of
Terra stronghold, those same founders and leaders blew up their own
headquarters and buried themselves, making capture impossible. I humbly
regret to inform you that I was unable to completely carry out my duty."

Two recon battalions under Commander Konrad Rinser, going on
Wahlen's intel regarding entry and exit points, managed to infiltrate the
stronghold and commence their all-out attack. One of their tasks was
to pursue a group of independent Phezzanese merchants representing a
"flaxen-haired boy."

The black-clad pilgrims came at the fully armed imperial soldiers
with knives and small firearms. Dumbfounded by their recklessness, the

imperial soldiers nevertheless immediately returned fire, mowing down the religious fanatics and their primitive weapons, trudging over their corpses as they went deeper into the compound.

Normally, such unilateral slaughter would have intoxicated soldiers who lived for the taste of blood and flames. But their emotional stomachs were tested to their limits. While the believers, who'd been infected mind and body with fanaticism and thyoxin, were firmly in death's pocket, the soldiers vomited, laughing hysterically, and even burst into tears.

Upon reaching the eighth stratum below the surface, the imperial forces knew they'd stepped into the deepest part of this underground maze.

Even here, believers resisted with everything they had, and any warnings on the part of imperial forces to surrender were met with gunfire. After a failed third attempt, the imperial forces gave up on arresting the old founders, starting with the Grand Bishop, and chose to exterminate them all.

Despite their overwhelming firepower, manpower, and battle tactics, the imperial forces had just faced one of the toughest fights they'd ever waged, if only because the Church of Terra had home field advantage, and because none of the believers feared death. They filled the passages with water, drowning their own and enemy soldiers alive and even martyred themselves with nerve gas grenades, taking as many down with them as they could.

"Are they complete idiots?" screamed the imperial officers about these church believers who lacked any concept of death.

They weren't even killing each other. Rained upon by imperial gunfire, the church believers were committing suicide, burying themselves in the earth by blowing up the deepest parts of their sanctum.

"Did we really get them all?"

"Who knows…"

Such were the whispered exchanges among the soldiers afterward, feeling anything but proud of their victory. Every face was pale, overcome by shades of weariness.

The Grand Bishop, of course, didn't see the corpses of most of his followers, buried as they were beneath trillions of tons of earth. But nothing could bury all of their lust and malice. All terrain within a ten-meter radius of the stronghold caved in, crumbling the holy mountain from within.

When Julian first met this admiral called Wahlen, his complexion looked weak. Julian knew it was because of a serious wound, but seeing that his courageous countenance was undisturbed, he couldn't help but admire him deep down. And while, of course, Julian adored nothing so much as Yang Wen-li's "utterly unheroic" side, he felt a certain attraction to the different effect of an iron-tough fortitude such as Wahlen's.

"According to Commander Rinser, you helped out considerably in our capture of the Church of Terra's headquarters."

"Yes, absurdly enough, we were caught by Church of Terra followers, and while we partly had our own reasons, we were more than happy to be of assistance."

Because Julian deemed this Admiral Wahlen a man worthy of respect, it pained him somewhat to be hiding his true character.

"I'd like to give you a token of my appreciation. Is there anything you desire to have?"

"Only for us to get safely back to Phezzan."

"I'll be more than happy to compensate you for any damages you suffered from all this nasty business. There's no need to be modest."

If he refused, he might raise suspicion for being too frugal. Julian was careful in shamelessly receiving the commander's good favor, calculating the exact amount of damages and presenting it to Admiral Wahlen the next day. He also said they should reward Captain Boris Konev. A single optical disc was all the recompense he needed.

Everything was recorded on there. The history of Earth, a planet which had lost its hegemony over humankind by vindictively stitching its desire and malice into a veritable Gobelins tapestry of power spanning nine centuries.

This had been passed on to Admiral Yang's hands, and had been useful in Julian's long journey all the way to Earth. Julian had led the imperial forces, clearing away human and material obstacles, and that had led them to finally discover the "reference room" he'd been searching for. Knocking down knife-wielding fanatics left and right, they made it to the unexpectedly modern data room, where it took five minutes to gather the required information. Although they managed to wipe the remaining records so they would not fall into imperial hands, the data room got buried anyway, which meant they'd ended up doing twice the work for nothing.

As Julian stepped back from Wahlen, standing at the edge of the cliff and looking down on the caved-in terrain, Boris Konev stood next to him.

"Underneath all that lies the bodies of believers."

"To a religious cult, nothing's cheaper than the lives of its followers. It's the same with leaders and their citizens, tacticians and their soldiers. Worth getting angry over, maybe, but not being surprised about."

Julian found it increasingly difficult to condone Boris Konev's harsh words. Then again, Boris was in a foul mood, having lost an important crew member in the melee.

"You once said Admiral Yang was different."

The captain shrugged his shoulders.

"It's fine to like Yang as a human being. I do, too. It's only natural to respect him as a tactician as well. But the tactician leads a cursed existence. Yang himself knows this, I'm sure, so it's nothing for you to get worked up about. You know it, too, so I forgive you for criticizing soldiers."

Olivier Poplin was watching them from a short distance.

"That Julian's a mystery to me," muttered the ace pilot under his breath, leaning his head to one side.

Even he, and elders concerned with Julian, seemed compelled to appoint themselves as the boy's guardian.

"It's his virtue," responded Machungo, with an expression that was clichéd yet persuasive. "You don't usually find it in one so young."

His body was wrapped in several places with geliderm, an ultra-thin plastic membrane used as a bandage, which gave him the appearance of a hulking zebra. Although no one within the Church of Terra surpassed his strength and fighting abilities, his body's surface area was broad enough to have sustained an unenviable amount of shrapnel.

"Virtue? Hmm, he's got a lot to learn."

Poplin shrugged his shoulders. He was quick-witted and agile, even on land, and had emerged unscathed from the battle with hardly a tear in his clothing. Fighting with his feet on the ground was extremely undesirable to him, but his style had earned even Machungo's respect.

"How can he have come of age without having at least ten or twenty affairs under his belt?"

Their voices didn't reach Julian's ears, and so the boy's flaxen hair blew in earthly winds at the top of the cliff.

Julian had come to Earth with one goal in mind. But not once thereafter did he ever desire to return to Earth. Wherever it was he needed to return, live, and die, Earth was most certainly not it.

Julian wasn't alone in thinking that way. To most people, Earth belonged to the past. It was fine to regard it as a museum. But reviving it as a center of power politics and military affairs did humanity not one sliver of good. As Yang Wen-li had once quipped, "Our limbs have grown too much for us to return to our cradle." Although humanity's past was on Earth, its future was destined to unfold elsewhere.

On August 1, the Wahlen fleet's first wave left Earth and charted a course for the imperial capital of Odin. *Unfaithful* cut a gallant, if modest, figure in tow. Both Julian and Poplin were of the same mind that they might as well have a look at the enemy's home base, seeing as it was on the way.

II

At around the time of Wahlen's report, the intel coming in from the Free Planets Alliance capital of Heinessen was exceedingly ominous.

Commissioner Lennenkamp had been abducted, and many related incidents shocked the empire's senior statesmen. Even after escaping the grip of death on more than one occasion and conquering many fixed-star worlds, the empire's bravest generals were by no means accustomed to being surprised.

Along with the official report, an urgent addendum came from Admiral Lennenkamp's subordinate Captain Ratzel to his old friend Neidhart Müller.

Müller's sandy eyes filled with deep color.

"Are you claiming that Admiral Lennenkamp acted unfairly as commissioner?"

"Whether for the nation's senior statesmen or for a superior to whom he was obliged, he overstepped his bounds. By his misguided actions, Admiral Lennenkamp tipped the scales when they were already balanced."

According to what Ratzel had said, Lennenkamp had put his faith in an anonymous tip, despite having no evidence to back it up, and coerced the alliance government into arresting Yang Wen-li. If true, then he'd crossed the line both publicly and privately.

"Would you be willing to testify before an official assembly?"

"Whether by court-martial or trial."

Müller nodded at Ratzel's confidence, and with that information in hand, appeared before an assembly of top military leaders.

In the hallway leading to the conference room, he ran into Wolfgang Mittermeier. Ratzel spoke of his testimony as they walked side by side.

"I see. There was something shady going on behind the scenes after all."

Mittermeier clicked his tongue, lamenting the shallowness of Lennenkamp's heart.

Lennenkamp himself, of course, had only done what he did out of loyalty to Emperor Reinhard. But from where Mittermeier and the others stood, the impatience of his step and the myopia of his vision were troubling.

Wolfgang Mittermeier, also known as the "Gale Wolf," was a true military man. It had been his long-cherished desire to battle heroic enemies on an equal footing, but he was fundamentally opposed to torture.

At the council meeting, only those officials ranking higher than senior admiral could attend, with one exception. Emperor Reinhard had a slight fever and abstained from the meeting, but expected a full report on the results of their free debate when it was over.

Müller, who always demanded to speak first, presented Captain Ratzel's complaints.

"This concerns the dignity of the empire, particularly the impartiality of its stance. Without fixating on the empire or the alliance, we would prefer it if you could come up with something that the public can agree with. If I may give my own opinion on the matter, I think the first thing we need to do is determine the whereabouts of those who seeded the situation with their anonymous tip."

Commander in chief of the Imperial Space Armada Mittermeier backed up Müller's sentiments.

"It would seem that Captain Ratzel is correct. We must protect His Majesty the Emperor's dignity, first and foremost, by punishing these shameless informants. If we can prove that Yang Wen-li's actions were out of legitimate self-defense against an injustice being forced upon him, that might just give us enough to piece together the rest."

Without revealing one iota of his own strategy, von Oberstein interjected.

"He was only trying to eliminate Yang Wen-li as a danger to the future security of our great nation. Maybe he couldn't help but resort to subterfuge."

"Was our nation founded on subterfuge?!" yelled Mittermeier with every fiber of his being. "No, it was founded on fidelity. If we don't aim for that much at least, then how are we to explain to our soldiers and citizens the significance of this new dynasty? Yang Wen-li might be our enemy, but he's also universally renowned. How do you plan on justifying to future generations that we eliminated him not with honor, but through betrayal?"

"A splendid speech, Marshal Mittermeier. Need I remind you of your involvement in the plot to purge Duke Lichtenlade two years ago? Does it still pain your conscience?"

An uncontrollable rage burned in Mittermeier's eyes. Where did the very ringleader of Duke Lichtenlade's purge get off bringing *that* up? Before he could say as much, the man sitting next to him raised a hand lightly and restrained his colleague.

It was secretary-general of Supreme Command Headquarters, Marshal Oskar von Reuentahl. A keen light emitted from his mismatched eyes, clashing head-on with the light shooting out from the secretary of defense's artificial ones.

"The purge of Duke Lichtenlade was an even contest. One step behind, and we'd have been the sacrificial lambs. We shouldn't be ashamed just because we attacked first. But is that what happened this time around? Aren't we trying to charge a retired soldier living a comfortable civilian life with a nonexistent crime? Why should we involve ourselves with the shameless criminals of a self-interested alliance? With all due respect, Defense Secretary, is this the kind of disgraceful behavior by which we must abide, regardless of the philosophy it's based on?"

Von Reuentahl's eloquence was not only keen, but also consistent with the sentiments of most of the men in the room, and so he was met with murmurs of agreement all around.

Artist-Admiral Mecklinger spoke up.

"If the relationship between Yang Wen-li and the alliance government is irreparable, might it not behoove the Imperial Navy to extend a welcoming hand? We should appeal to him against further mischief, and dispatch investigators right away to deal with the situation. I'd be happy to leave for the alliance capital of Heinessen under those auspices."

"It seems you've failed to grasp something here." Secretary of Defense von Oberstein showed no signs of being uncomfortable in the hot seat. "My problem with Yang Wen-li's crime has nothing to do with the anonymous intel, but rather with the fact that he and his men managed to abduct Lennenkamp, His Majesty the Emperor's official representative, and get away with it. If *that* crime goes unpunished, how do you expect to maintain the dignity of the empire and His Majesty? I'd like you to bear that in mind."

Mittermeier opened his mouth again.

"It pains me to say this, but Lennenkamp must at least be held accountable for carelessly trusting an anonymous tip and taking it upon himself to try and execute an innocent man without a shred of evidence. If we're going to come out of this with our dignity intact, shouldn't we disclose the truth and make up for any mistakes we may have made?"

Chief of the Domestic Safety Security Bureau, Heidrich Lang, was against this.

"Senior Admiral Lennenkamp was graciously appointed by His Majesty the Emperor. Your Excellency Commander in Chief, to punish His Excellency Lennenkamp would harm the reputation of His Sacred and Inviolable Majesty the Emperor. I would advise you to take that into consideration."

"Silence, you pathetic boor!" The reprimand came not from the lash of Mittermeier's tongue, but von Reuentahl's. "So now you're going to block the commander in chief's sound argument not by your own opinions but by His Majesty the Emperor's good name? Don't try to be more than you are! Why should the chief of domestic safety be allowed into a meeting restricted to senior admirals and above in the first place? Not only that, but you have the gall to interrupt a debate among marshals? Know your place. Get out of my sight this instant! Or would you like to ride my boot on the way out?"

Lang turned into a fluorescent-colored sculpture. Had he been entitled, he would have been disgraced, but he was lacking in the grace department, thought Mecklinger. Lang at last looked to von Oberstein for support, trembling slightly and not getting what he was asking for.

"Leave until this meeting is adjourned."

At the secretary of defense's words, Lang coldly and mechanically bowed. Then, with a gait as deflated as he was, he left the conference room, a wave of derisive laughter nipping at his heels. In his pale heart, he decided it was von Reuentahl, when in fact it was Kessler and Wittenfeld.

Lang waited in a separate room until the conference was over. When von Oberstein showed up an hour later, he'd abandoned his usual composure. Lang's face was covered in a flop sweat, and he couldn't stop the handkerchief in his hand from trembling.

"Well, I have *never* been so humiliated. Actually, if it was only me I wouldn't even care, but to drag Your Excellency's name through the mud as well…It's like they were showering us with abuse."

"Von Reuentahl wasn't the only one who didn't care for your line of reasoning. I didn't, either." Von Oberstein was indifferent. He had no intention of going along with Lang's treacherous sedition. "I was careless in allowing you to attend without the others' consent. It seems neither the secretary of the interior nor the military police commissioner approve of you being close to me."

"It's not like you to be concerned about such things."

"I don't mind being despised. But I *do* mind standing in the way of others."

Lang turned his handkerchief inside out and wiped his sweat again, narrowing his eyes.

"As do I. Even so, given the aggressiveness of Marshal von Reuentahl's conduct, shouldn't we slap him with a demerit, just in case?"

Von Oberstein's expression was completely blank. Lang didn't know what lay behind it until von Oberstein's clear speech broke the silence.

"Von Reuentahl was indispensable in the founding of this nation. Lennenkamp cannot hold a candle to His Majesty the Emperor's trust in von Reuentahl. Surely you know better than to follow Lennenkamp's bad example and disavow others without evidence."

Lang's eyes filled with oily light as he bared a few teeth from his twisted mouth.

"Understood. Then allow me to seek out that evidence. Incontrovertible evidence…"

Since the previous dynasty, Lang had shown exceptional ability in two areas. Punishing the guilty, and pinning crimes on the innocent. But he'd carried these out as official duties, and never out of a personal desire for revenge. Or, at least he shouldn't have.

But now, for the sake of his severely wounded reputation, Lang was seized by an improper and useless determination to seek out the young heterochromatic admiral's weakest point and bring him down.

III

A slightly feverish Emperor Reinhard was laid flat in bed, his attendant Emil seeing to his every need.

Reinhard thought it might be due to bad genes, but according to Emil, with all the wars and government affairs demanding his attention, it would be strange if he *didn't* feel under the weather from time to time.

"If it were me," said the emperor's future physician, "I'd be at death's door."

"Either way, I've been feeling rather fatigued these days."

"It's because you work too hard."

Reinhard smiled gently at the boy.

"Oh? Are you saying I should neglect my duties?"

Even the smallest jest made Emil turn bright red, and so the emperor always sported with him as he would a small bird. Only, this small bird sung in human speech, occasionally voicing wise things.

"Please forgive my impudence, Your Majesty, but as my late father used to say, a strong flame burns out quicker. So please, try to take it a bit easier. I mean that."

Reinhard made no immediate reply. What frightened him wasn't burning out, but the thought of smoldering away in vain. A distinction Emil was probably too young to understand.

"In any case, right now you should be focusing on taking an empress and having a family."

The boy was obviously relating something he'd heard secondhand.

"It's hard enough protecting me. I wouldn't want to burden my guards further with an empress and crown prince to think of."

That was generally about the extent of Reinhard's sense of humor. As a joke, it was as flat as he was, and a shallow expression of his true feelings. Emil didn't care for it.

Reinhard's grand chamberlain entered to announce the arrival of Defense Secretary von Oberstein. Now that the council of the military's highest leaders had reached something of a conclusion, he'd come seeking Reinhard's approval. Because the emperor was still sluggish from fever, he welcomed his guest in the lounge adjacent to his bedroom.

Von Oberstein briefed him on the details of the council. The backlash against Lennenkamp's rash actions was unexpectedly severe, and many insisted on an investigation into the truth of the matter. But because the alliance clearly lacked the ability to maintain its own order, they motioned to prepare their troops to be mobilized at a moment's notice. Von Reuentahl said nothing about banishing Lang from the conference room.

"It's my fault for appointing Lennenkamp in the first place," Reinhard muttered. "To think he couldn't hold down his station for even a hundred days. I suppose there are those who will only be able to demonstrate their abilities when I have them on a short leash."

Several faces, both living and dead, lined up in his mind.

Von Oberstein ignored the sentiment.

"But this gives us carte blanche to completely subjugate the alliance, does it not?"

"Don't overstep your bounds!"

The violence in Reinhard's voice was as intense as his good looks. He was suddenly furious. Von Oberstein bowed, less out of fear than out of a desire not to get a sick person riled up. Reinhard caught his breath and commanded that, out of consideration for Lennenkamp, Admiral Steinmetz would act as proxy for the high commissioner and that they negotiate with Yang Wen-li.

"We must hear Lennenkamp's testimony. Only then will we know how best to deal with Yang. Keep close watch on the alliance government's movements, and if any disturbance should arise, Steinmetz is to employ whatever countermeasure he deems necessary."

With this, he dismissed his secretary of defense.

Reinhard's state of mind was never simple. While he couldn't suppress a loathsome anger toward Lennenkamp's disgraceful behavior, Reinhard was the one who'd placed him in an important office unbefitting of a mere military man. Although von Reuentahl was the first to enter him as candidate for that seat, Reinhard had also voted for him in the end. The final responsibility therefore lay with Reinhard alone.

Or maybe I expected Lennenkamp to fail all along, Reinhard thought to himself. When he learned of the rioting brought on by Lennenkamp's tragic failure, Reinhard had to admit that every cell in his body throbbed with excitement. After sitting on the throne for only a few days, he'd already begun to feel the suffocation of a solemn equilibrium. In the end, his throne was nothing more than a golden cage, and it seemed his wings were too big to fit.

As an architect, Reinhard was possessed of abundant genius. Two years ago, he'd crushed the Coalition of Lords, purged Duke Lichtenlade, and grabbed dictatorial power by the reins. Since then, he'd brought about major political, social, and economic reforms. The noble class, which had monopolized privilege and wealth, lost five centuries' worth of undeserved glory, while the people enjoyed the benefits of a tax system and due process. The mansions and castles of nobility were converted into hospitals, schools, and welfare institutions, becoming an integral part of the metropolitan landscape.

Those reforms were ones he'd cultivated in his heart since he was a boy.

But while Reinhard was happy to see them realized, none of it exhilarated him. Good government was his duty and responsibility, not a privilege. He'd endeavored to be one who doesn't neglect the requirements of his position, a great ruler who becomes such by acquiring power rather than having it handed to him. But were harmony and stability somehow incongruous with his original intentions?

Reinhard had caught himself thinking that power was no longer necessary. What *was* necessary to him was something else entirely. But he was deflated by the fact that he had yet to hold that something else with his own hands. He knew it was something he'd never regain. He saw nothing but war ahead, and for the first time felt renewed. Only in the heat of battle could he believe that his own life was replenished.

Reinhard would likely be remembered for all time as a belligerent emperor. That thought fell lightly like first snow in his heart, but there was no way to change who he'd been born to be. He was never one for bloodshed, but for the collision of grander purpose and ingenuity. He called his chief private secretary, Hildegard von Mariendorf, who'd returned to the imperial palace, to take down an edict.

While working on the edict, Hilda came to realize that perhaps Reinhard *needed* a rival in his life. She felt a touch of anxiety over this tragic thought. She wanted nothing more than to point the compass of his vast life force in the right direction, more for his own sake than for the empire's. Or maybe, she thought, he'd reached the top too quickly, even if it was good for him to encounter an enemy who, like Rudolf the Great, could become a great object of his denial.

She herself admired Yang Wen-li's abilities, and couldn't bring herself to hate him.

Reinhard read over the letter he'd dictated to her, but suddenly flashed her a roguish smile.

"Fräulein, did your handwriting get stiffer while you were under house arrest?"

Another questionable joke.

On August 8, Emperor Reinhard's edict went out as follows:

The imperial headquarters will relocate to Phezzan. Odin is too far from alliance territory. Count von Mariendorf will govern as my regent on Odin.

Furthermore, Reinhard ordered that among his ten cabinet ministers, his secretaries of defense and works would follow him to Phezzan, where they would be transferred to new offices. Among his highest-ranking officers, Kessler (commissioner of military police and commander of capital defenses), Mecklinger (who as the newly instated "rear supreme commander" reserved the right to inspect almost the entire former imperial territory), and Wahlen (now en route back home after fulfilling his duties on Earth) were the only ones staying behind on Odin. The nucleus of the empire, in particular its military power, was relocating to Phezzan—and not, he added, temporarily. Marshals Mittermeier and von Reuentahl were the first to learn that the young emperor intended to relocate the capital to Phezzan.

The transfer was to be completed within a year, at which time the emperor himself would move to the imperial capital on September 17. Marshal Mittermeier was set to leave before that, on August 30, while Marshal von Reuentahl and the other admirals would be traveling with the emperor.

After withdrawing from the emperor's presence, Mittermeier discussed these developments with his friend.

"Phezzan, huh? I see. He's thinking on a whole other level. Perfect for absorbing that land into the new territory and ruling over it."

Von Reuentahl nodded silently, mulling over a private matter. Because he was a bachelor, he was fine with departing from Odin at any time, given the proper battle formation. But then there was Elfriede von Kohl-rausch, that violent young woman who'd become a fixture in his house. Would she follow the man she supposedly hated all the way to Phezzan, or would she steal his valuables and go into hiding? Either way was fine with him. It was up to her.

"Even so," Mittermeier spat out, "His Majesty's error wasn't using Lennenkamp but von Oberstein. That bastard may fancy himself a loyal retainer, but at this rate, he'll eliminate those he doesn't get along with, one by one. And in the end, he'll bring about a rift in the dynasty."

Von Reuentahl moved his mismatched eyes in his friend's direction.

"I'm with you on that one. What worries me is the fissure I see between His Majesty the Emperor and von Oberstein. Who knows what might happen when *they* don't get along…"

Von Reuentahl couldn't suppress a bitter smile, as this level of concern was strange even for him. Didn't he himself at one time desire a supreme position with many subordinates under him? But there was surely a method behind such madness. There was something disconcerting about watching a man he valued so highly be degraded as a puppet, not unlike von Oberstein.

IV

When Julian thought of Yang on Earth, did a butterfly effect cause Yang to sneeze in rapid succession? No official record could confirm that.

Yang, who'd let João Lebello go free and taken the late Helmut Lennenkamp hostage, boarded a cruiser dubbed *Leda II* and left the planet Heinessen. Joining him were Frederica, von Schönkopf, Attenborough, and his former subordinates, now released from house arrest. It was July 25. Attenborough served as the cruiser's captain, but using Lennenkamp as an excuse, he'd succeeded in obtaining a large amount of weapons and provisions from the alliance government. Leaving plans for what was to follow up to Yang, he whistled, every bit the good-humored space pirate.

Frederica G. Yang switched out her floral-patterned apron for a black beret and military uniform, standing valiantly by her husband as his assistant.

At the time of their departure from Heinessen, Yang thought of paying respects to Admiral Bucock, but gave up on the idea.

The retired, convalescent commander in chief of the space armada had also earned the suspicion of the alliance government. Even a one-on-one meeting was too risky, as it might compromise the old admiral's already-frail position. In any case, the day would come when they would meet again, and so Yang suppressed this desire.

Yang did, however, get in touch with Vice Admiral Alex Caselnes. He was a man whose affiliations had always been clear, and if Yang didn't contact him, he might arouse suspicion of some pre-existing secret pact between them. Once Caselnes, who until then had been nominally banished to rear services headquarters, knew of the situation, he contacted his family. He tore off his insignia and placed it on his desk, throwing himself under Yang's command.

"Without me there," he said, "that blasted Yang will never make it."

Admiral Rockwell, knowing he'd be left behind as acting general manager of rear services, tried to dissuade him from leaving, but Caselnes looked at the admiral over his shoulder, only snorting through his nose.

Former chief of staff Murai, Vice Commander Fischer, and Deputy Chief of Staff Patrichev were no longer on Heinessen, but attached to their respective frontier posts, making it impossible to contact them.

In the summer of that year, the Wiliabard Joachim Merkatz fleet had secured 464 warships and 80 flagships. What the fleet lacked in organizational balance, it made up for in its advanced firepower and strength.

And while it was diminutive in manpower, many highly experienced soldiers with actual combat experience joined the battlefront. They were, of course, too proud to swear allegiance to the Galactic Empire, but as Lieutenant Commander Hamdi Ashur, who held highest rank among them and was known for his superiority as a fleet tactical operator, was led along the bridge of the Merkatz's warship *Shiva*, he deferred completely to Merkatz's right to command.

"While I don't disagree with you about flying the flag of revolt against the empire, under what pretense does this fleet operate? Is it democracy? Another dynastic dictatorship like the Lohengramm Dynasty's? Militarism, even?"

As Commander Bernhard von Schneider looked back at Merkatz, the exiled guest admiral signaled for Ashur to continue.

"I know it's rude of me to say, Your Excellency Merkatz, but you once held high rank yourself in the Imperial Navy. Furthermore, while I was banished to another country, you served as secretary of defense for the legitimate imperial galactic government. The purpose of the legitimate government should've been to restore the inherent authority of the Goldenbaum line, but I cannot be a part of such a goal."

The newly recruited soldiers stirred uneasily behind him. Not only because Ashur was their commanding officer, but also because he'd proven himself to be a charismatic character.

"Allow me to be clear on that point. The purpose of this army is not to restore the Goldenbaum Dynasty."

"I hear that you never go back on what you say, Admiral. I believe you. But, while it may not be my place to say so, when it comes to rallying soldiers dedicated to democracy, your good name, Admiral Merkatz, lacks a certain attraction."

"Then who would you recognize to lead this anti-imperial volunteer army?" responded von Schneider.

Ashur slightly tilted his swarthy, virile face.

"Admiral Bucock has the requisite accomplishments and popularity for soldiers of democracy, but at his age it's hard to imagine him as a flag-bearer of the future. Successive former directors of Joint Operational Headquarters, Sitolet and Lobos, are men of the past. And so, I would hope for a younger man with his own charisma and dignity."

"Admiral Yang Wen-li?"

"Don't jinx his name. In any case, this isn't something we'll see realized today or tomorrow. I will follow your command for now, Admiral Merkatz. You can count on me."

Because they lacked the requisite number of men for the number of ships they had, Ashur consented when asked to assist in operating the fleet and readied his men for the task. Von Schneider muttered as he watched them go.

"That one certainly has a lot to say. Seems reliable enough, at any rate."

Merkatz gave a rare bitter smile.

"He's right, you know. I'm not qualified to be a flag-bearer of democracy. About two or three years ago, I was battling democratic forces as a soldier of a despotic nation. If I were to take up democracy as my flag this late in the game, then future generations would regard me as a man without integrity."

"Your Excellency, aren't you reading too much into this? Everyone knows your hand was forced by the circumstances, and that you always tried to make the best of things regardless."

"However posterity chooses to me, the truth of the matter is no one but Yang is capable of uniting the soldiers of democracy. That's why even his own ally, the alliance government, is afraid of him."

Their actions sourced rumors of irresponsibility. They never imagined that Yang and his clique would escape Heinessen.

Merkatz quickly changed the subject.

"And His Majesty's whereabouts are still unknown?"

By "His Majesty," Merkatz wasn't referring to the young golden-haired sovereign Reinhard von Lohengramm, but the Goldenbaum line's thirty-seventh emperor, Erwin Josef, enthroned at five years of age and kidnapped at seven. Von Schneider ashamedly hid his gaze.

"That is correct, I'm sorry to say. I know it's hard to hear, but under the circumstances any investigation is next to impossible."

Merkatz knew this. If they'd managed to repeatedly escape the Imperial Navy's detection, then there wasn't much point in launching an official investigation or search. The powerless Alliance Armed Forces couldn't make light of Steinmetz's ability to rat out an enemy.

Nevertheless, that Merkatz was fixated at all on searching for the former child emperor was because he knew there'd been a fault line in the boy's mind before his disappearance. His ego had frequently erupted, even drawing blood from those tasked with caring for him. With every such drop of blood shed, the human spirit had faded away from the Goldenbaum crest. Although such erratic violence was in his nature, it was a crime of circumstance that it wasn't corrected, and that had been the responsibility of the adults around him.

Restoration of the Goldenbaum royal line was hopeless. To begin with, the human spirit didn't desire it. What Merkatz did wish for was that Erwin Josef would grow soundly in body and mind, and that he'd live out a peaceful life as an anonymous citizen under whatever political system he found himself in. But this would probably be even more difficult than the pipe dream of restoring the royal line. And yet, he wanted to make it a reality. This, and to give Yang Wen-li the essential military resources he needed to make his grand reappearance on stage. *These are the last two jobs I need to finish before I die*, Merkatz thought.

On the bridge of the cruiser *Leda II*, the Yang fleet's three vice admirals—Caselnes, von Schönkopf, and Attenborough—handled their commander with sharp tongues, as they had even at his recent wedding.

"I can only hope that Yang Wen-li's star power will stretch its own limits," said von Schönkopf. "Not that he's even aware of it himself. It's hard enough just getting him to stand on the other side of the curtain."

"You speak like a teacher worrying over a bad student, Vice Admiral von Schönkopf."

"Actually, I once thought about becoming a teacher. But I hated being given homework."

"But I assume you like giving it?" chided Caselnes with a laugh.

Here was a man who, despite having an honorable post as director of rear services on a distant planet, had rejected it with a snort and come along for the ride. Losing his superior administrative skills would be a seed of regret for the Alliance Armed Forces after losing Yang Wen-li.

"Even so, Vice Admiral von Schönkopf, you were able to see through the government's vicious trick under the intense pressure of having next-to-no intel."

In response to Caselnes's praise, von Schönkopf attempted an unbecoming expression.

"Well, maybe the government just didn't think that far ahead. Or maybe it was just my wild imagination."

"Oh, *now* you tell us."

"That's right, Vice Admiral Attenborough. And at this point, it doesn't matter whether it was true or not. I'm as sure now as I was then that the alliance government was involved in a malicious conspiracy. It's not like I lied to you or anything."

"Even if you did fan the flames."

Despite his sarcastic retort, Attenborough suddenly grew anxious as he rewound the film of reminiscence.

"Are you sad that things turned out the way they did?"

"Far from it, Vice Admiral Caselnes," said the youngest of the three, shaking his head.

"I'm only a greenhorn, not yet thirty, and yet people are already calling me 'Your Excellency.' That's the blessing and the curse of being under Admiral Yang. We'd better hold him accountable for that."

Alex Caselnes took off his black beret and looked up.

"People call us a 'rebel force,' but from where I stand, we're nothing but a bunch of runaways."

The other two made no objection.

Whether one called him a marshal, leader of a rebel force, or a runaway, Yang Wen-li was Yang Wen-li. Bridging the gap between his commander's chair and desk with his outstretched legs, a black beret covering his face, he hadn't stirred in over two hours.

Sitting not five meters away from her husband, Frederica G. Yang was demonstrating contrastive diligence by compiling data on the cruiser *Leda II*, the Merkatz fleet, and Yang's "rebel force," so that they would have a tactical plan ready at a moment's notice.

Since rescuing her husband, Frederica hadn't thought about the future. All she knew was that whatever path Yang Wen-li chose, she would walk it as his better half. Yang, on the other hand, still had no clear idea about what to do after escaping from Heinessen. He hadn't been the one to instigate all this mayhem in the first place.

"Yang and his wife know how to defend themselves," concluded Dusty Attenborough, "and yet they haven't thought about the consequences. If only we could give their ambition a shot in the arm."

Attenborough had grasped a part of the truth, but from where Yang sat, there was no reason to be criticized by one of the ringleaders who'd led him around by the nose.

And while the resistance had remained on the planet Heinessen, taken hostage by the alliance government and occupying imperial forces, they too would be swallowed up into Heinessen's billion citizens. In the end, Yang had been pushed aside by the government he was supposed to serve, his only option now to run away.

The existence of Lennenkamp, dead and stored inside a body preservation capsule, was the only thing standing between them and total annihilation. When Lennenkamp's death was made public and he handed over the body to the Imperial Navy, a new danger was sure to befall them.

Nevertheless, many renowned generals before him had passed through the doors of purge and exile by the very motherlands to which they returned safely from the battlefield. One significant achievement was enough to make a million people jealous. The stairs got narrower the higher one climbed them, and led to more serious injuries when one fell.

In a certain ancient empire, when a general was arrested for treason, he asked his emperor about the nature of his crime. The emperor averted his eyes.

"My courtiers all say you orchestrated a rebellion against me."

"That's not true at all. Where's the evidence?"

"But surely, you've at least *thought* about rebelling against me?"

"It never crossed my mind."

"I see. But you *could* rebel if you wanted to. That's crime enough."

Those carrying bigger swords had to be careful about getting cut from the other direction. In the end, the sword itself was a third force to be reckoned with.

Just because one built a third force didn't mean one could maintain it. As in Yang's fundamental vision, if political and economic power didn't go hand in hand, then the candle of rebellion would quickly burn out. Where should they put their base? How was he ever going to stand up to the Alliance Armed Forces, let alone the Imperial Navy? When should he officially announce Lennenkamp's death? And what about supplies? Organization? Diplomatic negotiations...?

He needed more time. Not to die in obscurity, but for ripening and fermentation. Time that Yang couldn't have. It was more indispensable to him than power and authority.

Yang had many short-term goals. Linking up with Merkatz to establish a chain of command with a unified republican army. Welcoming Julian back from Earth and obtaining information about the Church of Terra. And after that? Although he'd taken João Lebello hostage and forced Helmut Lennenkamp to take his own life for the sake of avoiding an undeserved death, how should he exercise that right?

These vague imaginings appeared as translucent figures in Yang's consciousness. He accepted that universal hegemony was Emperor Reinhard's alone. To make up for it, he would establish his republican autonomy on a frontier planet in preparation for the inevitable erosion and collapse of the Lohengramm Dynasty. There he would nurture the sprout of a pan-humanist democracy. The time needed for growth and qualitative advancement of such democratic ideals was much longer than any he needed for himself.

Once humanity was intoxicated by the drug of a sovereign nation, no social system would exist in which the nation didn't sacrifice individuals. But social systems in which the sacrifice of individuals by nations was difficult to achieve seemed to live up to their intended value. Not everything would be accomplished in Yang's lifetime. But he could sow the seeds. He was no match for Ahle Heinessen and his ten thousand–light-year march.

Even so, Yang was more aware than ever of his own unavoidable omnipotence. If he had any ability to predict the future, it was in his ability to make the tactically impregnable Iserlohn Fortress a base of democratic government, despite having to abandon it in order to save the Free Planets Alliance, and to guarantee his freedom of movement.

But there was no use in regretting it now. For starters, during the Vermillion War that followed, he'd ignored the government's order yet was unable to finish off Reinhard von Lohengramm. In the end, Yang acted to the best of his abilities. He, too, wanted the intelligence and resources of the Phezzanese.

"Phezzan, huh?"

Yang was unaware that Emperor Reinhard had designs to relocate the capital to Phezzan and make it the center of the universe. Neither did he know that Phezzan was intimately connected to the Church of Terra, and had, in fact, acted as its puppet. But it was an indispensable element in his long-term plans. Ideally, he thought, he could use Boris Konev as an intermediary to borrow the power of independent merchants. But that, too, would have to wait until Julian returned. Yang interrupted his walk through a maze of speculation as he took the beret off his face.

"Frederica, a cup of black tea."

He then put the beret back on his face. No one could hear the words he muttered under it.

"Two months, just two months! If things had gone as planned, I wouldn't have had to work for another five years…"

After being set free by the "rebel force," João Lebello naturally wanted to negotiate with an enraged Imperial Navy, but before that gave the following instructions to the national defense committee.

"I want a letter reinstating Admiral Bucock to his former position. We might just need him if we're going to mop up Yang and his gang."

Although Lebello was anxious about plowing a one-way course to villainy, his sense of duty to protect the alliance's independence and sovereignty from the empire's coercion had only grown stronger. Future historians would likewise recognize that he drew a line between the elites who tried to deceive Yang Wen-li. Ultimately, Lebello believed in his country, whereas Yang didn't. Perhaps the wall had grown too thick between these two who would ideally have worked together. But Lebello was truly reluctant to have his accomplishments remembered by posterity only in relation to Yang Wen-li.

As the reflected stars twinkled in her indigo eyes, Katerose von Kreutzer, called Karin, stood on the observation deck of the warship *Ulysses*. Her cheeks were flushed from having just finished her training, her pulse slightly elevated above normal. With one leg stretched out straight and the other slightly bent, her back was barely touching the wall—just like her father, as her mother used to say. She thought it was annoying. Who didn't strike this pose at some point? If she were a man it wouldn't matter, but as a woman, she didn't take kindly to being likened to a man she'd never met.

Karin crushed the paper cup that had contained her protein-enriched alkali drink. She tried to shake off her father's imagined face, only to replace it with another. Having only just met that flaxen-haired boy two years her senior, she was reluctant to remember him.

"What's so special about that weakling anyway?"

Muttering an insult she didn't necessarily believe, Karin returned her attention to the vast ocean of stars, as yet unaware that, somewhere along those waves, her father's cruiser was making its approach.

The year SE 799 had already proved traumatic for humanity, and it still had a third left to go. No single year in history, it seemed, had ever been so greedy about giving time to breathe. Whatever it was that had been set in motion, people had no way of knowing if the cards were in their favor. They were all sick of war, but not yet used to peace.

On August 13, an autonomous entity in a star system near the Iserlohn Corridor declared its secession from the empire-ruled alliance.

El Facil.

ABOUT THE AUTHOR

Yoshiki Tanaka was born in 1952 in Kumamoto Prefecture and completed
a doctorate in literature at Gakushuin University. Tanaka won the Gen'eijo
(a mystery magazine) New Writer Award with his debut story "Midori no
Sogen ni..." (On the green field...) in 1978, then started his career as a
science fiction and fantasy writer. Legend of the Galactic Heroes, which
translates the European wars of the nineteenth century to an interstellar
setting, won the Seiun Award for best science fiction novel in 1987. Tanaka's
other works include the fantasy series The Heroic Legend of Arslan and many
other science fiction, fantasy, historical, and mystery novels and stories.

HAIKASORU
THE FUTURE IS JAPANESE

TRAVEL SPACE AND TIME WITH HAIKASORU!

USURPER OF THE SUN—HOUSUKE NOJIRI

Aki Shiraishi is a high school student working in the astronomy club and one of the few witnesses to an amazing event—someone is building a tower on the planet Mercury. Soon, the Builders have constructed a ring around the sun, threatening the ecology of Earth with an immense shadow. Aki is inspired to pursue a career in science, and the truth. She must determine the purpose of the ring and the plans of its creators, as the survival of both species—humanity and the alien Builders—hangs in the balance.

THE OUROBOROS WAVE—JYOUJI HAYASHI

Ninety years from now, a satellite detects a nearby black hole scientists dub Kali for the Hindu goddess of destruction. Humanity embarks on a generations-long project to tap the energy of the black hole and establish colonies on planets across the solar system. Earth and Mars and the moons Europa (Jupiter) and Titania (Uranus) develop radically different societies, with only Kali, that swirling vortex of destruction and creation, and the hated but crucial Artificial Accretion Disk Development association (AADD) in common.

TEN BILLION DAYS AND ONE HUNDRED BILLION NIGHTS—RYU MITSUSE

Ten billion days—that is how long it will take the philosopher Plato to determine the true systems of the world. One hundred billion nights—that is how far into the future Jesus of Nazareth, Siddhartha, and the demigod Asura will travel to witness the end of all worlds. Named the greatest Japanese science fiction novel of all time, *Ten Billion Days and One Hundred Billion Nights* is an epic eons in the making. Originally published in 1967, the novel was revised by the author in later years and republished in 1973.